MORE BY THE AUTHOR

THE RAVEN'S JOURNEY

Book 1: See Me
Book 2: See Me Revealed
Book 3: See Me Go
Book 4: See Me Believe
Book 5: See Me Overcome
Book 6: Hawk
Book 7: Ronan
Book 8: Stolas

LOOKING THROUGH THE SHADOWS

The Underbelly
After the Wreckage
We Always Fight

I S.P.I.

I S.P.I. Mischievous Magic (Volume 1)
I S.P.I. Spicy Sorcery (Volume 2)

SHORT STORIES & MORE

Where Realms Collide
Unnerving Descent
Unnerving Eclipse
Unnerving Wicked
Super: Unexpected Heroes Arise
Rise Reflection
Rise Resurrection
Rise Revolution
Rise Recreation
The Space Between Us
The Pulse (The Haunting of Orchard House)

Michelle Lee on the Web

Michelle on Facebook at
tiny.cc/MichelleLeeWrites

or write to
MichelleLeeWrites@gmail.com

THE RAVEN'S JOURNEY
BOOK THREE

SEE ME GO

Michelle Lee

BLUE FORGE PRESS
Port Orchard, Washington

For Saira
Strength comes from
doing what needs to be done,
and you have it in spades.

For Kristen
You finally get Ronnie.

SEE ME GO

Michelle Lee

Chapter One

onnie screamed, "Lightning!" They were still in the house! Adrenaline flooded Ronnie's body and he took off for the house, Aedan yanking him back.

"Let me go! They are still in there!" Ronnie shouted.

Oh fuck! The house was on fire. Flames leaping towards the sky as the dry wood crackled and burned. Ronnie struggled against Aedan and the mounting fear he would lose everything that mattered to him. He gripped Aedan's arm, his fighter strength taking over, and he pulled hard.

"Let me go now. I will hit you if I have to." Ronnie's voice was deadly. Aedan dropped his arm. Ronnie turned back towards the house seeing Smitty stumble out, the camera still strapped to his shoulder. Shaking and coughing from the now billowing smoke.

Ronnie ran over and stepped under Smitty's arm, lifting him to support his weight and dragged him back to Aedan. "Where are they?" Ronnie demanded.

Smitty choked, trying to get clean air in his lungs. "Basement. Jax isn't in control. Airiella was hurt by the guy."

Fury tore through Ronnie with a force equal to a

major earthquake. He turned, and as he headed back to the house lighting struck again, the bolt strong enough to lift him and toss him backwards like he was nothing. Lying flat on the ground he stared as smoke filled the night sky, the flames giving it an eerie glow.

Ronnie's head was ringing, and he was vaguely aware people were shouting at him, that firetrucks had arrived, help was here. He got up, staggered and started forward again when movement from both Aedan and Smitty caught his eye.

Both were heaving violently. Aedan hadn't been in the smoke, that didn't make sense. He paused, wasting precious moments he needed. "What's wrong?"

"She pulled Jax's energy." Smitty's fear slammed into Ronnie.

Ronnie bolted and reached the house as the guy stumbled down the front steps. This fucker was why his angel was hurt. Ronnie threw a punch with his full force behind it, his intent to cause pain, smashing the guys face. He crumbled to the ground, out cold. The cops could deal with this asshole. Out of the corner of his eye, Ronnie saw Aedan stumble, his face pale as he shouted, "Go!"

Headfirst he ran into the smoke-filled house trying to get a glimpse of anything. A raven sat at the stop of the stairs, cawing softly, and his gut knotted. Flames licked at the walls all around him, and he hardly noticed. He pulled his shirt up over his face and charged down the stairs, pausing as he saw her trying to get Jax up the stairs. Then she dropped. Neither of them was moving.

"No!" he screamed. He flew down the stairs, the raven landing on Jax, like it was telling him to take Jax. Indecision tore at him. Trusting the raven, he grabbed Jax under the arms and drug him up the stairs, coughing. He got him to the front porch where Aedan was waiting and handed him a water.

Ronnie poured it over his shirt and tied it around his face, while Aedan called for help as the firetrucks pulled up. He bolted back down the stairs and wasted no time in gathering Airiella up in his arms and getting the hell out of there. The smoke was thick now and his lungs were burning.

Timbers crashed down behind him, sparks burning his bare skin as the house went up like kindling. He stumbled on the top stair, the heat from the burning walls too close for comfort. He fell to his knees and couldn't find the air his lungs needed to get up.

Fuck that. No way was he giving in. With strength he didn't know he had in him he got up and ran for the front door, falling through it, barely managing to turn his body so he didn't land on Airiella who was not moving. He didn't need to add crushed to her list of injuries.

People were there, he felt hands on him, an oxygen mask replacing the wet shirt, someone trying to take Airiella from him and panic kicked in sending a surge of adrenaline through him. "No!" he yelled through the mask.

"We need to help her, sir," a fireman told him. "She's not breathing, let her go."

Aedan was there, gently pulling Airiella from him, his eyes showing the fear that Ronnie was trying to fight. He let go, and they took her, her body totally limp, no signs of life. Aedan helped him get back to a safe distance. It was like watching what was happening through someone else's eyes.

He saw medics working on Jax, Airiella was getting CPR, Smitty on a stretcher being checked and breathing oxygen through a mask. Ronnie let Aedan lead him to an ambulance as they looked at the burns on his back, applying ointment and bandages as needed, keeping the oxygen on him.

Smitty's eyes were wild as he watched them work on Airiella. The adrenaline rush over, Ronnie dropped, sagging into the medic behind him as grief took over his body. The weight of it too much for his body to bear. The entire team almost died because some asshole set them up.

Father Roarke came up on his side. "We have to get to a church as soon as she's breathing again. She can't hold that energy for long," he whispered in Ronnie's ear.

"Father, they're doing CPR on her. She's already

gone." Ronnie broke down.

"Have faith, son. She's not gone. Not yet. See the bird?" he pointed to the raven sitting above Airiella. "She's still here."

Ronnie shrugged off the medic patching up his back. "I'm fine."

"Leave the mask on," the medic advised with a warning look and left him alone.

"How do we get her to breathe then?" The scene was surreal. Smoke around them, the night sky burning, people rushing around them trying to contain the fire, police questioning the crew, Jax and Airiella hanging in some sort of limbo.

"I don't know much about this connection thing, but maybe it's through that," the priest suggested.

Ronnie stood, drawing the attention of Smitty and Aedan. He gestured with his head towards their angel lying lifeless on the ground. Smitty got it, and started to move, startling the people around him. Ronnie pointed to the mask letting him know to keep it in place.

Aedan hadn't caught on yet, but followed. Jax was still out, so they kneeled on the ground at her feet, leaving room for the medical personnel to keep working on her. The each put a hand on her leg, sliding their fingers up under her jeans. Ronnie prayed it would work.

Chapter Two

Winnie was in front of me, crying. Where the hell was I? There was nothing here. It was gray. Everywhere and everything was a muted gray. "Winnie? Where am I?"

"Dead," she howled.

"What?" That wasn't right. Cold seeped into my bones. No, no, no, no. "Jax?"

"He's alive. They all are, but you aren't! Why Airy?!"

"Winnie slow down. Why what?" It wasn't clicking in my head.

"You died before the energy release, I don't know if you will come back from that," Winnie howled.

"How did I die?" What was I missing? I remembered everything. I got Jax to the stairs, then nothing. "No air. I couldn't breathe," I said numbly, last piece falling into place.

She nodded numbly at me. I felt the energy I pulled from Jax still in me. Trying to plant roots. "Ronnie pulled you out."

"I'm not dead, Winnie." I was sure of it.

"Airy, you aren't breathing. That equals dead."

I wasn't dead. I couldn't be if this shit I pulled was still trying to plant roots. "Winnie, listen to me. Look at me. Am I glowing?"

She pulled her wet eyes up and really looked at me. "Yes, kind of. Not like normal though."

"I'm not dead!" I shouted at her and grabbed her shoulders to shake her. Wait...I could grab her shoulders?

"You can touch me...Airy! If you aren't dead you will be soon!"

Yeah, she was right. That couldn't be good. I felt for the raven and found it still there, but not in my mind like it was before. How did I see from it before? I closed my eyes and felt for her and then latched on and opened my eyes.

I wanted to close them. Smoke was thick in the air as firefighters fought back the flames on that house of horrors. Jax was not conscious, I knew why, but he was also bloody. Maybe it was my blood, I didn't know.

Directly below, three people were working on what I knew was my body. The raven made a small sound in her throat. "Tell me what to do," I told her telepathically.

"Live," she sent back to me.

Well, that just explained everything to me right there, damn raven. I saw Ronnie and Smitty headed towards me, both wearing oxygen masks, their movements slow. Aedan trailing behind them. The kneeled at my feet and touched me. The raven made another sound.

An unknown voice spoke. "You will never defeat me. Killing me means killing your love. Can you do that? Can you sacrifice your love to defeat me? I am him. We are one."

Who the hell was that voice? Focus Airiella. The connection. I closed my eyes and went back to Winnie. She stared at me silently with tears streaming down her face. "Don't you dare give up on me now, you damn ghost."

"Your glow is fading," she said forlornly.

I closed my eyes and put my hands on my legs where they had been touching me. I focused there, on what it felt like when their skin was against mine. I let their words flow through me, all the beautiful things they've said to me, their kisses. I felt their love. Their desire for me to come back to them.

Winnie gasped. "Whatever you are doing, keep doing it!"

I let the love I feel for them fill me, pushing against the darkness that was trying to take me down. "Fuck off, darkness, I'm not yours." The taste of them against my lips, how it felt to sleep nestled up against them, cocooned in the safety of their arms. "See that, darkness? I belong to them."

I heard the flapping of wings again, and coughed. My lungs burning, body screaming in pain. Stomach cramping as I tried to heave. Oh, the joy of living.

Smitty froze. She moved. He saw it, it wasn't his imagination. "Breathe, baby girl," he whispered into the mask.

She gasped for air her body going rigid beneath their hands as she fought. They snapped an oxygen mask over her face and Smitty bowed over her foot as pain washed through him. She was back, but she was hurting. Fuck, she was hurting bad.

He saw Aedan reacting the same as him and he knew the connection had worked, it brought her back to them. Only now, they were going to have to lose her again. Father Roarke came up behind him, "She has to get to the church, we don't have a lot of time," were the whispered words in his ear.

Fuck. How were they going to make that happen? They were surrounded by medical personnel and police. They weren't going to just let them take her. Smitty stood and pulled off the mask. "How?" he gestured all around them.

"Tom, and me. I'll cite religious beliefs and Tom can say they have a personal doctor waiting for her," he thought out loud.

"Crafty old man, lying is a sin you know," Smitty retorted. "She's already injured, I don't think it will be that easy."

A car came careening up the road at that moment, and Smitty saw Taklishim and Degataga getting out and rushing over. "They'll help," Father Roarke said with a gentle smile.

Smitty didn't know much about what abilities they had, but he put his trust in them because there wasn't much else he could do. "Do what you need to do, and tell me where you want us to put her."

Father Roarke nodded at the two council members in signal of something, Smitty didn't know what. The priest pointed at a sedan parked close by. "That's mine, get her in there. Only one of you can come." He walked off to find Tom to start pushing.

Smitty swore. Ronnie stood up next to him. "I heard. I'm going."

"Ronnie," Smitty warned.

"No. I'm going. There's no argument. Aedan needs to stay with Jax and you can be of more help here than I can."

Smitty gave in. "It's not easy, man."

"Neither was this." Ronnie pointed to Airiella laying on the ground.

"Let's get her up then," Smitty said giving in.

The medical team that was working on her put up a good fight, but once the higher ups told them there was a personal doctor waiting for her they stepped aside. The three of them got her up and laid across the backseat. Smitty took his mask off and put it around her face and placed the oxygen bottle on the floor of the car next to her.

"Love you, baby girl. Come back to me soon, you hear?" he whispered into her ear.

She didn't even move. Smitty's heart broke at the sight she presented. Breathing, but barely, bloody, soot covered, burned and bruises forming. He was almost glad he wasn't going to witness this, but the urge to not be away from her was strong. Ronnie climbed in the passenger seat and closed the door, his face set in stone. They passed Father Roarke headed to the car.

"Take care of her," Smitty said, fighting the emotions down.

Father Roarke took off like a bat out of hell, and Smitty walked over to Taklishim. "Do I want to know what you are doing here?"

"Helping. Jax is going to need a bit of healing, you all probably do. Dega is manipulating the energy here to try and stabilize it. It's broken here, the earth is sick. Then both of us are going to do some in depth talking with that man that just tried to kill you all. On live TV."

"Shit. My camera was still on?" Smitty hadn't even thought to turn it off.

"It's quite popular on the internet already. And yes, this was a set-up. Onida saw the truth." Taklishim was barely holding in his fury, and Smitty took a step back.

"How did she know this guy had something going on?" Smitty was baffled.

"She didn't. He, the backer, was trying to make it a flop. I think Jax caught on judging by the questions he was asking the guy," Taklishim said as he resumed walking.

Tom came rushing over. "Art, this is a disaster. I'm chartering a plane for you guys to take back when Airiella is released from the doctor's care."

Smitty was momentarily confused. Taklishim nudged him. "You just loaded her up for the personal doctor that was on standby."

"Right. Okay. Ronnie will let us know when they are on their way back. Sorry. Long night." This was getting confusing.

"They want to take Jax to the hospital since he's still out. Should I let them?" Tom worried looking back and forth between Smitty and Taklishim.

"No, he'll be fine. Taklishim and Degataga will see to him," Smitty reassured Tom.

Aedan came up. "Tak, is she going to be okay? The pain running through me is damn near unbearable."

"You need to believe she will be." He pointed to the raven above them. "If you can see that, she's still with you. She's watching over you right now, even as she fights."

Smitty's eyes welled up with tears, he had to face the fact he wasn't strong enough to keep his emotions in check. "Aedan, find out when we can go."

"Not yet. Police want to talk to us first. The crew is breaking down the tents and Tom is on the phone arguing with the backers. He's getting us a plane."

One of the medics came back up to them. "We'd like to look you both over a little more thoroughly before we go. Also, I think you need to sit down." The guy was older than them, kindness showing in his eyes.

Smitty gladly sat on the stretcher and accepted the blanket and oxygen they handed him. Tom came back over with the coat Airiella had been wearing. "Probably a good thing she took this off before she ran in there."

Smitty clutched it to his chest and gave in to the tears, Aedan sitting next to him trying to be stoic but succumbing to shock. They both sat there gripping the coat she'd been wearing as if it were a lifeline to her. Thankfully Jax was unaware of the shit going on around them at the moment.

Chapter Three

My body was bouncing, every movement hurt. I was in a car. Where was I going? What was on my face? Oxygen mask, my brain clicked on. Fire, smoke, Jax. My stomach heaved and I rolled to my side, I didn't want to choke on my own puke.

"Hang on, angel, we are almost to the church," I heard Ronnie say.

Church. Oh god. The energy. I tried to sit up and groaned. He couldn't see this, it would hurt him so much. God, how much of this energy did I pull? My joints felt like they were coming apart. Maybe that is the injuries from that guy beating the crap out of me? I couldn't tell, the energy was making my head fuzzy and my ears ring.

The car stopped and I felt Ronnie lifting me out, and as much as I tried to not let him know it hurt, the groans escaped anyway. His beautiful face was covered in soot and tear tracks. I forced my arm up, my body protesting every inch, but the need to touch his face was strong. I ran my thumb under his eyes.

"Love you," I whispered.

"I've got you. We will get through this, angel. I love you so much, you damn brave, foolish woman." His tears dripped on my face as he kissed my head. His eyes held mine as he carried me inside, so gently and carefully.

"Ronnie, you need to prepare mentally for this," I heard Father Roarke say. I wanted to apologize, but I knew he didn't want to hear that. And I *really* didn't want him to get mad at me and drop me.

I saw Winnie floating over Ronnie's shoulder. "It's going to hurt, Airy. Your color has faded so much." I could tell. I was starting to not feel like me. "I can't help him like I did with Smitty, you haven't bonded yet."

"It's okay," I whispered. Ronnie thought I was talking to him.

"Will there ever be a time when you don't run head first into a life-threatening situation?" he asked me, his voice cracking and those green eyes, perfect emeralds, staring down into mine. "I'm so mad at you I could scream, and it makes me feel like an ass because you are all busted up and not okay."

Good question. I didn't have an answer for him, and it was hard to talk anyway. I just kept my hand against his cheek, needing to touch him. He was so incredibly beautiful. He should have been the angel, not me. The pain in my body was getting worse, and I couldn't keep it from showing on my face.

"Fight it Airy," I heard Winnie say, but the buzzing in my ears was so loud. I smelled the candles, then I was moving. I winced as Ronnie laid me on the ground. I must be in a circle. I felt a dribble of something on one of my hands, then the other and pain shot through so intense I arched off the floor, a scream ripping through my throat, the coppery taste of blood filling my mouth.

I heard voices, but I couldn't hear what they were saying. Out of the corner of my eye I saw Father Roarke leading Ronnie away from me and sitting him down. Ronnie nodded, his eyes glued to mine, and Father Roarke came back.

I knew what that meant. The holy water in a cup came next. "It's for Jax," I told myself. "You helped him. You kept him from killing. It's worth it. You love him." Father Roarke was saying something to me again, but I kept losing focus. The pain was front and center as that energy was taking me apart. Drink. He was telling me to drink. The mask was gone.

Guess I didn't need it if I was going to die again. The water might feel good on my throat, at least it will wash the taste of blood and ash out of it. I saw Winnie hovering near Ronnie. She'd find Smitty or Aedan if he needed them. "Thank you." I whispered before I swallowed.

I was right, the water felt good on my throat, but it was short lived. I thought my vocal cords had been too damaged from the choking and smoke inhalation to scream. I was wrong. I heard it over the buzzing in my ears, my voice echoing the sounds of hell in this small church. I had a swift thought of gratitude that I couldn't see the expression on Ronnie's face. The screams were what hurt Smitty that most.

The pain consumed me in a fire hotter than the one I just escaped. My limbs had a mind of their own as they tried to twist away from me, snapping and breaking, bending in ways a contortionist couldn't even move. Blood filled my eyes, my throat, my nerves felt like they were exploding. I think I even was throwing up blood, but it was too hard to tell what was happening. It was all extreme pain. Then, nothing.

Aedan had just finished giving his statement and was heading over to Smitty. Degataga and Taklishim, who were pulling some serious strings somewhere, to secure an interview with the guy who caused all this, met them where Smitty was sitting in the open hatchback of their SUV.

They'd gotten Jax released, against all orders from medical personnel, and they had him laid out in the third row of seats. He still hadn't budged, made a sound or shown any signs of life other than breathing. Aedan supposed that was good enough for now. He was still with them at least.

He was going to have nightmares like Jax did for the rest of his life. The sight of the lightning striking that house with Smitty, Jax, and Airiella in it would haunt him for years. Just like the picture of her lying lifeless on the ground covered in soot and blood would. The entire night had become a living nightmare, and somewhere, Ronnie was facing another.

Along with all of that came the violent blasts of pain that kept coming across the connection to him and Smitty. He wasn't much of a drinker, but damn did he need one right now. He'd talked to Mags briefly on the phone who had been watching and lost her mind when she saw the pieces that'd been aired from the basement and from the waves of pain that had been hitting her as well.

"Hey, who's Chris?" Smitty asked, his voice strained.

"I don't know. Why?" Aedan barely had the energy to keep standing.

"Whoever it is, keeps calling Airiella's phone. Every five minutes." Smitty looked down at the phone again, slightly jealous.

"Airiella's phone? It's not on her?" Aedan couldn't make sense out of his thoughts.

"It was in her coat pocket." Smitty held up the jacket he hadn't let go of since they had driven away with Airiella in the back of the car.

"Is that the friend she went and visited yesterday?" He couldn't remember her name.

"Shit. You're right. What do we do? I can't keep ignoring it. If that was me calling, I'd want some sort of answer." Smitty jolted as the phone rang again.

Aedan held out his hand. Out of all of them, he'd been through less than they had. He felt like a tool for not running in and helping his brother, friend, or Airiella. Father Roarke had held him back, telling him she'd need him to be out here.

"I'll answer the next time she calls."

Smitty silently handed the phone over right was it ringing. Aedan answered. "Airiella's phone."

He listened to a frantic voice on the other end and cringed at the shrill tone. "No, this is Aedan." He paused, listening. "I don't know, she left with Ronnie and the priest. She was breathing when she left. One of us will call when we learn something. Sorry, I don't have more to offer you." He hung up and handed the phone back to Smitty.

Degataga and Taklishim joined them after another argument with the police. "No word yet?" Taklishim asked.

Smitty shook his head no. Aedan didn't even have the energy to do that as another bout of pain tore through them both. "What do we do now?" he asked doubling over.

"Go back to the hotel," Degataga said. "All you can do it wait for it to be done."

Taklishim stepped forward, "One of you ride with Degataga, I'll drive the other car. You guys aren't in any condition to drive."

As Smitty went to hand the keys over, he doubled over and fell out of the SUV and Aedan stumbled. Then the most horrific scream Aedan had ever heard tore from Jax, and Aedan's heart stopped beating. Degataga and Taklishim flew into action.

Taklishim pulled something from his pocket and was rubbing it inside Jax's mouth. Degataga was chanting something and Smitty sobbed. "Baby girl, what have you done?" he was repeating.

Aedan fell down beside Smitty as his world crumbled around him. "What's happening?" he choked out.

"She just died," Smitty cried.

Ronnie now very clearly understood what Smitty had meant when he said he couldn't ever explain the horror of what he had seen. Father Roarke had told him to brace himself, that she would come back and that she would need him. He said it would be hard to watch. He hadn't said he would want to die along with her. He hadn't said the amount of pain she would be in would literally break her.

SEE ME GO

Ronnie heard bones snapping amidst the screams that haunted Smitty. He heard the agony in every echoing cry that tore from those beautiful lips. He heard her back break, her body went so rigid fighting that shit that lived inside Jax. Bloody tears fell out of her eyes. She was crying blood.

He broke inside a million times, each move her body made, Ronnie broke with her. His every cell screaming at him to save her. The sight of her burned into his eyes, a vision of absolute suffering. He couldn't even hear Father Roarke's prayers anymore. Just the screams that spoke of a pain Ronnie hoped to never know. A sound that begged for death to just make it stop. A sound seared into his memory.

His body shook and stomach cramped, tears fell unchecked, his own cries lost among the echoes of the echoes. She was vomiting blood, choking on it, and there weren't enough ways for Ronnie to think of to apologize to Smitty for his attitude after he'd seen this. And when it stopped, so did Ronnie's heart. He lurched to his feet, swaying like a drunk man on a boat in a storm at sea. The silence was worse. Smitty had been correct again, it was so much worse.

He fell to his knees, sobs tearing him open at the sight of the blood dripping from her eyes, ears, nose and mouth, her body once again, deathly still. She'd died for them. Again. He crawled across the floor, to be stopped by a shaking and pale Father Roarke. Ronnie saw his lips moving, but he couldn't hear them over the sound of his heart shattering.

"Ronnie, Ronnie, look at me. Ronnie," came the faint sounds of the priest. Ronnie tore his eyes away from his angel and tried to focus on the priest, but he couldn't.

"Ronnie, it's not over." Father Roarke shook him.

"How is it not over? She's dead," Ronnie screamed. "Kill me. She's not going alone."

"Faith, son. Have faith. She will be back. The miracle happens next," he said as he sat down next to Ronnie lending his support. "I know that was hard to watch.”

“Hard?!” Ronnie shouted, his voice breaking. “It fucking killed me!”

Grief took him so hard he threw up. Black bile spewed all over the floor. He didn’t care. It didn’t matter now. He rested his head on the cement floor where feet away his angel died for the second time that night, and he’d watched it happen in the most horrific way he could think of.

He heard Father Roarke moving around and then half pick him up off the ground. Ronnie let himself be led to a pew where a bottle of water was stuck into his hand. “Drink, son.”

He couldn’t. He watched through a haze as the priest cleaned up his mess. Ronnie had lost every person he had ever loved, except Jax, Aedan, and Smitty. He wanted to believe Father Roarke, and maybe somewhere in his mind he did, since Smitty had been through this. But his eyes and heart were not matching with what his brain was processing or hearing. He wanted to die with her. If he’d had a knife, he would have stabbed it through his heart, it would have hurt less than what he just watched play out.

“Ronnie, look.” Father Roarke’s gentle words fell on his ears.

Ronnie lifted his head and shot to his feet, almost falling over again. She was floating. The glow coming from her skin the most brilliant light he had ever witnessed. Her body was putting itself back together before his eyes. The sounds were no less horrifying than when they had broken.

“Believe Ronnie. You call her angel, but she really is one. How else can you explain this? She *will* come back to you, son. What you are seeing, is love. Her body is purifying itself. The love she feels for you all brings her back. That is what I believe.” The priest made the sign of the cross over his heart and whispered a prayer.

“How?” Ronnie’s legs shook and then the floor was coming up to meet him. Instead the priest caught him and set him down gently.

“Given my faith, I’d like to believe it’s God, healing

his warrior. The truth is, I don't know. She's a living miracle. Why else would I be here? This was worse than the times before, that seems to be the pattern, I imagine she pulled quite a bit from your friend." Father Roarke sounded so calm and awed, and Ronnie couldn't understand how he could be that way.

Ronnie broke down again. His heart was so confused. He understood why she hadn't wanted him here. He also now understood why she asked Smitty last time, that he was the less emotional choice and she relied on his reason. He now understood why Smitty had changed. Ronnie himself was changing as the seconds turned to minutes. But understanding all those things didn't help him right now.

She did this of her own free will. She put her body through pure torture to save them. "How long does this last?" Ronnie's rough whisper was barely heard. He wanted to hold her, touch her, breathe life into her. He wanted to hand her all the pieces that broke inside him at watching this and ask her to put him back together, make him stronger.

"Depends on the damage she took on. It appeared to have been a lot. I think we almost lost her on this one. I was gravely worried." The Irish lilt to the words made it seem less harsh. They hadn't almost lost her, they *had* lost her. Twice.

The raven Ronnie saw earlier appeared next to him on the pew, making him flinch at the sudden movement next to him. He looked between the bird and his floating angel who still had no life in her body. "You make her okay, please? Bring her back to me." He felt like an idiot talking to the bird, though the raven had her eyes. "I don't know what to believe anymore raven, I just know she owns my heart, and I need her to breathe. Please help her."

Ronnie broke down once again, this time feeling love wash over him that he swore felt like Airiella. The raven hopped closer to him and cawed softly. Ronnie held out his arm and it hopped up his arm landing on his bare shoulder, not using its talons. This beautiful black bird with his angels' eyes leaned its head against Ronnie's face, then launched, landing closer to Airiella.

"You can't go in that circle until the glow stops. That's my gut instinct anyway," the priest explained. "I wouldn't let Art in there until she was done."

Ronnie had no plans to leave her side no matter what. They would have had to bury him with her if she hadn't made it. He moved his exhausted body as close to the circle as he could get before Father Roarke protested. "Ronnie, drink some water before you pass out."

Ronnie drank. He had no idea how long it was before she came down, but it was no short period of time. He battled the fatigue that was trying to shut him down, determined to be what she needed. It felt like hours before he heard a gasp of air through those glowing lips.

His eyes teared up again as her body lowered back to the ground, the glow fading. He glanced over at the priest who nodded at him and he threw himself at her, pulling her over on him and held her as he cried, her hair covering his face. She smelled like blood and smoke, but she was alive. She came back to him. The raven cawed again, then disappeared.

Smitty hung up the phone and through raw, burning eyes looked over at Aedan who lay in one bed, watching Jax lay in the other. He was in Aedan's room back at the hotel. Neither had showered yet, waiting to hear about Airiella.

After the scream, Jax hadn't made another sound. Hearing Airiella's scream coming through Jax's lips had done a number on him. He mentally shook himself. "Father Roarke is bringing them back here. He said it was really bad. He thought he was going to lose both her and Ronnie."

"Ronnie? Why?" Aedan looked confused. "Is he hurt?"

"Like I said before, it's not something I can explain. Seeing it, man, it fucking kills you. Hearing that it was worse than last time and given how much more emotional Ronnie is than me, I get it." Smitty shuddered, his body shaking the bed.

"She's okay though?" Aedan was worried.

"She hasn't woken up yet. She's breathing. Ronnie is glued to her. I was too. When they get back here, don't push him. He might not be okay yet, and he will need time with her. Fuck, I still don't think I am over it." Smitty pulled his arms over his eyes as if it would block the memory.

"I can say I don't want to feel her die again. That was pretty fucking awful." Aedan's tone was bewildered.

"Let me put it this way, that scream you heard from him." Smitty pointed at Jax. "That was nothing compared to what I heard coming out of her. That should give you a small idea of what it's like. People who torture prisoners of war have nothing on what happens to her body. She willingly puts herself through this. For him. For us. Think about that."

Smitty stood up as his words sunk in to Aedan's head. "I don't want to see it," he whispered.

"No, you really don't. I don't think we will have much of a choice in the matter though. No one should go through that alone. I'm going to go shower before they get back. You should do the same. He'll be fine for a few minutes. When I'm done, I can come back and we can try to clean him up so he doesn't stink up the room."

Aedan nodded and stood, taking Smitty's advice. Smitty went back to his room and collapsed on the bathroom floor and cried. She was alive. They'd figure out the rest later. For now, that was all he cared about. When he could move again, he stripped off his clothes and turned the water as hot as he could tolerate without triggering a memory of the flames coming for him in the stairs as he escaped while that valiant woman fought for them. Died for them. Again.

Chapter Four

Aedan showered as quickly as possible, took his clothes and wadded them up in a garbage can. He never wanted to see them again. He checked to see Jax hadn't moved yet and grabbed his phone to call Mags.

"She's alive. Not awake, but Father Roarke is bringing her back here. I'll call Tom to see when the flight he chartered can bring us back. We need to get out of here before people figure out where we are," Aedan rushed out.

"I felt it Aedan. I felt her die," Mags choked. "All that pain, how much she suffered."

"I know baby, me too." His eyes clouded with tears again. "Jax hasn't moved yet, either. I'm so scared right now I don't know what to do. I'm going to have nightmares. I'm afraid to sleep, but so exhausted I'm about to pass out."

"Lay down, love. Call me when you know when the flight is coming, so I can come get you. I need to see you all. Just bring them home to me." Mags paused. "Social media is going crazy. Everyone is trying to figure out who she is."

"Fuck, we need to get out of here. I'm gonna hang up baby, I need to call Tom." Aedan needed to do something to keep his mind off what was happening around him.

"Love you Aed."

"Love you more, Mags." Aedan hung up, shaking. His fingers fumbled around the screen as he tried to bring up Tom's number.

He finally got it and dialed. "Tom, how soon can the flight leave to get us home? We need to get out of here before people figure out where we are and storm the hotel."

"Tomorrow morning is the earliest I could get. The company said they could leave at 6:00 AM. Want me to confirm? How are they?"

"Yes. Chances are Jax and Airiella will still be unconscious." Aedan's eyes slid to Jax again.

"Do I need to arrange medical transport?" Tom sounded exhausted.

"No, I've got Taklishim and Degataga, I'll ask them to help." He didn't need to ask, he knew Taklishim was going to keep an eye on both of them.

"I'm so sorry, Aedan. Never would I have thought anything like this would have happened." Tom sounded wrecked. A feeling Aedan was all too familiar with at the moment.

"You don't even know the half of it. Thanks for the charter. Text me what time we need to be there and the address." He needed to feel Mags and he was so far from her.

"You have all of us supporting you Aedan. It's only the one asshole that isn't. The other holdouts have now changed sides after seeing what was shown on the internet and TV. I'll send you the info."

Aedan slid the phone into his pocket and packed up everything in the room before going over to Jax. "Be okay, Jax." He started pulling the clothes off Jax, noting the burns that had been overlooked. He went into Jax's room to grab a set of clean clothes, and all the extra towels and washcloths.

He also packed up all Jax's stuff and brought it to his room. Smitty was back by the time that Aedan was soaping up some washcloths and between them they got him mostly cleaned off and treated some of the burns that had been missed.

They washed his hair as best as they could but it still smelled like smoke. Aedan knew they couldn't do much better than they had without drenching the bed. Smitty left to go pack up all Ronnie and Airiella's things.

Once all the bags were packed, they called the front desk to request the use of the service elevator that took them to the garage, so they wouldn't be seen and the loaded up all the bags in the SUV. Aedan texted the crew to tell them to get on the first available flight out of here they could and head back to the studio.

By the time that was done, Aedan was running on fumes. Smitty forced an energy bar down his throat and they sat there waiting for the call that Airiella and Ronnie were here. Aedan had cleared use of the service elevator again to get them up here without being seen.

The call finally came, and they met them down in the garage. The sight of Airiella's limp body hanging in Ronnie's arms like a rag doll made his knees weak. The amount of blood streaked all over her was nightmare inducing alone. Ronnie looked traumatized, much like Smitty had warned he would.

Smitty offered to take Airiella to give Ronnie a rest but he wasn't having any of it. Smitty didn't push, just followed closely behind. They went to Aedan's room first so Ronnie could see that Jax was still breathing and ease his mind of that burden. Then Ronnie just used Jax's room.

Aedan looked at Smitty who was staring with haunted eyes. "Is that what you expected?"

"It's worse." Aedan saw that Smitty was suffering just as much as Ronnie was.

Aedan dropped to the bed unable to process anything else. "We need to be at the airfield by 5:00 AM." Smitty nodded vacantly, then left going into Jax's room. Aedan set his alarm and passed out.

Chapter Five

Smitty recognized the devastated gaze Ronnie had. He wasn't at all prepared for the sight of Airiella. Not even last time prepared him to see her so battered. The bruises around her throat were vivid, even through the soot and blood all over her.

He followed Ronnie into Jax's room. "I'll run a bath. Try to get her as undressed as you can, I'll help and get her in there with you. Clean her up, wash you. Get the smoke smell out. I've already packed all the bags; I'll bring the extra clothes in while you are in there. Here's the toiletries." Smitty just went on autopilot, thinking only of getting them more comfortable.

Ronnie nodded, no sign of the playfulness he usually displayed. "I get it now, Smitty. I'm sorry for not understanding, for pushing you, being an ass."

Smitty nodded woodenly, the apology hadn't been necessary. "No words can describe it."

Ronnie just shook his head and started undressing her, pulling his clothes off as well. With Smitty's help, they got her undressed. "Get rid of all those clothes, I never want to see them again."

"You got it. I'll help you with the burns on your back when you're done. The hot water will hurt," Smitty warned.

"Pain has new meaning for me now." He said it so quietly. Smitty knew Father Roarke wasn't far off when he'd said he thought was going to lose them both.

"Day at a time, bro," Smitty said gently. "I wish I had never seen it, but now I also know that I was meant to in order to understand the gift she is."

He held her while Ronnie climbed in. There were nasty burns and ugly bruises marring her body, and Smitty fought back tears. "I need to go grab you more washcloths."

He lowered Airiella into the water remembering when he did the same thing for her. "Does it get easier?" Ronnie struggled to say.

"No," Smitty said honestly. "It comes up at the worst times. I'll be right back with the washcloths."

He practically ran to Ronnie's room, the only one left with any clean linens and grabbed them all, stopping to grab the clean clothes for both of them as well. It had been almost two days she was out last time. He wondered how long it would be this time.

He knocked to let Ronnie know he was back and brought in the washcloths and towels, setting them on the toilet. "Clean clothes are on the bed. We have to be at the airfield at 5:00 AM. So, get as much rest as you can."

"I'm afraid to sleep," Ronnie admitted.

"I was too, but touching her helps. Keep your skin touching hers. I'll sit out there until you are ready to get out, then I'll leave you alone."

Smitty knew Ronnie would need the alone time with her, the memory of it still fresh in his mind. He'd do his best to keep everyone away until it wasn't so raw for him. Smitty laid on the bed and waited, fighting to stay awake until Ronnie called him. He grabbed her out of the tub and sat on the toilet rubbing her skin dry while Ronnie dried off.

Between them they got her in the sweats Smitty left out, but left her shirt off so Ronnie could have the skin contact. Smitty cleaned the wounds on Ronnie's back, bandaged them as best as he could and left them alone.

His heart was beating a mad rhythm as memories assaulted him. Coupled with the day's events he was barely functioning. He set his alarm and waited for sleep to take him, knowing the nightmares would be following.

Ronnie saw the bruises all over her body and they served as reminders that she had taken a beating before the church. Not that he would ever forget the sight of her laying there dead. He hadn't been down there for the beating part though. He could only see what was on the screen when he'd gotten out. What he'd seen had been bad enough.

At least she smelled like her now. Ronnie had used her soaps, lotions and hair care products on her to get rid of that smoke smell and the endless amounts of blood that had dried on her skin. The hotel was going to have to burn those towels and washcloths. Ronnie shifted again, his body way past burnt out.

He'd thought laying curled around her would be enough, but it wasn't. He moved so he could pull her on top of him. He was trying to be as gentle as he could, though he had no way of knowing if he was hurting her or not.

He propped some pillows behind his back and felt better with her laying on him. Her skin finally warm and feeling like life again. He was helpless to stop the tears that kept falling, and he was starting to hate them. He wanted more reasons to laugh and smile. More reasons to laugh and smile with her.

Seeing her like this, right now, was not an inspiration for happiness. He had to grudgingly admit she looked peaceful, but the bruises all over told a different story. At least when she healed, the bullet wound on her body had mended itself closed. The scar fresh and pink.

Ronnie dropped another kiss on her forehead and breathed the scent of her in. He thought about her friend Chrissie, and what she had said about Ronnie, and her having a future together and it made him cry harder. He didn't even want to think about not being with Airiella.

His arms unintentionally tightened around her and a groan broke through her lips. Startled Ronnie let go and looked to see if she was waking up. She wasn't. He'd just used too much force. He kept his arms down and held her hands instead and listened to the steady cadence of her breath blowing against his chest. He drifted off to sleep.

Winnie paced. Airy had been so broken, and so close to joining Winnie on this side that it had scared her senseless. She was nestled on top of Ronnie now; she would be okay. She wasn't so sure about Ronnie though. He looked pretty destroyed. He'd kept it together and taken care of her, with patience and love despite the evident struggle going on in him.

Jax on the other hand, she worried about. He'd lost the necklace he had been wearing in that house so Winnie could see him now. She could feel inside him again. He was hurting bad. Airiella had managed to pull about half of that energy out of him and she hadn't had time to be gentle about it.

Winnie shuddered at the thought. She took way too much for her own safety. Winnie ruffled Jax's hair while he laid there. There wasn't a whole lot she could do for him to ease the pain. She wasn't sure that there was anything that anyone could do to ease that for him.

She could still feel the love Jax had for her, even stronger though, was the love he had for Airiella, and that gave Winnie so much hope. She'd save him. She'd save them all. The evidence of that lied in Smitty and Ronnie now.

Seeing what they had seen, they were now firm believers that all things were possible in the power of love. Smitty had grown empathy, Ronnie had grown faith. Mags was pregnant against all medical odds. Aedan, he hadn't tumbled all the way over the edge yet like the others had, but he was close.

Jax was starting to believe there could be happiness in his future. He had a long way to go though. He still wasn't fighting for himself. Sure, he'd fought to save Airiella from that guy, but he still gave into the darkness to do it. His heart might have been in the right place, but the choice could have been better.

Winnie went back to Airiella and stroked her hair in the way she liked. Maybe she'd try in a little bit to reach her. She wanted her to rest some more first though. That energy had been brutal on her this time. Her screams penetrating both sides of the veil, casting a pall that many spirits had felt.

There was no hiding what she was anymore. All those that Winnie hoped never learned of her, now knew. They'd heard her. They'd felt what she had done when she killed that energy. Some were scared, others were angry, and some just in awe. The dangerous ones would come for her. Like they had when they used that guy.

Winnie stroked Ronnie's face while he slept and he shivered and pulled the covers up over them both. She was happy he knew love. Airiella was his first real love besides her, and now he knew the lengths she would go to in order to protect them, what she could do. She kissed them both and then popped out to watch over Jax until Aedan woke up.

Chapter Six

edan was jarred awake when the alarm went off and he wanted to throw his phone through the window. He was still mentally raw from the day before and his body was sore. He flipped the light on and checked on Jax. No change. At least they had dressed him last night. That would make it easier on them all this morning.

He got up and called down to see if they, by any chance, had a wheelchair laying around somewhere. They were going to check for him, but they also warned him that news crews were camped out in the lobby.

Shit. They'd found them. Aedan rushed around making sure nothing was left in the room and texted Smitty and Ronnie. He wasn't sure Ronnie would get the text, but Smitty would check on them. There was a knock at his door and Aedan looked through the peephole. Taklishim.

He threw open the door. "Press is in the lobby."

"I saw. They don't know who Dega and I are, so we went down and grabbed coffee and some food." He held up a coffee and small plate of food.

"You're a lifesaver." Aedan grasped the coffee gratefully and sat down to eat.

"No change in him?" Taklishim looked Jax over and checked the burns on him, swapping out a few bandages.

"He hasn't even moved," Aedan worried.

"He's in pain. His soul is damaged," Taklishim answered, his eyes closed as his hands hovered above Jax's torso.

"Damaged how?" Aedan came over to look down at Jax.

"When she took the energy from him, she just pulled. It was rooted in him; those roots were ripped apart. He will be okay, but his soul is trying to heal itself. He needs her, but she is still healing too." Taklishim rested a hand against Jax's forehead.

Aedan shifted. "Is she okay?"

"Physically, her body healed when she was reborn, the marks are still there and the newly healed wounds still hurt her, but as with Jax, her soul needs to heal. There's something else you need to know." Taklishim stood and faced Aedan.

"Tama and Onida called me. They both talk with the spirit realm. They know who she is now, the spirits. They also know he," he pointed to Jax, "is a tool they can use to get to her."

Aedan's heart began to beat loudly in his ears. "What do you mean?"

"Things will be harder."

Aedan gave a dry bark of laughter. "Harder? Than yesterday?"

"That was the beginning. That guy was used by a spirit, not a demon, a spirit born of anger," Taklishim explained.

"He wasn't after Jax?" Aedan didn't know if that was good or bad.

"No. He used him to get to her. Jax was a bystander. The energy in Jax didn't like being used, I don't think Airiella would have been hurt by Jax. That guy wanted to take her light though." Taklishim tried to word it gently.

"Kill her, you mean," Aedan put it bluntly. Bad, it was bad. Jax was going to continue to be manipulated by this energy and was now a target. Airiella was going to continue to get hurt.

Taklishim nodded. "They don't see her as a person, they see her light. What happens when you shine a light in the shadows?"

"They go away." Aedan got it now. Terrifying was picture that was painted.

"He's more himself now, but his necklace is gone. So is Airiella's. Kalisha is making new ones, they'll be sent to the house in California."

Another knock came on the door and Aedan peeked through the hole again. An employee with a wheelchair. "Thank God! You are fantastic. Thank you."

"My pleasure sir, anything else I can do for you?" The young kid asked.

Aedan thought, "We can use the service elevator again, right?" The kid nodded. "Okay, great. The towels and washcloths that we used last night are pretty ruined from the soot and smoke we had on us. Can you let the management team know they can charge that to us?"

"Sure, I don't think it will be a problem though. Can I ask you something?" The kid looked nervous.

Aedan tensed, but agreed. "Sure, what?"

"Is he okay?" he nodded into the room.

"Jax?" The kid nodded. "He will be."

"Thanks. Can I get an autograph?" he asked shyly.

"Sure, what do you want me to sign?" This part Aedan was used to.

"My shirt." The kid grinned and pulled up his work shit to expose a white undershirt. He handed Aedan a marker. Aedan wrote Shadow Seekers, then signed his name.

"Knock on that door there and tell the guy that answers I told him to sign your shirt too." Aedan smiled at the kid. "Thanks for your help."

Aedan shut the door and wheeled the chair over to Jax. Taklishim helped get him into it. "Where's Degataga?"

"He dropped off a plate and coffee for Smitty, then was going to go get another for Ronnie and check on

Airiella. He's probably in there now." Taklishim adjusted Jax so he didn't pitch out of the chair.

"Should I not go in there?" Aedan felt a desperate need to make sure she was still breathing.

"My saying no, is more for Ronnie's sake than hers." Taklishim gave him a look.

"Then I should be asking if Ronnie is okay?" Aedan reworded his question.

"He is, Degataga is checking his burns, but mentally he needs more time." Taklishim's voice was gentle but firm.

"What happens in there? Why was Smitty so traumatized? I am guessing Ronnie is the same way now." Aedan pushed for answers to explain what was happening to his team.

"The worst pain you can imagine being inflicted on your body, mind, and soul. Then death. Then the miracle." Taklishim closed his eyes. "I've seen a lot of things, bad things, here and in the spirit realm. That was the worst. I'm sorry, I can't give you more details than that. I can only repeat what I saw with my own eyes, what I heard. What she feels is a different story. It affects each person differently on a personal level. When Tama, Onida, and I left that room last time, each of us were different for our own reasons. What you need to understand is, if you see it, you are watching your own version of hell play out before your eyes on someone that means a great deal to you. There is nothing you can do to stop it."

Aedan sucked in a shaky breath. "Why does she do it?"

"To save you. For love," Taklishim simply said.

Degataga came in through the connecting door. "They are ready. Ronnie will carry her. He doesn't want to let her go yet."

"What about Smitty?" Aedan asked.

"He's with them. You have a secure way down?" Degataga checked on Jax.

"Service elevator, it takes us directly to the garage. Smitty and I moved our SUV close to the elevator last night."

"We will follow you." Taklishim guided him towards the door.

Degataga pushed Jax, and Aedan left the key cards in the room hoping he'd never have to come back to Kansas.

Smitty got settled on the plane next to Ronnie, he needed to be close to Airiella too, but still give Ronnie his space. He had only let go of her to go to the bathroom, and even then, he refused to put her on the bed. He handed her to Smitty.

Not that Smitty was complaining, feeling her warm body in his arms did wonders for his aching heart. And not one of them was about to tell Ronnie to leave her alone. All it took was one look at his face. Smitty knew he'd had a similar look when it had been him.

He'd helped get Jax in a seat and buckled up. Degataga, Taklishim, and Father Roarke were all on the plane with them and Smitty had questions. Once they got underway, he started in.

"I know you talked to the guy last night, what did you learn?" Smitty began.

Taklishim leaned forward. "How much do you know about us?" He gestured between Degataga and himself.

"What tribes you are from, and that you are powerful, you'd have to be, to be on the council. I don't know specific abilities, but I have heard through the grapevine that you are both medicine men," Smitty answered.

Degataga nodded. "In our culture, there are three worlds. Below, middle and above. Us, here, this is middle, we all live and exist here. Below and above are what Christians associate with heaven and hell. Tama, Onida, Taklishim and I, we can see in the other worlds. Talk with them, interact."

Taklishim added, "It's what I call the spirit realm."

Degataga went on, "When we talked to this man, we

used both planes of existence. I asked questions here, Taklishim asked questions in the other world. So, on the camera that was in the room all they would have seen was me asking questions."

"It is in the other world that the answers came from. Aedan, that is the information I gave you earlier," Taklishim explained.

Smitty looked at Aedan, "You knew?"

"Not all that, just was Taklishim told me this morning before we left. Sorry, I forgot," Aedan apologized.

Smitty looked over at Taklishim, his face was calm and ageless though Smitty could see secrets were hidden there. "What did you learn? And can we fight it?"

"I like that you ask if you can fight it. I'll get to that. Dega and I will work with Father Roarke to get better answers, but we think short term, we can give you a path that will help." Taklishim moved his mouth in something similar to a smile. "That man was possessed with a spirit. It was not a demon. He had been this spirit for many years now, no human soul left to speak of. I can tell you, this is probably why Airiella pulled from Jax the way she did, it was all she could reach. A raven, or angel, can only affect human emotions and souls. She can feel the energy of things not of this world, but she can't change it."

"Why would she have pulled from Jax then?" Smitty was missing a piece. He knew only she could fill it in, he just needed to try to understand better.

"She wanted to save me," came the weak response from Jax's dry throat.

Smitty flipped around, "Jax! Glad to have you back, bro, you okay?"

"It hurts," Jax croaked. Aedan handed him a bottle of water and Smitty watched him struggle to get it down.

Degataga removed a tin from his pocket and held his hand out for the water bottle. Smitty saw Jax freely hand it over and Degataga mixed some of the stuff from the tin in and mixed it up. The water turned a murky brown color, and Jax didn't hesitate to drink it all. Smitty was impressed.

"She didn't want me to have the mark of killing someone on my soul. She chose saving me over saving herself." Jax's face showed the heartbreak he was feeling.

"She always will," Smitty told him, hoping it would ease some of the pain.

Taklishim watched the exchange carefully. "You will heal Jax. It will hurt less, she will help you." He looked back at Smitty. "His answer is what I expected had happened. She did the only thing she could think of to help the situation. Without that energy in Jax having a conscious body to work with, it couldn't affect its surroundings. That man didn't want Jax, he wanted Airiella. He wanted to kill the light in her."

"He wanted her dead." Smitty blanched.

Degataga joined the conversation after studying Jax more carefully. "In the other worlds she appears as light. For some spirits that is comfort, and her love and warmth draw them to her. For others, it has the opposite effect."

"What happens when you shine light on a shadow?" Taklishim broke it down.

"By killing the light, they save themselves." Smitty put it together.

"Correct," Degataga said. "Not all intentions are malevolent. It's preservation. Then you have those that are intent on causing harm. It's not all black and white. Spirits can be persuaded to change sides or take sides, just as humans can."

"Was this guy bad?" Smitty wanted to clarify.

"Yes," Taklishim said. "It was a spirit that fed off negative emotions, chemical dependency, and darkness. It's unclear to me how he became aware of Airiella, he wouldn't give that information up. Jax was just a tool to him, one he could use to get to her. He had hoped that by activating that darkness in Jax, that Jax would hurt her. He didn't count on Jax going after him. She's had an effect on you Jax, that shows improvement."

"Not enough, I wasn't able to hold it back," Jax answered glumly.

"I think it's more that you didn't try, you just

diverted the attack to the man instead of her. Or the energy let you knowing he would be an easier target than Airiella," Taklishim amended.

Smitty noticed Ronnie's undivided attention focused on Jax, waiting to hear what he said. He knew if Jax wasn't careful or honest, Ronnie would walk away from Jax after what he'd seen happen.

Jax looked at Ronnie, and Smitty knew that Jax understood. Holy shit, Jax was more Jax than he'd been in a long time. "When I had my first real conversation with her, the first sentence out of her mouth was she had been hoping that for once someone was coming to save her instead of it always being her saving someone else. But that she didn't think I was the one who would save her, instead I could destroy her. Down there in that basement, letting that shit take control of me and focusing on that guy was the only way I could think to try and save her. I wanted her to know she deserved to be saved."

Ronnie was trembling, Smitty forced himself to stay put, this was between them. "You couldn't have known what she would do. In your situation I probably would have done the same thing. I don't blame you, Jax."

Smitty saw something ease in Jax's eyes, and he realized that Jax thought he had lost Ronnie. Smitty looked between the two. They were both ghosts of themselves right now, the changes they were being put through was hard on them.

"Did this guy think he'd be able to control the energy in Jax?" Smitty went back to looking for answers.

"He did. Since it's mainly compromised of negative emotions, he thought he would be able to feed off it to strengthen himself. He said that it fought him and was intelligent. We knew that though, because it keeps adapting," Taklishim continued. "She pulled a great deal from Jax. From my own look at him, it appears she pulled about half of it."

Jax was crying silently, his shoulders shaking, his face bowed in shame. It pulled hard at Smitty. "What does that mean?"

"Well the last time, when you and I were there," Taklishim explained, "she had pulled the small amount from Dr. Stone, and then a small amount from Jax. I don't think what she pulled from them was even half the amount she just pulled."

Smitty shuddered at the memory, and looked over at Ronnie. Fuck. No wonder he wasn't letting her go. Ronnie wouldn't meet his eyes, they'd both seen things they wouldn't ever want to talk about. He gave a sad smile.

"Where do we go from here?" Smitty leaned forward letting his head hang down.

Degataga spoke, "Jax's soul is damaged right now. From what we can tell, the only thing that will help fix it, is her. It's a part of who she is. What we learned from that man, about what is in Jax, is, that energy is a make-up of all the emotions Jax has stuffed down from the things he has dealt with in his past."

"You are telling us that Jax created this?" Aedan was dumbstruck.

"Not completely," Taklishim added. "That's where it started."

"Jax," Degataga looked at him, "you need to use the stuff I sent you." Jax didn't respond. Smitty didn't think this was the time to push him. "Your past is colliding with your future in a way we can't really predict given your choice of field work. The empath abilities you have attract the negative emotions around you, due to what you have inside you already. It feeds off it, and grows. It learns the patterns and behavior that strengthen it, and that is what it calls."

"That doesn't tell me how we can fight it," Smitty interrupted.

Father Roarke spoke softly, "You can't. All you can do is love him."

"Bullshit!" Smitty yelled. "That's all we have been doing and it hasn't helped at all."

"That's not true," Degataga said calmly. "He's still here. The love you guys have for each other has kept him going. Without it, I believe he would have killed himself."

Ronnie broke down in tears, and Aedan visibly shook. Smitty glued his eyes on his friend. "Jax, have you considered suicide?" Smitty wasn't sure he wanted to know that answer, that he could deal with it. The look on his face was all Smitty needed to see, and he ground his teeth together in fear.

"Okay, so why is it worse now?" Smitty moved on, not knowing how to process all this.

"Airiella," Taklishim answered.

"Wait, you just said she would help him, how did she make it worse?" Aedan piped up, happy to be off the suicide remark. Shit, they all were, though Ronnie was still crying.

"She didn't make it worse. It wants to fight the changes she's brought out in Jax," Degataga clarified. "Jax, have you felt more you lately?" Smitty saw his slight nod. Degataga looked at Smitty. "Love."

"There's a lot we don't know. But now that we have had the chance to question that guy, we know a lot more about what we are dealing with. Jax is highly susceptible to negative emotions and energy. Every location you go into, there is a chance that what is inside him will grow, or open him for possession or attacks. This energy is calling it." Taklishim wasn't holding anything back. "Scientifically speaking, it's great because it gives you the evidence you need to prove to those with closed minds that there are other answers out there that they don't want to accept. Personally speaking, Jax is living his own private hell."

Degataga leaned forward resting his elbows on his knees. "Jax, emotional healing is a hard journey. It's painful, time consuming, it leaves scars and it changes you. There is no denying that. There is a balance to life that within you has shifted so far to one side that you have a very hard fight on your hands. Given the baggage you carry from losing Winnie, the guilt you feel over it you are going to be forced to face some ugly truths. If you want to live, if you want to have a chance at a future with someone that is willing to die for you, you have to face them. Emotions are a powerful thing, they carry the ability to manifest absolute horror, but they can manifest miracles and joy like you've never felt. Airiella is living evidence of that. There will always be good and bad, it's the way of life. This has to start with you. If it doesn't, and you die, it doesn't end. You will have unleashed this energy onto the world and she will spend forever trying to find it and remove it."

"That's a bit of a guilt trip he doesn't need right now," Smitty broke in, needing to defend Jax.

"It's not a guilt trip, Art," Father Roarke said. "It's the truth."

"This energy already exists though. In the natural balance of life, there is already darkness in people, didn't you just say that?" Smitty was trying to apply reason and it wasn't working.

"This energy in him, is new. Add in the work with spirits, demons, and other entities you encounter. The empath abilities amplify things in him to that energy, and you get this. What others have is a darkness. We all have a darkness to us, even Airiella," Taklishim explained. "If that energy in Jax was able to get through and plant itself in her, darkness like you have never seen before would become rampant in the world. Think on the level of hatred you saw in the holocaust. Just more. This energy in him has evolved from just being his own emotions. Its alive and has its own agenda."

Smitty saw the bigger picture. Judging by the look of terror on Jax's face, he did too. "We can't help him?"

"You can, but you don't fight hate with hate. You fight hate with love," Father Roarke broke in.

Degataga softened his tone, "Positive reinforcements. Small changes to start restoring balance. You've seen it in Airiella. Her struggles to overcome the emotions she carries from her past. The same applies to Jax. The most important difference is she is willing to face it and fight it. Jax, no one can make you do that. It's got to start with you."

"I get it," Ronnie said, his voice numb. "I've been battling this with her. I get it, Jax. You know you've got me."

Smitty realized then that more had been happening he hadn't been aware of. Smitty gestured to Airiella, "Any better ways to deal with this? If she pulls it all out of him what happens?"

"I don't know." Taklishim sounded frustrated. "The best we have been able to come up with is the holy water works because Jax does have faith in God, and this all started with him. So, because of that belief that resides in him, that holy water works to purify his soul, it's an effective strategy. There are still those of us that think salt water may work too, but it has to be the sea, an ocean. We haven't found any recipes passed down through our tribes using plants from the earth that will kill this. My own personal belief is Jax will come to great harm if she pulls the rest of this without him fighting for himself. I think it will kill him; it's rooted so deep inside. If she pulls it, his soul might shred. That's why we keep pounding it into you Jax that you have to start fighting for yourself."

Aedan bit back a sob threatening to come out and Smitty saw he was still shaking. "I can't claim to understand any of this. Logically, the words make sense in a literal meaning, but applying it is another side."

"Because your eyes haven't seen what ours has," Taklishim told him.

"You know she is different, but you haven't seen the miracle take place," Father Roarke added.

"You felt what she went through, right?" Degataga was a little less gentle now, his patience growing thin.

Aedan grudgingly admitted he did, Smitty *knew* he felt it. "How did it feel to you when she died?"

Aedan glared at Smitty. "You know damn well how it felt."

"I know what it felt like to me, not to you."

"Like a part of me was lost."

"Has she ever shown you what it feels like when she pulls an emotion from you?" Ronnie asked quietly.

"No, I've felt her share emotions," Aedan said.

"Have her show you what it feels like. It will give you a little bit of a better idea of what Jax feels." Ronnie didn't leave much room for argument. Aedan nodded.

Smitty looked back at the two medicine men. "Is that all?"

Degataga and Taklishim shared a look that set Smitty's teeth on edge. "No," Degataga started. "But Taklishim will have to explain it."

"She's known now. In the spirit worlds. The scream you heard from Jax when she died, it echoed across the realms. They know what she can do, who she is. They will come for her, the ones that want the light gone. Tama and Onida said that there is much chatter about it, and they are watching."

"Can we fight that?" Smitty asked tightly.

"The same way you fight them now. These spirits aren't what Jax has. But they can and will try to use him. Exorcise them, move them on before they can hurt anyone."

"Fucking great," Aedan mumbled.

"Look for human possession, she doesn't have to go through this," he motioned to Ronnie and Airiella, "to fight these."

"The lightning will ash any of the energy from Jax that possesses a human or figures out a way to manifest." Degataga added, "She shouldn't feel guilty about that either. Those that is uses are already marked for the below world, their souls already gone."

"She can feed it love and the energy will die?" Jax asked quietly.

"In a newly affected person, I would think that would work," Taklishim said carefully. "In you, it would just buy time. It all has a cost for her, it takes a lot of energy to get rid of this. Regular spirits she can release whatever she pulls in the normal way she did before without the pain and dying."

"The last thing I would need to say," Degataga added, "is be careful with her blood. Her blood carries power, can form connections, can heal, and can likewise be used to destroy. Chances are, the spirits that are after her, will want her blood."

Smitty shifted. "Some part of me wondered if that was true."

"She bled on the man in the park during her interview. He has since been healed. Seen the light, he says," Taklishim added. "Kalisha thinks if we use her blood on charms for you all, it might be a more powerful protectant for you. I am against this right now, charms can be taken, and blood magic borders on things I'm not comfortable with."

Smitty agreed with that. "If we can get the stuff in Jax beat back and eliminated, the part that does this," he gestured at her limp body, "goes away?"

"That's our belief," Degataga said.

"The battle doesn't end there, you will still have things to deal with, but I imagine that most of it will be part of your show. The only other caution I would have, is whoever is behind the guy from yesterday in the spirit realm. He could be a problem. We are looking for signs of who it might be."

By no means did Smitty feel like they were in for an easy time, yet he had to admit if they could get this stuff with Jax dealt with they wouldn't have to keep watching her die. That was the positive and he hoped it was true.

"I take it that means I am not the end of her journey here then?" The look on Jax's face broke something in Smitty. He was afraid to hope for a future. That was where him and the guys could help Jax. They could help him see he was worthy of her love. Shit, of their love.

"None of your journey's end with this," Taklishim said. "Your roles are important to the world. The way you show the evidence, both sides of the equation is important to the balance of everything. Your work needs to continue. Where hers ends beyond that, I can't see. I can see that she needs you, just like you need her. The same for all of you."

Smitty had a lot to think about. He had answers to some of his questions, and he started to plan out a method for them to help Jax. The change in him she brought about gave him a new look, and he'd fight to keep what they shared.

Chapter Seven

Ronnie got up from the seat, cradling the woman he loved more than life itself to his chest, and forced himself to hand her over to Smitty. The relief on Smitty's face when he held her almost made Ronnie smile. He wasn't there yet.

"I gotta pee. I want to talk to Jax for a moment too. That cool?" Ronnie fidgeted, needing to take her back in his arms.

"Perfectly fine with me. Go do what you gotta do."

Ronnie took care of his bladder first, and grabbed an apple from the kitchen area he passed. He sat down next to Jax. "She showed me a little what it felt like to take something from someone. She also explained to me that what I felt was nothing even close to what you would feel. So, tell me, how are you right now? That couldn't have been easy to hear."

"It wasn't," Jax agreed. "Did she really die?"

Ronnie choked on the apple he was chewing and felt sick. "Twice. She died getting you to the stairs. The raven sat on you when I got there, telling me to take you first. I got you out and went back for her. She was gone already."

Jax shook and gripped the armrests with his hands. Ronnie knew he was trying to rein in the emotions, but maybe he needed to let these ones out. He reached over and unbuckled Jax's seat belt and pulled him up and to the corner of the plane. He made sure Airiella was still in his sight line.

"Stop holding it in. That's part of it. She does the same thing. She's struggling the same way you are."

"Why would she do that for me?" Jax's lips were pulled in this mouth as he bit them.

"Really? Come on Jax." Ronnie let the sarcasm fly. He was still too raw to sugar coat anything.

"When was the second time?" his voice a whisper that made Ronnie think of a scared child.

Ronnie broke out in goosebumps. "Getting rid of the energy she pulled from you." Ronnie closed his eyes. "Look, I can't lie to you. It was the most fucking brutally, awful thing I have ever seen. I also know that if you don't make effort to fight for yourself, I will walk away. That shit she went through can't be for nothing. I've stuck by you through everything, I don't regret one part of it. I won't watch you let this destroy you though. And I will fight her tooth and nail on doing that again if you aren't making an effort."

"How do you beat back the fear?" Jax asked quietly.

"I don't. You think she beats it back?" Ronnie was astounded. "She told me she is scared all the time. It terrifies her. She does it anyway, out of love. You can't honestly sit there and tell me that you haven't felt the love that radiates out of her."

"I've felt it. It scares the hell out of me," Jax admitted slowly.

"Yeah, well it scares her too. You saw a fraction of what she's been through, first hand, as she tried to face it down. Jax, I will help you every step of the way. Besides her, there is no one I love more than you. We can't fight this for you, though," Ronnie pleaded.

"I know. That was shoved at me enough that I get it. Right now, I just feel like there is a hole in me and it's bleeding. I don't know how else to explain it. It fucking hurts. Like a thousand times worse than Winnie dying."

Ronnie winced. "Want me to bring her back here with us?" He didn't want to share her right now, but for Jax he would.

"What if I hurt her again?" Jax paled significantly at that thought, and he had been pale already.

A bitter laugh escaped before Ronnie could catch it. "I'm sure you will. Fuck, I think we all will, but she would back each of us into a corner if we argued with her because we were afraid to hurt her. As for right now, if you hurt her on this plane, I'm going to knock your ass out and throw you out the door to see if you know how to fly."

Ronnie stood up and walked back to Smitty who handed her back reluctantly. "Sorry," Ronnie mumbled.

"Trust me, I understand," Smitty said quietly, a sad look in his eyes.

Ronnie held her close for a moment before walking back to Jax and settling her across both of their laps. Jax slid his hand up her pant leg so he was touching her skin and watched him visibly relax. "Maybe if I had seen what you saw it would force my hand," Jax thought out loud.

"No. I'm not sure you'd ever be able to see it. You're out cold when she does it. Besides that, it damn near killed me. I can't tell you how many times my heart completely stopped and the sounds tore me apart. Jax, I know Smitty doesn't like to talk about it, but when the screams stopped, I wanted to die. I couldn't handle the emotions that shredded me to pieces. If I'd have had a knife, I would have ended it."

"You look pretty wrecked," Jax admitted sadly.

"I was nothing but an empty shell with the screams of her dying echoing through me. And when it stopped, I wanted them to start again, because at least then I knew she was alive. That killed me even more, to think that I was wishing the pain back on her for my own selfish reasons. When she started to heal, you could hear her bones moving back into place, and she glowed with the most amazing light. So bright that my eyes felt like they were burning, but

I couldn't look away. Warm light that shone down on all the broken pieces of me, showing me in clear detail, how much I needed to work on myself. I saw every failure, and I also saw her love putting those pieces back together in a way I didn't think possible. She floated there in the air, I'd never have believed it if I hadn't seen it. Her broken body healing itself, glowing like starlight, and somehow, with her not even breathing, she managed to fill me with love."

Jax crumbled forward, jabbing her knees into his eyes and Ronnie saw Smitty stand unable to stay away any longer. "You told him?" Smitty was pale and trying not to shake.

"Yeah. I can't lie to him Smitty." Ronnie watched Jax fall apart.

Smitty kneeled, his hands resting on Airiella too. "This is her power Jax. She breaks us so we can rebuild with love. I don't know how else to put it."

"It's not her that breaks us, it's what she's willing to do for us that we won't do for ourselves, that is what breaks us," Ronnie corrected. "She finds worth in us, even if no one else does, or we can't."

"I didn't save her at all, did I?" Jax cried quietly.

"No," Ronnie said honestly. "I understand why you did what you did, though. Like I said, with the roles reversed, I probably would have done the same. Your heart was in the right place."

"Jax, she's told me so many times now that she would die over and over again to save us, to save you. You need to fight for yourself so she doesn't have to do that." Smitty was blunt. "That's how we save her."

Ronnie saw it sinking in and he leaned his head down into hers. Even like this she was healing them bit by bit. "I saw her glow," he heard Jax's hoarse whisper.

Aedan saw them all gathered at the back of the plane and he couldn't join them. His brain refused to believe the fantastical things they had said. The proof sat there on the plane with him, yet he couldn't make it mesh.

He fully believed in her abilities, kind of hard not to, he'd seen them in action. He even believed in the connection and now better understood the power it held for her. Whatever Ronnie and Smitty had seen, didn't gel though.

He was absolutely scared shitless that he would have to see it, and it would turn his world on its head. But there was also a part of him that recognized he would never believe it until he saw it. It was undeniable that Smitty was changed by it, and while it was still too soon to tell with Ronnie, he felt a difference in him.

Logic and science, those were his strengths. This was neither and he felt utterly useless. He knew Mags would jump in feet first, and now that she was pregnant, it scared him even more. As the plane taxied to the hangar he grabbed as many of their bags that he could carry and waited impatiently.

He wanted off the plane and to hold Mags in his arms. Something that felt normal, safe and rooted him in life. The moment they opened that door, he was outside breathing in the fresh air and looking for her. His eyes caught the golden hair flowing behind her as she bolted towards him catapulting herself into his arms.

The bags all fell around him as he felt something in his gut release. If this was how they felt about Airiella, he got it. He loved her too, but Mags was his life. He felt her tense in his arms. Ronnie must be out with Airiella.

She tried to push away and move that way but Aedan held her tight. "Don't go. Not yet. He's not ready to let her go yet. Smitty went through the same thing."

"She's not moving, Aedan. I thought you said she was okay," Mags accused.

"She's alive. She's healed. It's internal that is healing. It's why Father Roarke said she's still out." Aedan didn't know if he believed it, but it's what he told her. "I just want to go home. Well, the temporary home."

She nodded resolutely and helped him gather up

the bags and get them loaded up. "We won't all fit in one car."

Aedan nodded to a second one that was pulling up, Tama behind the wheel. "Ronnie will ride with Airiella in that one."

Mags looked unsure as she watched him head that direction. "Are you lying to me? Or keeping things from me?"

"No, I'm not lying. They said she will be fine. We learned more on the plane. I'll fill you in when we are alone." Aedan loaded the bags in the car.

"The internet is calling her a hero. The footage shown is intense. Have you looked at it yet?" Mags asked as she watched Ronnie get in the other car.

Aedan shook his head no as Smitty and Jax approached. "Didn't have time. I'll look in a while. It can't be worse than what I saw while being there."

Mags took his hand in hers. "Let's go. You all look exhausted." She cupped Jax's cheek as he gave her a little hug before getting in.

"Take us back, boss," Smitty told her weakly and leaned his head back.

They were all together, that had to mean it would help, Aedan told himself. Maybe they should all lay together in a pile like they had in Jax's room. Maybe he'd ask Smitty about it. He needed time with Mags first.

Ronnie was stressed. It had been a little over two days since they got back. No change. Smitty had been bringing him food and Ronnie was close to losing his damn mind. He carried her back to her room since it had the biggest bath tub. He'd asked Mags to prepare a bath for her like one that she would take.

Ronnie could care less if he smelled like a girl, he was getting in that damn flowery water. Smitty said he thought it would soothe her. Ronnie would do anything. Mags passed him as he walked in her room and he paused so she could whisper words of encouragement into

Airiella's ear. He didn't even snarl at her when she gave her a little kiss.

He just needed her back. He wouldn't even care if she yelled at him about being possessive and not sharing. Anything at all would ease his mind. Taklishim, Degataga, and Tama had been by every day to check on her. They all said she was fine. He didn't know how they could say that, this wasn't fine.

He growled as he stepped into the tub holding her. This wasn't fine, he thought again. He settled her between his legs and reached for the shower head so he could wash and rinse her hair. Thoughts of her running her hands through his hair, through Jax's hair flew through his head.

He did that for her. Massaged her scalp as he washed, then conditioned her hair. He thought she moved, but it was probably the water. He washed her, massaging every inch of her skin, rubbing life into it and he heard a moan.

He froze and waited, but there was nothing else. He took his time after that, the close proximity of her naked body having a profound reaction on his own. "Damn it, wake up Airiella."

He drained the tub and stood up carefully and dried them both off. He grabbed the jasmine lotion Jax had gotten her and buck naked, went back to his room, closing and locking all doors. Time to see if the fingers that had been called magic before could work it again.

My first thought as I started to wake up was that I liked the song that was playing. The second one was that whoever was touching me needed to keep doing it. I smelled jasmine and wondered if heaven smelled like jasmine. The aching in my body firmly told me I was not in heaven.

Rather than opening my eyes, I just enjoyed the massaging touch. I knew it was Ronnie. Their touches all tingled in different ways. Plus, if it had been Smitty the connection we shared would have told him I was awake.

I had a habit of waking up naked when around these men, right now though, I didn't care in the slightest. My last thought had been a pain so intense that it had felt like my body was ripping itself apart, filleting my skin open and pouring acid on my nerves. Thank God that was over.

"Please Airiella, come back to me." I heard the ragged edge to Ronnie's voice and felt bad for not letting him know sooner.

"I thought you called me angel, are you mad at me?" I tried to speak but my throat wasn't having it.

"Oh fuck! Angel!" I found myself being crushed to his very naked body. Definitely not going to complain about that.

Until I felt him sobbing. Oh no. I remembered Smitty after I woke up last time. It would have been worse for Ronnie. I pried open my eyes, and was immediately happy he'd had the blinds turned down. The little light he had on stung. His face though, I'd let my eyes burn if I got to see his beautiful face more.

I moved my arms to hug him and stifled a groan at the movement. No magic juice from Degataga I guessed. "Ronnie, I'm okay. I'd never leave your beautiful face," I whispered.

He chuckled and in a teary voice, "I missed you."

"Water please." Jeez, my throat hurt. Fire. I'd been in a fire. It all came back. I tried to sit up but Ronnie was holding me too tight. When he let me go, he handed me a funny colored water, I raised an eyebrow.

"From Degataga, they've been checking on you every day. He had said it would be soon that you'd wake up," Ronnie said quickly.

The magic juice that would take that pain down a few notches. I'd gladly sip brown water for that. Only I didn't sip it. I downed it. "He's here? Where are we?"

"Back in Cali. Taklishim, Tama, and Degataga are here along with Father Roarke." Ronnie's eyes were raking over me.

"All of them? Why? Is Jax okay? Smitty?" I worried.

"Everyone is fine. All worried about you. The live

show created a bit of a media storm and we needed to beat feet out of there as soon as we could. It's been two and half days since you've moved." Now the pain in his voice was as naked as he was.

My throat was only partially soothed by the magic juice. "More water please."

"Take it easy. It's been a while since you've had food, your stomach might revolt a little," he told me softly and handed me a fresh water.

I swallowed more water, slowly this time knowing what he said was true. "How bad was it?" I touched his thigh. That glorious, hard muscled and naked thigh.

"Bad. I understand Smitty's reaction now, and fully forgive him for the way he acted. I haven't left your side."

"You look tired, are you having nightmares?" He kissed me, gentle at first, then with overwhelming passion and it was a good thing I was already sitting, that kiss would have dropped me. All of my nerve endings lit up, but not in pain, in the most delicious heat. I groaned into his mouth, needing more.

He pulled away from me and gave me a wicked smile. "I have you naked in my bed, why the hell would I have nightmares in that situation. You are lucky you aren't sticky right now."

There was the Ronnie I knew. Just as quickly though, his eyes became haunted again and filled with tears. "I'm okay Ronnie." I leaned against him soaking him up.

"Angel, that was the scariest shit I have ever seen in my life."

"Didn't Father Roarke warn you?" I stroked him hand over his skin.

"I'm not talking about that. That part was beyond scary, I'm talking about seeing the lightning hit that house and go up in flames with you, Jax, and Smitty inside it. I'm talking about the shit I saw on the screens in the tent. I'm talking about running down those stairs and seeing your lifeless body lying there surrounded by flames."

"I remember it now," I said quietly. "You brought

me back though.”

“The other part, that was pure hell.” He rubbed his hands up and down my arms. “Jax asked me what it was like. I couldn’t lie to him, so I told him as best as I could so he got the general feeling of what I was talking about.”

“Is he okay?” I asked.

“Physically yes. Emotionally, no.” Ronnie didn’t hold back.

“Nightmares?” I wondered.

“Not recently, Taklishim gave him something to help him sleep.” Ronnie dropped a kiss on my head.

“And Smitty?” I knew he would have struggled.

“Hovering. Keeping his distance because I gave him the same, he gets it. Aedan doesn’t get it at all. Mags has been keeping the peace.” I smiled at that.

“You made it through,” I said as I laid my hand on his chest.

He covered it with his own. “Barely. Father Roarke had a few moments of doubt.”

“Don’t downplay it for me, Ronnie,” I demanded.

“I thought I was going to die. If you hadn’t started breathing again, I would have demanded they bury me with you.” He took a shaky breath in. “I told Jax that it was like every scream you made broke me, and when you died everything in me shattered. Then when you glowed, you shone so bright that it showed me all my broken pieces and all my failures. It felt like none of them mattered because you loved me anyway and you put me back together with your love.”

“Ronnie, that was beautiful. Hard to hear, nonetheless beautiful.” Tears pooled in my eyes.

“What is beautiful is you, sweetheart. All that shit showed me just how much I love you, something I didn’t think was possible. It showed me that I have the capacity to love. Real love. The thought of never getting to tell you how much you mean to me and how much you have changed my world, my life, scared me to death. There is no one on earth that has impacted me the way you have.” Ronnie’s words washed over me.

I didn't even know I was crying until he touched my face. "Angel, you healed me when you healed yourself. All that shit from my past I was holding on to, it was gone in an instant watching you heal. Every wound on your body that fixed itself before my eyes put one of my broken pieces back together in a way I can't explain, other than it's how you see me."

"Ronnie, it *you* who is healing *me*. When you say things like that, those holes inside me fill up," I told him.

"Words have power, it's true. But Angel, I intend to back those words up with action. Please tell me your body is healed," he whispered against my hair.

"I'm sore, but the wounds are all healed, I think. Now that I drank the magic juice, the pain is receding. Why?" I frowned.

"Because I'm about to show you how much I care," he growled and flipped me over covering me with that glorious naked body of his.

"Okay," I purred. "I won't argue." I pulled his face down to mine and sucked on his lower lip, watching his pupils dilate and eyes darken to the color of a forest.

"Tonight, you are mine," his voice rasped and I sunk into his kiss. He trapped my legs between his and brought his knees up to my hips, holding me in place. "Tell me now if something on you hurts because I intend to touch every inch of your body."

Heat pooled in my belly and the connection between us sparked a visual spark. "Nothing I can't handle. My throat is the worst," I added. "Start now. Touch me," I begged.

He sat back on my thighs and ran his fingertips over my throat. I knew it had to be bruised, I'd seen the other bruises scattered all over as I moved. He leaned forward and brushed a kiss across my throat, so gentle and soft.

He sat back again and lifted my left arm, kissing the healed bullet wound first. Then up and down my arm to the tips of my fingers. He did the same with my right arm, across my collarbone, sucking lightly at the base of my neck on each side.

He trailed his lips up across my face and kissed me again before he got up off me and started again at my feet, working his way up one side and down the other. A slow tease that was driving me insane. He skipped right over where I wanted his mouth the most and went up my belly, paying attention to each breast before flipping me over.

He kneaded my back with his hands and followed with kisses and sucked at my skin at the base of my spine, his teeth grazing over sensitive parts of my skin I didn't know I had. Down the back of my legs, his tongue tickling me along the way.

This was entirely way too one sided. I wanted my hands on him. When I went to move, he held my hands in his. "No angel. This is my time. My way." His husky voice setting fire to the parts of me he had ignored.

He turned me back over and pushed my thighs apart and settled between them. "Ronnie, please."

"I do like hearing that, but not yet. It'd be over way too soon angel." He kissed me again, pouring his heart out into it, his love covering me whole, freeing my hands when he cupped my face. I traced his chest with my fingers letting that spark we shared tingle his skin like mine did. I brushed my thumbs over his nipples lightly enough to tease.

"No baby, if you touch me, I'm going to give in to you." He moved my hands back up and put them under the pillow. "Leave them there. I'm not done yet."

"As long as you understand that I will get my turn," I challenged, the need in my voice apparent.

He nodded and slid back down my body, dipping his tongue in my belly button and nipping his teeth on my hip. He slid his hands up under my ass and lifted me off the bed, his eyes hot on mine as he breathed me in. "Sweet like honey," he growled and slid his tongue up me.

Fuck, yes. He was a God. My hips bucked as my back arched up. "Ronnie," I mewled pathetically.

"Yes angel." He licked again. "What do you want?" He flicked his tongue fast over me, then blew lightly across the swollen little bundle of nerves. Oh god. I wanted more but I couldn't speak. He sucked lightly then rapidly licked and blew again, then back to a suck. In no time at all, I exploded on his tongue.

A hoarse cry tore from my mouth, my hips twisting violently as he lapped at me, one orgasm crashing into another. He let me come back down and roamed back up my body, sparks flying between us, he bit a nipple and my body jumped. "So fucking beautiful that I almost came," he rasped and bit the other nipple.

He crushed his lips down on mine again and I wrapped my legs around him, trying to pull him into me. He rubbed himself along me, allowing my body to slide along his hard cock, but not letting me have it. I was wild with need. He slid a hand along my belly and one under my back, then flipped me again and pulled my hips up.

He ran himself along my folds and as I was about ready to cry in frustration, he slid slowly in, holding my hips still so I couldn't move. Slowly, he tortured me until he was fully buried in me. My breath coming out in gasps, his just as ragged. He was huge. I felt every twitch he made deep in my body, every nerve burning with the need he ignited in me.

"Fuck angel, you are so tight, this isn't going to last." He growled. He slid his hand around my hip bone and found the still extremely sensitive bud, wringing a harsh cry from me as I thrust backwards on to him, needing him to move. "Not yet baby," he ground out, swiveling his hips, making him rub against that spot inside that others never seemed to find.

He worked with his fingers as he started to move, slowly at first, then a little faster. His skilled fingers quickly bringing me to another earth-shattering orgasm that had sparks lighting between us, that connection with him begging to be made.

He pulled out and spun me around. "I need to see you when I come." He kissed me again and didn't go slow this time as I wrapped my legs around his hips, pulling him to me. Holy hell this man was magic between my legs as he rode me straight into the strongest orgasm that I think I've ever had, and he toppled right over that edge with me as I clenched around him. The waves so powerful I couldn't even make a sound.

The room lit up blue around us as the connection flared to life, his emotions slamming into mine as mine did him. It was incredible and potent, like I knew it would be. He kept sliding in and out of me as it went on and on, the air shimmering around us, both of us brought to tears as it ended.

I threw my arms around him and poured my soul into a kiss that I hoped told him everything he needed to know. He held me as we shook in the aftermath of what had to be the best sex of my life. No offense to Smitty, because he was damn good too.

The connection I had with Ronnie was mind-blowing. "You might not be let out of this room for a week angel," Ronnie gasped.

"I'm okay with that," I said into his side. "I don't doubt your abilities in bed anymore."

His laugh was the best medicine for my soul. "I can't believe you had doubts. I'm legendary," he joked. "Angel, I don't think there is anything more special than what just happened." His face was serious.

"It was amazing, Ronnie. I've never felt anything like that before."

"Stay put," he got up, slipping out of me. My body aching to have him back. He came back with a washcloth and cleaned us both up. "I think they all know you are awake now."

"Why do you say that? I barely have a voice," I said, confused.

"I have one, and I think we made the power flicker," he nuzzled me.

"That was our connection," I told him, tracing the ink on that sculpted, magnificent chest.

"You felt that with all of them?" he said in wonder.

"No, not like that."

"Even anything close to that and I'm surprised Smitty let you out of his sight. Aedan has Mags, so I get that one, but still, damn," Ronnie growled.

"It was different for each of them, nothing like what you and I just experienced. That's us. Only us, Ronnie." I put my heart out there for him to feel.

"I love you so much, angel." He pulled me into him.

"I felt it Ronnie, I know what you feel." I tapped his chest. "You should be able to feel me now."

"I do, and it's incredible. You aren't hiding anything, I can feel it all." His eyes shone as he looked at me.

I climbed on top of him, straddling his hips and kissed his cheeks, his chin and his forehead. "It's all there for you to see, you sex god."

His hands settled over my hips as I felt him come to life beneath me. Perfect, my plan was working. It was payback time. "Sex god?"

I nodded at him as I slid down his body. "My turn." I leaned over and bit his nipple, flattening my tongue over it and licking it. He bit back a groan, and I did the same to the other one. "Don't move." I gave him a wicked smile as I used his words against him.

"Angel, you are playing with fire," he warned.

"Good, I've never been afraid of a little heat," I told him, using the very tips of my nails I dragged them down his chest just enough to make goosebumps break out, then traced each one of those ridges with my tongue.

It turned me on to see his face fill with desire. "Fucking incredible," he whispered, but didn't move his hands. I turned my nails to his sides, dragging them down and watching as his belly jumped. Next were his thighs, his coarse hair tickling my palms, legs muscles tense under my hands. No nails this time, I used the tips of my fingers to trace the contours of the outsides of his thighs, then up along the insides.

"You are a girl's wet dream," I told him, dropping a kiss on his stomach. His breath hissed between his teeth as I ran my tongue over his balls, feeling them tighten. I sucked one in my mouth and rolled my tongue over it, then did the same to the next.

"Oh fuck," came the quiet moan, his body quivering.

"Do you have any idea how hot that is? How much it turns me on to see you trembling like this?" I licked up his cock and his hips jerked. "To feel you move like that under me? To hear your voice when you moan like that?" I ran my tongue over the head of his cock.

His body was taut, his gaze locked on mine. "I'm yours," was his rough cry as I sucked him down, letting my teeth graze the head, my tongue rubbing the sensitive spot under it. His mouth was open and his breathing jagged and sharp as I played with him. Learning what drove him crazy.

I hollowed my cheeks and bobbed up and down a few times, his hips bucking, his arms bulging as he strained not to move them. "I love doing this to you," I told him, sucking the head of his cock while I pumped with my hand. I cupped his balls with my other hand, tugging a little then moving to rub my thumb under his sack, massaging the sensitive spot behind it.

I sucked him back down my throat fast while I did that and the cry that tore from him was a good indication he was close. I slowed down and he made a wild noise in the back of his throat. "I'm not done with you," I taunted him and climbed back up him, sliding down on him, grinding my hips into him in a slow rotation that rubbed him against that delicious spot inside me.

"Angel," he begged me.

"Touch me, Ronnie," I said. His hands were on me in an instant, his thumb rubbing circles over me as I rode him hard. We came fast, but no less intense than the first time, the room once again lighting up with that brilliant connection.

Wrung out, I laid on his chest. "That's a god given talent right there, angel," he managed to get out between breaths.

"You liked that?" I smarted off.

I loved it when he laughed. "You brought me up and down the ladder so fast my head was spinning."

I got up, needing to clean off, "I'm going to clean up, and I need food. Probably only soft food, but I need something."

"I'm coming with you, and I have some stuff up here already. We aren't leaving this room tonight." Ronnie followed me.

I smiled at that. I wasn't ready to be away from him yet either. We showered and ate apple sauce, there was nowhere I'd rather have been then right there with him. Ronnie told me all about the things that Degataga and Taklishim told them on the plane, and we talked into the night quietly about how we could help Jax.

"Ronnie, I have to ask before we go to sleep, what does the connection make you feel?" my voice was getting sleepy.

He thought about it for a moment, "Life, I'd say. Before you, I was alive, but it felt more like going through the motions. This may be insanely good sex talking, but now, if I touch this," he reached to the connection between us, "I feel life. What do you feel?"

"Vulnerable. Not in a bad way," I clarified when I saw his expression. "You make me feel like it's okay to be that way. That even though you know the ugly truth about me, it doesn't matter. It's a piece that has been missing from my life. This," I ran my finger along the connection, "might be one of the most important things I've been missing. You had it all along."

"Do you mean that?" the raw hope on his face hit me hard.

"With all my heart. You've seen a truth in me no one else has. You shone a light on it, and showed me that it was okay. That you still found beauty in it. What can be more precious than a love that sees the scars and doesn't flinch away from them? Ronnie, this is a gift. It scares the hell out of me, but I wouldn't ever trade it for anything."

"Fuck, angel. You slay me. The gift is you."

I fell asleep with him holding me. We didn't need to say anything after that. I knew the depth of his feelings, and he knew mine. He made me incredibly vulnerable, and it did scare the hell out of me. I was honest though, it was a gift.

Chapter Eight

Jax knew Airiella was awake. The sounds she was making had him hard enough to cut a diamond. He was jealous, but not because she was with Ronnie, but because it wasn't with him. He knew she needed Ronnie, he knew she needed all of them, himself included.

He was genuinely happy for Ronnie, and he certainly sounded happy. Jax was just glad to hear she was back with them. He'd thought a lot about the things she'd told him about the connection, how it's different for each person. He'd also thought about if he'd be willing to share her. He thought if it was just Ronnie, he'd be okay with it. Maybe even Smitty. He couldn't do it with all of them.

He felt it was a pipe dream anyway. He knew she wanted him; he even knew she loved him. He felt that it was just because of what she was. She was made to love; it didn't mean he deserved it. Not after what he heard on the plane.

She'd died for him three times now, or was it four? Saved him countless others. What had he ever done for her? He'd made her dinner once, bought her a coat, and a pillow, and the lotion. Oh, and clothes because some crazy person stole all hers. No math can make that add up.

Jax rolled over, his heart still feeling raw and exposed, his soul broken. The intensity of the feelings he had for her made him want to run. He felt more like himself now than he had in years. He was able to think clearer, get control of his emotions quicker. And fall in love faster and harder.

He pulled out that tin from Degataga he had promised to use. Not yet. She just got back to them. He was afraid it would pull her under with him, like hers did to him. It's not like she didn't already know, it was the shit that was in his nightmares.

Ronnie said she had the same struggles he did. Jax didn't see it though. He'd caught flashes of something, he didn't know what it was. His skin itched with the need to crawl into bed with them. He wouldn't do that to Ronnie. He couldn't. But he wanted to.

He had to do something. He got up and changed his clothes. He'd go for a run. It had been a while since he'd done that. He placed his hand on the door that connected their rooms, the two people that completed his life. Jax needed to learn to fight for himself, he needed to do it for them. He pushed himself away from the door and went for a run.

Smitty heard Jax leave and went to follow. Airiella was awake now, he'd heard the sounds coming from Ronnie's room. That's all he cared about. Jax was running! Holy shit! Maybe they'd gotten through to him. Smitty threw on some sweats and shoes and followed.

A run would do him some good too. Jax was moving faster than Smitty thought possible but he didn't care. It just made him push himself harder. The night was cool, but not cold. Clear sky, and a giant half-moon lit the earth. It felt good. Jillian would be arriving tomorrow, too. Despite all the shit he'd heard on the plane, he would have a couple days of relaxing.

Smitty closed in on Jax in a burst of speed as they ran down the street of the neighborhood, hidden driveways among the trees becoming a blur. Their feet pounding the pavement in the same rhythm so Jax didn't hear him coming up. "Hey!" Smitty huffed to let him know he was there.

Jax glanced over and gave a weak smile. Smitty was breathing hard and didn't bother to try and talk. They just ran it out. On and on they went, eating up the miles. The nervous energy, fear, anger, betrayal from the money man, sexual tension all bled out with each step.

Smitty followed Jax's cues and slowed when he did, sped up with him and stopped with him. Their breathing labored as they both bent at the waist, resting their hands on their thighs before stretching out.

"Any idea how far away we are?" Jax staggered out between breaths.

Smitty shook his head no. "Just walk for a ways." They stretched their muscles out before starting an easy walk back the way they had come. Once Smitty's lungs calmed he looked at Jax, "Damn dude, that was a hell of pace you held. Thought I was going to pass out."

Jax grinned and Smitty's heart flipped. That was all Jax there. "You must be slowing down in your old age."

"Old age? We're the same age, you ass." Smitty shoved him.

"Yeah, but I make this look good," Jax joked.

Smitty stopped and grabbed Jax in a sudden hug. "It's good to see you, Jax."

"Not all the way yet, but so much closer now." Jax said it quietly, though he didn't detect any of the self-pity that had been there before. Maybe he *had* run it out. "I just needed to move. The sounds were getting to me, and it had been too long since I'd run. Gave me a thought that maybe doing this was a start to fighting for myself."

"It is, good start too. Pretty sure that whatever demons you were running from got left in the dust way back there somewhere. I struggled to catch up to you." Smitty started walking again.

Jax chuckled. "The demons never leave me alone. Hoping to change that."

"Joking aside, Jax, you can do this. I believe in you."

"Fear is a pretty big inhibitor," Jax told Smitty in an honest tone.

"When we started this show, you stared fear right in the face. Granted, sometimes you sent Ronnie to stare it in the face while you watched. You didn't let it stop you though." Smitty worked on the positive reinforcement angle.

"Because I wanted to die," Jax put it bluntly. "I was challenging the spirits to just take me."

It stopped Smitty in his tracks. "Are you being serious?"

Shame colored Jax's cheeks as he nodded. "The suicide statement was accurate. I think the only reason I didn't do it was because I am too much of a coward."

Smitty started walking again. "I'd rather not think that you didn't do it because you were a coward. The Jax I know wouldn't do it, because he knew it was the wrong choice. You need to start giving yourself credit. This run, and owning up to wanting to die are great steps."

"I don't have rose colored glasses on right now." Jax faced backwards and walked that way. "I left them at home."

"You know why Airiella is so good for us?" Smitty decided to push him a little.

"Well, the sounds Ronnie was making tell me she's great in bed." There was a hint of jealousy there, Smitty didn't fault him for it though. He'd been jealous too.

Smitty shoved him in a playful manner. "That she is. I'm talking about in everyday stuff. For me, she challenges me to find the good in the situation. That's what she does. That shit she goes through after she pulls that energy? First things out of her mouth are asking about everyone else. She's finding the good in the middle of all the shit."

"I need to find the good," Jax stated.

"Yes, that's how you start to fight this for yourself.

Find the good in what is making a situation bad for you," Smitty advised.

Jax stopped. "Just how far did we go?" He looked around. "Okay, tonight I was jealous that it wasn't me in there with her. The good in that was Ronnie was happy. It made me think though, that I don't deserve that. For the life of me, I can't see why I would."

Smitty listened to what he wasn't saying. "You think she only wants you to finish the connection and not for anything else?"

Jax gave a tight nod and started walking again. His strides a little longer as the doubt in him crept up. Smitty sped up and tried to think of a way to push it back in a positive light. Telling Jax to not be an idiot wasn't exactly positive.

"When she chose me, it felt like I was the experiment, she was just testing the theory out on me because I was the only one available. I wasn't going to complain, because the sex was incredible, and the feeling of the connection being made, as it came to life was like *nothing* else I had ever experienced before. Neither of us knew what would happen or come of it. When I started to understand that I now had some of her empath abilities, I could feel what she was feeling."

"This helps me how?" Jax sounded frustrated.

"Let me finish. She knew what I was feeling and she told me why she picked me. She didn't calm me down or pull anything from me to get me to believe her, I could just hear it in her voice. In the emotions that she willingly opened and offered to me. It dispelled all my fears. Maybe if you are feeling that way, you should talk to her," Smitty suggested.

"Make myself sound more pathetic than I already am?" Jax scoffed.

"It's not pathetic, Jax. It's honesty. Not one thing you have said or done has scared that woman off. You've made her mad and hurt her feelings, yes. She can also tell when it's the energy affecting you and that those words aren't really you. She can see your heart. She sees you,"

Smitty argued.

"She's told me that before." Jax's tone was soft. "I just don't understand why she still wants me. I see me, and I wouldn't."

"This is where you are her are eerily similar. She feels the same way you do. She's afraid if we know too many details of her past that we will run screaming from her. That we will find her ugly, or stained, as she put it to me." Smitty tried to wipe the hurt from his voice when he thought about how she felt for herself. "She doesn't see herself in the same way that everyone else does. Neither do you. It's something that hurts me deep, because I can't hold a mirror up and tell either one of you to look. You will just see what you want."

"She really feels that way?" Jax was incredulous.

"She does. Breaks my heart, too. Out of all of us, I think Ronnie is the one who has made the most progress there," Smitty added.

"He is a persistent bastard when he's trying to make a point," Jax grumbled.

"It's out of love, at least," Smitty snapped, trying to bring Jax back into the moment. He'd known this road was going to be hard for Jax, he wasn't wrong. "Let me tell you what I see in you. It's nothing I haven't said before, or wouldn't tell anyone else."

"I'm listening," Jax said.

"You are one of my brothers. We share successes, we share losses. Despite what you think about what you call failures, or saying you wanted to die, you keep going. Not out of fear, but out of belief in what you are doing. Losing Winnie may have pushed you to start this show, harder than you had been, but it was a path you were already on. I see the grief in you, and I see the guilt you layer over everything you do. You aren't being fair to yourself on some of the things. I also see you going out of your way to help women, or girls, that are being abused in some way. I see that need in you to make things better for them, even if they don't know it's you."

"What if it's just out of guilt that I'm doing it?" Jax

asked.

"Why would it be guilt? You didn't hurt anyone that way," Smitty tried to point out.

"I did though. I was a complete ass to Winnie the day she died." Jax spoke the words that he'd been so afraid to say.

"Jax, being an ass and being abusive are different things," Smitty said with frustration.

Jax sat down on the curb of the sidewalk. "I kept Ronnie from being with her."

Smitty sat down next to him and thought about that. "Is that what started all this inside you?"

"I think so." He dropped his head and wrapped his hands behind it, resting his elbows on his knees. "I knew there were feelings between them, and even though Winnie and I had agreed we were over, I never really gave her a verbal go ahead to explore it. She'd told me she had strong feelings for him. I can't even say it was jealousy that kept me from doing it. I really think it was fear of change. I knew Ronnie would never approach me to ask if I would care if he started seeing Winnie. That's not who Ronnie is. It's what Winnie and I fought about that morning. She left my house livid, and went to see him, and being Ronnie, he wouldn't let anything happen between them. She left there mad too. I was on the phone with her when the accident happened. I heard everything."

"Fuck Jax. You've been holding this in for all this time?" Smitty was stunned. The guilt made absolute sense to him now. And the way him and Ronnie had fought. "You told Ronnie."

"Yeah. That's why things blew up. We've talked it through now, but the guilt doesn't leave. It's also part of why I am so scared to be with Airiella. I can't take another person from him, and the way I feel about her is so much more than I ever felt for Winnie. When she touches me, I see forever with her." Jax gave up the truth.

"Have you talked to either of them about that?" Smitty asked carefully. He knew given Jax's admission that this was shaky ground.

"I have. I'm the only thing in my way. Though Airiella did tell me that neither of us is ready to make that move yet," Jax said, still staring at the ground. "Probably because she knows how fucked up I am. She's seen the nightmares."

"Jax, if there is one thing I can say for certain about that woman, it is no one can tell her what she can or can't do. If she doesn't feel ready yet, there's a reason, and I doubt it's the one you just claimed. I personally think she is scared. I can feel what she feels, remember?"

"She's scared of me?" Jax completely misunderstood Smitty's statement.

"Not of you, you giant ass. Of what she feels for you." Smitty clenched his fists so he didn't punch him in the arm.

"Why?" Curiosity got the better of Jax.

"I think it's because you and Ronnie make her feel vulnerable. That's hard for her. With what she's endured, she has only ever relied on herself to get through it. Having us around, poking and prodding at those memories, making her admit feelings and details, exposes her in a way that I pointed out earlier. She feels ugly, she's afraid we will see her that way and now that she's bared her heart to us, she'll lose everything she's ever hoped for," Smitty told him quietly.

"Fuck. We are similar."

"Yeah, you are. When it comes to her, my suggestion is to listen carefully to what she says. She doesn't hold back the truth, and yes, sometimes it's brutal. Try and see through her eyes. It's made me see myself in a different way." Smitty sent up a silent plea of forgiveness for sharing her secrets.

"What if I can't share her?" Jax broke in to his thoughts.

"That was a struggle for me too, but I looked at it from her perspective. She chose all of us. Maybe she chose us because of some preordained connection none of us ever knew about, I doubt it though. She's strong enough that she could have walked away. She saw something in us she wanted to be a part of." That was the honest truth, and Smitty believed it wholeheartedly.

"I'm surprised you are so open minded about this," Jax told him, glancing at him out of the corner of his eye.

"Why? Out of all of us I'm the only one in an open relationship." Smitty wasn't following.

"Because you apply reason and logic to everything, and this defies all of that."

Smitty stood up, tapped his heart and his head. "She changed me. The two are more in sync now than they ever have been. Think about it. It's always her choice, whoever she is with. If she goes to sleep with me, and hears you having a nightmare, she chooses to go to you. Sometimes she waits until you settle down and comes back to me, others, she stays with you the whole night. It's always her choice. It never changes how she feels for any of us."

Jax stood and followed Smitty as they kept walking back to the house. "I just need to go with it, is what you are saying?"

Smitty nodded. "Yep. Big fucking leap of faith, bro. Totally worth it too. Aedan is having a harder time accepting things, maybe talk to Mags if you need more."

Jax snorted. "Mags will just browbeat me until I agree to whatever Mags thinks I should do."

Smitty laughed, "You have a point, but it's still out of love. She wants you to be happy. We all want you back."

Smitty spied the house up the road. Jax was lost in thought, and Smitty felt in his heart progress had been made with Jax. He'd learned more about what they both suspected was the root of this energy that grew in him. He smiled, wanting the moment to last so Jax was Jax. He reached out and shoved Jax again, making him stumble.

"Race you to the house," he challenged and took off running in a dead sprint.

Two seconds later a grinning Jax passed him, his long strides easily overtaking Smitty. Smitty gave himself a pat on the back while he was still able to move.

Chapter Nine

I woke up with a start, trying to figure out where I was, when it hit me that there were arms around me and I was naked. It was the naked part that threw me for a minute, and it shouldn't have. Reality crashed down around me as it all came flooding back. Biting back a groan of pain as I moved, I looked at Ronnie, sleeping peacefully and hoped like hell that this wasn't going to be an awkward morning after scene. We'd gotten pretty heavy into emotions last night.

I didn't regret it; it was pretty damn enjoyable. Boy had skills. I smiled remembering the multiple orgasms, then I couldn't hold back the groan of pain in my body now that the magic juice had worn off.

Ronnie woke up at that, "Angel you okay?" He mumbled, his voice thick with sleep.

Not wanting to worry him, I cupped his cheek and gave a weak smile. "Sore," I admitted.

He sat up and looked me over carefully, "Did I make it worse?" He asked softly.

"No, don't be ridiculous," I told him sternly. "I'm not fragile, and we were both in that together," I reminded him.

He gave me a sheepish look, "It doesn't look so good right now."

"My throat? Bruises? Or what we did?" I asked for clarification.

"Um, that feels like a trap, no matter what I answer," he joked. I rolled back to my side so he was spooning me again.

"No trap, I promise. But seriously, how do you feel about all of that?" I asked hesitatingly. His heart had been right out in the open all night and I wanted to tread carefully.

"Are we doing the where are we going with this talk right now? While you are naked pressed up against me?" Was that caution in his voice, or need?

"Shit, sorry. Want me to move and get dressed?" I asked, embarrassed. Why the hell was I feeling so weird about this when I had wanted it so much?

"Fuck no. Stay right where you are, angel," he growled in my ear. "We've laid together in bed how many nights now where neither of us has attacked the other? And before your twisted little brain makes something of that, it was in no way, shape or form a comment on me not liking the way you look, or feel, or taste."

Well hell, he had me pegged. "Okay, so..." I hemmed.

"Are you fishing for compliments?" Now there was a smile in that voice that was doing things to me again.

I knew I was blushing. I could feel the heat in my face. "No! My question was pretty straight forward, what are your thoughts on what happened? The connection, the emotions, what we shared?"

"What are yours?" He fired back at me.

I should have seen that coming. I blame sex brain. I sighed, "I don't regret it. Not at all. I think it was a release we both needed and could give each other freely. I like what we have, the friendship with you is the closest one I've ever had. You can touch me without me freaking out, the flirting is fun, there is no pressure. There is sexual chemistry.

Seriously, what is wrong with me right now? God, Ronnie, I'm sorry, I have no idea what my brain is saying. Look, there's some part of me that keeps telling me that being with you would be so easy, so natural, and so good, and I can't tell you how bad I want that. I know that this is forever for me. I *never* want to be without you. Then there's Jax. Every time I touch him, I feel it in a part of my heart that scares the living hell out of me, it's so overwhelming. I hate this feeling of being torn between you two, because honestly, I love you both so much. Shit. Can we just continue as we have been? Can you just pretend that no words just came flying out of my mouth?" I spewed out in a rush of verbal diarrhea. "Fuck, this vulnerable thing is hard."

"Angel, I feel the exact same way. Don't look down, look at me. I don't want what we have to be only this one night, but neither am I assuming because we declared our love that we are getting married, are exclusive, or that you don't have something going on with Jax. All of us know there's something between you two. I'm not going to stand in the way of that, and I also don't want to lose this. I'm going to be selfish and demand more of that, because, damn. I know it sounds awful to say we can share you, but you know what I mean by that. You told me that he and I were your strongest connections, and I am aware his is stronger than mine is." He got that same look I'd seen on Smitty's face that I could only call haunted. "We are coming back to the touching without freaking out comment though, later. I'm not ever going to use that vulnerability against you. Ever. For right now, I'm going to circle back to the sexual chemistry comment. Of course, there is, it's me, and I'm a sex God, you even admitted it. I know it, you felt it, don't deny it," he said tickling me.

Keeping my voice as monotone as I could make it, I said, "I faked it." Biting my tongue to keep from laughing. He went completely still behind me, then launched into a tickling attack trying to avoid the bruises.

"Liar!" He shouted at me as I squirmed away from him and dropped to the floor with a groan. "Shit. Angel, I'm sorry, are you okay?" His eyes went wild when he thought I was hurt. It was adorable.

I grabbed his shirt off the floor and put it on. I held my hand out to him for him to help me stand up, right as the door opened and there was Smitty. "Oh great, a party," I mumbled as Ronnie laughed and Smitty looked between us, his eyebrows raising.

"Nice shirt," he commented. Looked around me at Ronnie and said, "Jax is flipping his shit about this. The sharing part, that is. By the way, why did I have to pick the lock to get in here?"

Ronnie winced. "Hey, it was mutual, and I wanted to be sure that we weren't interrupted. Jax knows the score. So do you. Like any of us can actually get away with telling her what to do?"

"Hey! I'm right here you know!" I put my hands on my hips.

"I heard yelling," Smitty explained, "and I also wanted to check on baby girl, here, and you, Ronnie, to make sure you are okay," Smitty said giving Ronnie a knowing look and then looking at me. "You decent under that shirt of his?"

"Define decent. Ronnie liked what was under here, and if I remember right, so did you," I snickered. Ronnie howled with laughter.

"Dude, you just missed her telling me she faked it, right before you came in," Ronnie told him, laughing.

This time it was Smitty who howled. "Oh, baby girl, I love you to pieces. You can't fake those sounds though, because that would mean you faked with me too, and that is not something I care to think about. My ego isn't as big as his and couldn't take it. But, I do want to check you over so put some drawers on, you are distracting me." He stood there with his arms crossed giving me a look. The haunted expression lying under the surface of his face.

"I'd love to, but you are standing on them," I replied. Flushing as he bent over and handed me my boy shorts, I slid them on and said, "Let's do this." I held my arms out waiting for him to start his examination.

Smitty rolled his eyes. "A half-naked you in front of me saying let's do this, would have drastically different results if it weren't for the fact that I'm worried about touching you," he said laughing gently. My damn facial expression must have relayed something I didn't want to, and they get me in trouble sometimes, because both Ronnie and Smitty growled at me. "No. Stop right there." Smitty grumbled, holding his hand out in a stop gesture to Ronnie, but the words were for me.

"Look at me baby girl," he said as Ronnie got out of bed buck naked and distracted me. I hoped I hadn't drooled. I looked back at Smitty as Ronnie threw some sweats on. "What I said and what you heard were two different things. I look at you and see a beautiful woman, curves for days that I had more fun exploring than I want to think about right now. And obviously Ronnie, given the noises we heard, Ronnie feels same. Me being worried about touching you doesn't mean I don't want to touch you." He pointed to the tent starting to pitch in his pants. "Stop with the feeling ugly stuff. That shit you went through did a number on you and I don't know what hurts on you."

I nodded, shaken up by how much he got from my expression, and quickly realized that he could also feel my emotions from that connection. They both could. "Thank you for the reminder, I'm working on it, I promise." He pulled me into him carefully and hugged me tight, his chin on my head, my head nestled into his chiseled chest. Damn it, I was horny again. Or I needed to feel the connection with him. Or I just flat out wanted him. Maybe both of them. I slid my hands up his shirt and let it tingle for a minute.

"Now please put a bra on because I am still a man, and those are still fantastic boobs, with hard nipples, on a half-naked beautiful woman. And I need to look at you thinking with this head," he pointed to his face, "not this one," Smitty fired off, pointing to the now prominent tent and heading into my bathroom across the hall and walking back out with my bra. "Boobs go in there," he said as he threw it to me. "Stop feeling those dirty thoughts too, it's not helping."

"I heard someone say boobs," Aedan said as he walked in. "Just popping in to check on Airiella."

"Aedan better not be looking at any boobs that aren't mine," Mags said as she too walked in. "Oh, he can look at Airy's, I'm good with that." At that, the mouths of all the guys dropped open. She shrugged, "He's already seen them." Laughing she said to me, "Guessing everyone had the same idea of checking on you." Looking at Ronnie, "Most of us are dressed though." I saw the moment the figurative light bulb over her head went off. She swiveled her head between the two of us mouthing "WOW" at me. "Was it as good as he says?"

Smiling and not revealing anything, I shooed them out so Ronnie and I could finish our morning in peace. They could check me over later. "You didn't really fake it, did you?" He asked me shyly. Momentarily stunned he would even think that after those performances last night, I aimed for laughter to ease his worries.

"You'll never know," I fired back over my shoulder as I headed across the hall to my bathroom. I giggled at the expression on his face and took pity on him, motioning him in with me, "You can help me." I pulled the door shut behind us. "You know damn well that there was nothing faked about any of that." I touched the connection, "This wouldn't be here if it was. It takes two." I pointed to his heart, and then mine, "I wouldn't even know how to fake that."

"I knew it," he crowed. "I'm a sex god." He pulled his shirt off me and took off the underwear.

"Is Jax really worried about sharing still?" I searched Ronnie's face. No doubt I loved him or that he loved me, but I think we both knew that Jax was who I was supposed to be with.

"Don't worry about him. We'll handle it later. For as long as this feels right, we are going to enjoy it." He pulled off his sweats as I jumped in the shower before I jumped him again.

Ronnie joined me in the giant shower, with the light blazing, he looked over the bruises on my back, arms, chest and throat. He gently washed me and soaped up my hair, pulling the shower head down to rinse me, his touch as soft as can be. He dropped down in front of me and examined the bruises on my hips from where he gripped me last night, I kinda liked those ones. I put my finger under his chin and lifted it up. "No guilt, I like those ones."

Ronnie smiled, pushed me back against the wall and cleaned me a second time with his tongue. He's got mad skills. He had me shaking and coming in seconds. He stood up and hugged me, "Not fake." He smacked my ass and pushed me out telling me to dry off. "I gotta rub one out now."

"You know I can help with that," I said walking back in.

"No Angel, I don't want to hurt your throat anymore," he said gently.

I bent over in front of him, my ass snuggled up to his gloriously hard cock. "Get the picture?"

He got it, and 15 minutes later our shower was finally done and I was walking funny.

Chapter Ten

ags saw Airy came down before Ronnie did, she assumed he was checking on Jax. She ran over and threw her arms around Airy. "Tell me you are okay?"

"I'm fine," she said.

Mags touched the bruises around her throat. "Those don't look fine."

"I promise Mags, I'm okay, just sore."

"From sex? Or this?" she gestured at the bruises.

Airy laughed, "Both."

"Tell me, I've always wondered about him," Mags whispered, a naughty look on her face.

"I'm not telling you. Well, I'll tell you it was fucking fantastic, but nothing else," Airy grinned.

"Spoilsport."

"Where is everyone?" Airy looked around.

"Waiting on you in the TV room. I made them go away so you could eat something. Does it need to be soft?" Mags asked instinctively.

"I think soft is best, it's tender," Airy admitted.

Mags handed her a banana, "You still need to take it

easy. Puking would suck right now.”

Airy shuddered at the thought. “I agree. You haven’t told anyone yet?”

Mags put her hands over her belly. “No, blood test confirmed it, but it’s still too soon for any real examinations and I want to wait until at least a month in. Not too much longer. I have an appointment scheduled in three weeks.”

“That’s more than a month,” Airy pointed out. She closed her eyes and in case anyone walked in stood close to Mags, splaying her hand out across Mag’s stomach. “This new ability is kinda cool.”

Mags nodded, tears in her eyes. “This is the best gift you could have ever given me.”

“Hey, I have no sperm. Shit, I don’t even have eggs. This is on you two, not me,” Airy pointed out.

“You know it happened when we were with you,” Mags said softly.

“I do. I can’t explain how I know that, but I do. Makes it more special.” She paused, “I feel two, Mags. Do twins run in your family?”

Mags gasped. “T-Two? Twins? Two babies?”

“Yeah. When I’m touching you I feel three lives. Hang on, let’s do skin to skin, the connection is stronger that way.” Mags pulled up her shirt and placed her hand over Airiella’s. “Feel it Mags?”

Mags didn’t feel anything at first. “No, I just feel you, your skin is tingly.”

“No, go deeper. Concentrate. Feel the connection and like, imagine the threads that it uses and follow them into you. I’m not sure how to describe it. Without touching you I feel just that there is another life in you. When I touch you, I feel separate life forces that glow the same way.”

Mags did exactly as she asked. It took a few minutes but then she felt it and her knees sagged. Airiella groaned as she caught her, Mags quickly getting her feet back under her so she didn’t hurt Airiella. “I feel it, would Aedan be able to? He varies between believing it and not believing it.”

“I’d think he would be able to if he were open enough.” Airy shrugged. “Ronnie said he was having a hard time believing all this madness."

Mags nodded. "He is. I think it's fear."

"Well, go get him then," Airy said, eating the banana. "I'm going to drink some juice if we have any."

"I grabbed apple juice for you, I didn't want the acid in the orange juice to burn your throat," Mags said over her shoulder.

Mags popped her head in the TV room, "Aedan, I need your help for a minute please," she interrupted.

"Everything okay?" He stood up fast.

"Yes, can a wife need her husband for a minute without anything being wrong?" She propped her hands on her hips and raised her eyebrows.

She gave Smitty a look when he laughed and told Aedan the boss was mad at him. "What's up?"

"Come with me and open that stubborn mind of yours, you need to feel this," Mags told him, pulling him into the kitchen where a freshly showered Airiella was finishing a glass of juice.

"Feel what?" Aedan looked confused.

Airiella walked over and took Aedan's hand, placing it on Mags' belly, her hand covering his. Mags put hers over the top of Airy's. The connection between the three of them flared bright and it was easy to feel the lives in her now.

"Oh my God!" Aedan whispered. "Is that the baby? Wait, is that two babies?"

Mags nodded. "Twins, baby. We are having two." Mags eyes shone with the love she had for him.

Aedan looked dumbfounded at Airiella. "How are you doing this?"

She shrugged, "No idea, but it's pretty cool."

Aedan dropped to the floor and kissed Mags belly. "Oh my God!" he repeated, his face awestruck.

"Sshh, they'll hear you, you weren't ready to tell yet," Mags reminded him.

"I'm ready now. I can feel it, they are real." Tears fell as he kissed her belly again. He stood and dragged both of them to the TV room.

Mags saw Smitty jump up at the sight of tears on

Aedan's face, and she shook her head at him. He sat down slowly, not sure what to think. "I've got some news. Where's Jax?"

Aedan ran out of the room, "Jax!" he screamed from the bottom of the stairs. "Get down here now! I need you."

Mags bit back the laughter that was trying to bubble out of her as she held on to Airy's hand, not wanting to let go. Aedan's frantic scream had brought Jax thundering down the stairs and he was towed into the room by Aedan.

Mags let him lead, this was his show right now. She nodded at him. "Mags is pregnant! With twins! Airy can let us feel them! Jax, you are going to be an uncle!" Aedan was shouting.

He jumped over the chair to land in front of Mags and lifted her shirt. "Come here!" he yelled back to the room, not really caring who showed up. Mags laughed then, the moment perfect in her eyes. "Put your hand on her belly."

Airiella squeezed her hand. Mags suddenly hand all their hands on her, the first time she was feeling the connection flow through all of them. With the magic Airiella created, they all felt the little lives that were growing because of the love of this one woman.

Aedan was unapologetically crying, and Jax had tears in his eyes too. "I'm going to be an uncle." His voice was thunderstruck.

"Yes, you are. That means get your shit together, brother-in-law of mine. I want these kids to know how cool their uncle is," Mags said in her nagging tone, but was smiling at him.

"Congratulations, you nag." He pulled his hand away and hugged her. Mags got a round of congratulations from everyone, and settled down on the couch with Aedan so they could start their meeting.

Smitty knew Degataga, Taklishim, and Tama would be here shortly and he wanted to get the internet videos out of the way first. He pulled out his laptop where he already had them loaded up and played them. In the silence afterwards Smitty cleared his throat.

"Only Jax and Airiella can really fill us in on what happened after she sent me packing, which by the way, you need to tell me how you managed to do that, because it wasn't of my free will to leave you there," Smitty asked her.

Jax was struggling and last night's conversation flew through Smitty's head. He understood Jax was battling himself and trying to not feel guilty. Airiella watched Jax, and Smitty watched her, reading her expressions. He felt her frustration, but there was never disappointment, which he knew Jax thought was there.

"Um, well, the guy kicked my ass pretty thoroughly," she said, startling Ronnie with the admission. "I know the moves Ronnie taught me, but I froze." Smitty saw the look she threw at Smitty and his gut clenched, because he knew she was about to lay a harsh truth on them.

"My past reared its head in the back corners of my mind, and my body wouldn't obey the commands that I swear, I could hear Ronnie yelling into my head. I'll try to do better, but please understand, I'm battling some bad memories in that regard. The physically abusive relationships in my past dealt some psychological damage that Ronnie is helping me work on. Not just by training me, but by letting me speak the shit out loud. I know how hard it is to hear, because people tell me their stuff all the time, and I am sorry to burden you with that. Anyway, I think that's why I froze, and I think in those moments, because Jax saw some of those memories, it affected him and he reacted the only way he could. It's not his fault, and if anyone here wants to blame him, they will answer to me. Got that?" she dared them to argue with her.

Smitty smiled at the fierce tone that came out in her when she was protective of them. "No one blames him, baby girl."

She relaxed, "Good. I couldn't feel any emotions from that guy to pull. It was like everything was blocked from me. Jax was not in control, despite what he may feel, yes Jax, I can feel your emotions right now. He wasn't in control and that energy in him was violent in a way that scared the ever-loving shit out of me. So I did the only thing I could do and pulled it. It fucking fought me hard, and I wasn't expecting that. There were moments down there, I thought my skin was going to split in half and it was going to seep out of me. It all happened so fast, but when Jax dropped and the smoke was getting to me and the chicken shit guy took off, my only thought was to get him to safety because that ramshackle house was burning down around us. I let the raven go out of me in hopes that she could direct someone to come get him."

Smitty did his best to repress the shivers that tried to take control as he remembered the various emotions of her that he felt tearing through him. "How can we better help you? I'd rather not see you get beat up again."

"I really wish I had an answer for that Smitty, it would make my life so much easier. I can't even give good answers to people that seek me out for help in the same area. It takes time. Now that I'm actively working on healing those issues, I guess just keep doing what you are doing. Stop the patterns so I learn to break the cycle. It's hard." Ronnie pulled her onto his lap as she trembled.

"Jax, stop." She turned to look at him. "You told me we were more similar than I thought. So that means you are in the same boat as me buddy. Break the pattern. You didn't do anything wrong."

Ronnie stood and dropped her down gently next to Mags, and she cuddled up with Mags while Smitty tried to figure out what was going on. He didn't want another fight between those two. Instead, Ronnie pulled another chair over next to Jax and sat with him, lending support.

"We need to figure out how to help these two," Smitty continued. "That's *our* end game. We all need to step it up and find a way that works. We could have all died out there if it hadn't been for Airiella."

"Are any of you going to tell her what was said on the plane?" Jax asked sullenly.

Ronnie nodded, "I told her last night."

"When did you have time for that? The noises I heard were pretty constant." Smitty sighed. Jax was fighting the energy again.

"Jax," Ronnie warned. Smitty was surprised that it worked.

"Is there something I'm missing?" she asked the group.

"It's possible, if you try to pull all the energy out of Jax he could die," Smitty said bluntly.

She paled and gasped. "Nope. I need to spend some time with Degataga and Taklishim if that's the case. You said they are in town?"

Smitty nodded again. "They're on their way."

She stood up and knelt in front of Jax. "Hear this energy, I know you tried to talk to me, and I don't care what you think. You will not take him from me, from any of these people. I *am* the fucking storm that will end you."

Smitty's jaw was hanging open as she stomped off. "Well, um, let's no one threaten to kill Jax while she's around."

Ronnie snorted. "Don't threaten to kill any of us if she's around. That is one woman who could strike us all dead."

"You men are idiots. Don't threaten people period, and never piss off a woman," Mags said and followed after Airiella.

"Then there's always that," Smitty laughed. Jax got up and followed after them both.

Smitty leaned forward. "I wasn't kidding, we need to step up our game with those two. The more she heals, the stronger her abilities get. The more he heals, the stronger our team gets and we get him back to us. Think Pavlov. We need to reinforce the positive behavior. I ran with him last night and he shared some stuff with me."

"The working him out seems to be great for him, mentally," Ronnie said. "I'll keep pushing him there. The more aggression he bleeds off the better control he has.”

"I agree," Smitty said. "Aedan, positive comments to him. His guilt over every last damn thing that has ever happened will only feed this shit." Aedan nodded. Smitty felt a little better with this out in the open.

Jax kept his distance from her but followed. It stripped him bare when she fought for him like that. The fire and passion in her spoke to some part of him he long thought dead, buried in the repressed guilt he kept inside him.

She paced in the driveway; her arms stiff at her sides which told him she was tense. He longed to give in to the feelings she woke up in him, but he was still too afraid. It didn't seem possible that he could feel love like this for someone that pushed his buttons the way she did.

She equally frustrated him, and made him want to crawl to her groveling at her feet. She still ignited the anger in him, while at the same time making him punch drunk happy. Right now, watching her pace, the groveling was winning out. After her being out of commission for the past couple of days, he needed to be next to her.

He walked up slowly, he didn't want to set her temper off. "Hey, siren. Can you slow down a minute? I just want to look you over."

"It's just bruises," she muttered, but stood still. "You better be you."

"It's me. You silenced the darkness pretty quickly in there." He held up his hands in surrender and stepped closer. "I've been out of my mind with worry since that house." He reached his fingers out and ran them along her throat. The touch of her skin making his body jump to life.

"I'm so, so, so sorry Jax. I reacted without thinking of the consequences you'd pay." Her face crumbled.

No more tears, he couldn't see her cry because of him again. He pulled her to him gently. "I'm okay. Raw and broken-feeling, but okay. Because of you, I'm okay. I'm more me."

"How can I help?" Her voice was filled with angst.

"This helps." He held her, breathed her in. The jasmine and ocean scent filling his soul, her body next to his mending the cracks. He felt her hands slip under his shirt and slide against his back. The damage done from that shit being pulled from him began healing the moment she touched him.

"There's bandages back here, were you hurt?" She stilled her hand.

"Burns from the fire. Almost all the physical damage was done to you," he growled. There was no space between them and it still wasn't close enough for Jax.

"Physical wounds heal, I'm more worried about what I did to you when I pulled that energy," she told him softly, her words filled with concern. For him. Warmth bloomed in his chest.

"Whatever you are doing right now is healing that," Jax said roughly, his throat tight.

"I'm not doing anything," she protested, her cheek resting over his heart, her face tilted up looking at him. The sun caught her eyes perfectly and his pulse went wild with need. When the light hit them like that, they sparkled like a pool of water was on the surface, the gold specks flashing with that glow she had. Like starlight.

"Oh, but you are. It feels fucking fantastic." He tucked his chin so his lips rested on her forehead.

"The feelings you bring out in me petrify me," she whispered.

"Ditto, siren. Run for the hills scared, but I never get too far, because the need I have for you pulls me right back. It scares me even more. Even the thought of not being near you, or not having you in my life is enough to make me feel like I'm drowning, that I have no oxygen in my lungs." Jax's voice got tight.

Her fingers dug in to his back. "I'm going to figure this out Jax. Losing you isn't an option for me."

"What about Ronnie?" Jax felt the jealousy stir and pushed it back.

"What about him?" she asked confused.

"Um, you got pretty close to him last night, from what I could hear," he said sheepishly.

"Please don't." She pulled away from him and he tried to pull her back but she stepped away. "I'm madly in love with him." She searched his face for something. "If you bothered to look, you'd see I'm even farther gone on you."

Stunned by the admission Jax stood there frozen to the ground. "You're in love with me?"

She turned away as the gate opened and two cars came through. "You'll have to figure that one out for yourself. I can't make you see it." She walked towards the cars.

"Wait," he called out to her but she didn't stop or turn around. He saw Jillian get out of one of them and give Airiella an odd look. Airiella bypassed her though and went straight to the Native Americans that got out of the other car.

Jax's body was vibrating with something he couldn't name, and he tried to hold himself still as Jillian walked up to him and gave him a loose hug. "Hey Jax, glad to see you are okay."

"Hi. Smitty's inside," he said woodenly, not taking his eyes off Airiella.

"That's her, huh?"

"What?" Jax wasn't following, her surly tone threw him off.

"The one that changed Smitty, that's taking him away from me." Jax understood the tone then.

"Why the fuck would you think that? Because they had sex? Look how many people you sleep with and he never says shit about it?" Jax defended his friend. Smitty loved Airiella, and Jax knew he loved Jillian, though at times like this he wondered why. "Stop being so petty."

"How is it petty when he tells me that she changed him? How am I supposed to feel about it?" she challenged Jax.

"Knowing Smitty the way I do, I am 100% positive that's not all he said about her."

"No, he wants me to meet her, which makes me think this is more than a hookup," she tossed at Jax, her face screwed up in a scowl. It wasn't a good look for her and Jax felt himself getting pissed.

"It's not a hookup, it's far more than that, and if you pulled your head out of your ass and listened to the man you are supposed to love, you might understand better. She's changed all of us." Jax fought for control. Getting pissed when his soul was torn up wasn't going to be a good thing.

He saw Airiella shift away from Tama and focus on him, alarm in her face. Jillian of course missed it all, focused only on herself and the slight she perceived from Smitty. "You are all sleeping with her?"

Fuck, he flinched as he felt control slipping away from him. "Jax!" Airiella was running at him. "No! Fight it. Please." She reached for him and slid her hands under his shirt again, and the energy in him that fought her made his knees buckle. She groaned under the added weight falling on her and Jax fought to stay upright.

"Jillian, go see Smitty and leave me the fuck alone," Jax shouted.

Airiella's eyes got wide as she realized who Jillian was, and she gave her a weak smile but remained focused on Jax. Jillian huffed away and Jax faltered again, Degataga appearing at his side and taking his weight off of Airiella. She didn't release him though.

Instead, she lifted the front of his shirt and pulled it over the top of her head and put her cheek directly against his skin over his heart. He felt the warm wetness of her tears on his chest, his heart only beating for her as he passed out.

Winnie winced. Since neither Jax or Airy had necklaces on she was able to be there while they were outside. The mix of emotions flowing through the both of them was staggering. Jax had some pretty significant damage from when Airy had pulled from him.

It wasn't anything he couldn't get through with time, they didn't have a lot of that, though. Things had been shifting on this side of the veil since that last live show. She'd felt each of those Native Americans show up over here and search for answers.

Winnie hadn't been able to uncover much of anything other than they all knew who and what Airy was, which shook Winnie. Airy had a big target painted on her now, and in return, so did Jax who was the easiest to get to because of that darkness inside him.

It didn't paint a good picture. The bright spot for Winnie, was the connection with Ronnie was made. It made Airiella stronger, and if Ronnie took his necklace off, she'd be able to talk to him. While Ronnie wasn't Airiella's, what they shared was deep and everlasting. Theirs was a bond that would stand the strength of any storm.

Ronnie would be hers until Jax figured it out. Winnie had seen that much. She'd gotten glimpses of someone else in Ronnie's future and he'd looked happier than ever, she just didn't know who it was. Winnie watched as the two men carried Jax in the house between them.

Airiella stood outside with the woman, she remembered her name was Tama. She was the mate of one of the men, Taklishim, though Winnie couldn't remember which one of those he was. Degataga was the other one.

Torn, Winnie didn't know who to stick with. She figured Jax needed more attention right now, so she followed the men in the house and up to Jax's room where she saw Ronnie trying not to freak out again. Aedan paced while Mags touched Jax's forehead and brushed his hair back. Winnie used to love running her hands through Jax's hair. Thick and dark brown, always soft.

"He needs to take the mix I sent him," said one of the men. The one that didn't have the silver hair.

"I know. He knows. He promised me he would, Degataga," Ronnie said. Okay, that meant silver hair was Taklishim. Winnie should have remembered that.

Taklishim looked at Ronnie, "If you take your necklace off, you'll see her now."

Winnie jolted. She kept forgetting they could feel her presence, even if she didn't show herself. She silently thanked him, and hoped Ronnie would understand the meaning of that soon. It would be so good to finally talk to him.

"He should keep this on for a while," Taklishim told Ronnie, producing another necklace from his pocket. "Kalisha made it stronger and added some healing magic to it. We don't know if it will help him, but it won't hurt." Winnie felt a barrier settle around Jax and she couldn't see him anymore, not really. It was a lot stronger than the other one.

She left to go back outside where Airy was talking to Tama, who was putting another necklace on Airy. Well damn. That concluded her meddling for the time being. She knew Airy would take the necklace off eventually so she could talk to Winnie. If Ronnie hadn't figured it out by then Winnie would tell her to relay the message.

For now, Winnie would work behind the scenes, she'd try to aid the Native Americans how she could and seek out answers on her own. Or at least spy on the spirits that were chattering about Airy to see if she could learn anything useful.

Chapter Eleven

O kay, you have to help me figure this out," I said to the three council members sitting with me in the now empty TV room. Ronnie was up with Jax, Smitty off with Jillian, and Aedan and Mags out at the store.

"Your powers have grown," Tama said her face alight in wonder. "Fascinating."

Airy caught the subtle look that Taklishim gave Tama of deep respect and love. "Is it just Jax left that you have to connect with?" he asked me.

"Yeah. I'm a little afraid to go there with him. Ronnie's was so intense that I can feel him everywhere now."

"You are in danger, Raven. There's no easy way to say it. While you were resting, Dega, Tama and I have uncovered a little more in legends passed down. Onida talks with the spirits as much as she can to try and learn more too. We haven't sat idly by just waiting for something to happen," Taklishim cut straight to the chase.

"Seems more to me like it's Jax that is in more danger," I shot back. "And I need to know how to remedy that."

"Slow down, little bird," Tama said gently. "First, you drank the mix Degataga left for you?" I nodded. "How are you doing with the healing?"

"Slow, but I've made progress. Sometimes it feels like one step forward and two back."

"Will you allow me to check?" Tama asked.

I shrugged. "I don't think I have secrets anymore, do what you need to do." I felt a warm touch in my mind and dropped my walls. She was quick about it and nodded to me that she was done. I left my walls down anyway.

"You have made progress. The more you do, the easier it will be when you make that final connection. Not only that, but your abilities will manifest in many different ways." She took my hand. "Fear will always exist, it doesn't make you weak."

It kept catching me off guard how drastically different my life has become in such a short time, that so many people now knew things about me that those that are closest to me have never known. It's a strange feeling, and that vulnerability that Ronnie brought to life flares bright.

I tried to shake it off, "How does me healing help with connecting with Jax?"

Tama turned my hand over that she still held and traced the lines on my palm. "You are like no other human on earth. You may even be more powerful than those that have come before you. You aren't invincible, and from what we understand from the spirits, the amount of times you can come back may be limited. We aren't sure. What the stories tell me, is that there is a spirit who knows all about what you can and can't do. One so powerful that the spirits won't name it, and fear it's wrath. This energy in Jax might be of this spirit. For sure, it is something that Jax himself manifested, but its very nature called to this spirit and it gave this energy some of its own power. Granted, these are just stories, though many of them have a common thread."

"It's a demon then?" I asked, not really sure where she was going with this.

"No," Taklishim broke in. "Not a demon. I'm not

sure what to call it. Its nature is dark, its purpose is harm. And it wants you. We told you before, that you can turn dark. If you turn dark, that power will be used in the most vicious ways possible. This last go around you had, when you pulled it from Jax, your screams were heard in the spirit world. Those spirits that want out, that want to do harm, they know that energy now that you were releasing. And they know that energy does have the power to turn you. They want it. It will use Jax every chance it gets to try and harm you."

It struck me then how truly bad this situation had become. "Jax knows?"

Degataga studied my face. "You love him." It was a statement, not a question, but I nodded anyway. "Get him to drink the mix. If he doesn't start to fight for himself this isn't something you can fix. He has to heal. Emotions carry great power in all the worlds."

"And I can't just pull it from him?" This was seriously fucked.

"No. Not without risk. It has rooted deep in his soul, and when you pulled it last time, it tore his soul. We think that the connection with you can heal those tears, but I personally think you are right to be afraid to make that permanent yet. Not without him making an effort to fight for himself. It all boils down to emotions." Degataga held his hands out and I took them. "Being around you helps him."

"You have this magnificent gift; you are able to hold more emotions than any human has the capacity to hold. There is no one alive that can feel as much as you. Their bodies and minds aren't capable, it would destroy them, driving even the strongest insane. Yet for you, it is nothing. You wield emotions with an unmatched dignity and grace, can bend them to your will, take them on and in turn release it back out as pure energy. The very matter of all life. Your gift with emotions is so strong that through your connections, you allow them a tiny fraction of what you can do. This is an awesome power that you have, imagine it in the wrong hands." Degataga's voice held wonder and fear in equal measure.

"Okay, I understand that." He let go of my hands.

"You also have the ability to harness the elements. Energy itself. Remember when you were with me out on the mountain and the stream?" I nodded again, that was pretty cool.

"Wait, I thought that was you," I said. "I just fed energy to it."

"That is what I thought too, but you felt the energy of the water, if you can feel it, you can use it. It might not be something you have learned yet because you haven't healed enough, or maybe you need the connection with Jax. I don't know, but you have it. The lightning you manifest is evidence of that," Degataga added. "I also believe that your ability to use those elements is limited. My gut tells me that you can only use them when restoring balance."

"Ronnie said he found something that said it was God's justice? Used to serve justice for those who deserved it, or something like that," I remembered. "The lightning has only come when my life is in danger."

"There are many versions, Raven." Taklishim took over. "We don't believe you are of one faith. We think you are all faiths combined into one being."

"That's a god complex," I argued. "I certainly don't have that."

"I didn't say you had the power of God," Taklishim clarified, "just that your essence isn't rooted in Christianity beliefs alone. This energy shouldn't only react to holy water. In many beliefs, salt water is just as effective. Things like sage may be useful. We were hoping to try things with the guy we talked to, but he doesn't have that energy that Jax has. Experimenting on Jax wouldn't be good."

"Where does that leave this? I need to know how to get that energy out of him without killing him. Oh, and another thing, I heard a voice that I believe to be that energy. When I was releasing it last time, it told me that Jax and it were one and the same. That probably confirms the killing part, right?"

"It spoke to you?" Tama leaned forward, her eyes

intense.

"I think so. I was a little preoccupied, but a voice giving me that message was there. Not sure what else it could have been," I mused.

"It could have been the spirit," Degataga put in.

"I'd prefer to not think that. Wouldn't that mean it could get in my head?" The thought chilled me to the bone.

"Your necklace was gone and your walls were down," Taklishim told me. "That could have given it an opportunity. Either way, it's something we need to look into."

"Get Jax to drink that mix," Tama added. "That's how you help him."

"Did you know he showed up in my dreamscape, or whatever your call it?" I turned to ask Degataga.

He looked startled. "That shouldn't have happened."

"It did, he saw everything until towards the end when I became aware of him and spoke out loud. Ronnie went to wake him up. Is showing up in his something I can expect when he drinks it?" I didn't think that anything he would see was something I already hadn't seen from his nightmares.

"The connection you have with him is strong already if that happened. It may be possible, but this is the first I've heard of that happening before. Was it you that he talked about being in his nightmares?" I'd stumped a medicine man of great power, that didn't bode well for me.

"I don't remember, but it's true. I get pulled in. Sometimes I can tell right away and am able to wake up and try to head it off, other times I'm not pulled in until his emotions are crazy, and it's harder for me to wake up from those. Then there are times when he just screams or cries out and I hear it and go sit with him. There's not really a set pattern that I can see. Most of the time he doesn't even know I'm there."

"You do know that the raven is you, right?" Taklishim questioned me.

"I didn't at first, though I suspected. Now I keep

thinking it's an extension of me. Is that not right?" This crap was so confusing.

"I guess you could say that is a fair description. She is you, though. When she leaves your body, she is an extension of you, that is correct, though she is still you. She can be harmed which in turn will harm you, keep that in mind next time you run head first into a life-threatening situation." Taklishim raised an eyebrow at me. "She is your animal spirit."

"Aren't you a spirit warrior? Isn't it a little hypocritical for you to tell me not to run into danger when that's what you do? And didn't you just tell me that being me, I'm already in danger?" My mouth got the better of me.

"You and I are not the same, Raven. I was born a warrior. I am a skilled medicine man and have many powers you know nothing about. I know how to fight, it's not the same. You ran into a building and put yourself directly in the path of a spirit that wanted you dead without knowing it," Taklishim said angrily.

Feeling chastised, and with good reason, I replied, "Understood. You are wrong though, I knew it wanted me dead. I just needed to get them out of there and wasn't going to send in someone else to be hurt."

"You felt the intent?" Tama asked.

"No, I felt the danger. When I felt the atmosphere shift, I felt the lightning getting ready and that told me my life was in jeopardy. I'm good at reading signs," I explained.

"The fear you felt in the basement," Tama pushed, "the reason you froze, Airiella, that will heal in time. You have to fight it aggressively though. Tell Ronnie to get more creative when he trains you. He won't like it, neither will you, but it will pay off."

Taklishim stood, signaling the others that they were done. "One last thing, Kalisha has performed a binding ceremony on the one who planned that little trap for you guys. He won't be able to harm any of you, or ask others to harm you. It would come at a high cost for him." The thought bothered me because it sounded dark, yet I was relieved to not have to worry about things from that front.

"We will stay in touch." Tama touched my hand again. "Keep working on you. The beauty of your soul is deep and endless." She smiled kindly at me and I walked them out.

"Thank you," I told them gratefully. Degataga handed me a small bag with more tins. "Is this more magic juice?"

"Magic juice?" he gave me a confused look.

"That's what I call it, sorry," I said embarrassed. "The stuff that takes the pain away so I can move."

He laughed. "Yes, and more that can come in handy. I labeled it all and put directions in there. You truly are incredible, Airiella. Keep us informed of anything you learn." I waved goodbye and went to put my magic juice potions in my room. Then time to tackle Jax.

Smitty leaned back in bed after a vigorous round of sex with Jillian and allowed himself a smile. Things weren't great, but they were all under the same roof and that made him stupidly happy. Given everything that's been happening it shouldn't have come as a surprise to him that it was short lived.

There was a knock at his door, which told him it couldn't have been Ronnie or he would have just walked in. He made sure Jillian was at least wearing a shirt before he hollered out for whoever it was to come in.

The door opened slowly and Airiella stood there, her face unreadable, but her tone pissed off. "You care to tell me what the hell you said to Jax to get him pissed off enough to pass out?" she demanded looking at Jillian.

"What?" Smitty cried in shock.

"She pulled up at the same time Taklishim, Degataga, and Tama did and she was talking to Jax when I felt that shit in him stir up. I tried to stop it, but he passed out. He's still out." Airiella was definitely pissed.

"Shit. Was he him?" Smitty was terrified of the answer, Jax's soul was still torn up after she pulled from him, so another episode spelled disaster.

"I think so, but he went under fast. I tried Smitty, I really did," came her troubled response. "All I can tell you for sure, was it was in direct relation to whatever she said. It hit him fast."

Smitty looked over at Jillian whose face was stone cold at being called out. "What did you do?"

"Can we talk about this in private?" she ground out.

"I'll handle it, baby girl." Smitty gave her a look begging her to let him deal with it. "You okay?" He let out a sigh of relief at her slight nod and she left the room, closing the door behind her.

"Baby girl? Since when do you use pet names for strange females that you fuck?" Jillian snarled at him.

"This ends now, or we do." Smitty stood, hardening his heart. This wasn't what he wanted, but he couldn't have her at odds with Airiella because she was jealous. Not with Jax like this. It put them all at risk for some seriously bad shit.

"Are you fucking kidding me right now?" she howled at him.

"Not even a little. You know goddamn well how bad things have been with Jax. You saw the shit on the internet from the last show. You are extremely aware of the danger we were all in. And you purposely set out to start shit immediately upon arrival? What the fuck, Jillian, this isn't you!"

"Well it's not you to sleep around either!" she yelled back.

Smitty froze. Anger rose so fast in him that it was dizzying. "You've got a lot of nerve. Since we've been together you've had how many other side relationships? At least twenty that I can count. Never once did I pull any of this shit. I agreed to an open relationship because that's how you view life. I never agreed to a double standard where you can do what the fuck you want, and I have to stand quietly in the background. If that's what you are looking for, you can just go. I love you, but that shit isn't going to fly with me. Not now. I wanted you to come here to see the dynamics of the group with Airiella in it, to see how important she is to everything. I wanted you to meet her, so you would understand why she is in my life. You didn't give any of that a chance. You went straight for Jax instead."

"That's not how it was. He was out there when I pulled up. He was hugging your new little toy," she spat out.

"Jealousy doesn't look good on you, Jillian." Smitty said evenly. "I used to think you had an open mind. I haven't seen one shred of that since you've been here. It's pretty damn disappointing."

Smitty barely even flinched as his door flung open again and an almost glowing Airiella stormed into his room while a wide-eyed Ronnie stood helplessly in the doorway and quietly pulled the door shut.

Airiella pointed to the chair and told Smitty, "Sit down and shut up."

Smitty sat. He knew better than to argue with her when she was glowing. Her emotions were battering him right now and his need to protect her was boiling up. "Stop. Now. Smitty, I don't need protection. You," she looked at Jillian, "I am assuming are Jillian. If you had taken two seconds to introduce yourself to me, you might have seen I am not a threat to your relationship."

Smitty saw Jillian gearing up to argue and winced internally. "Jillian, for the love of humanity, shut your mouth."

Airiella didn't give her a chance to speak though. "Jax is laying in his bed, unconscious because of you. I am standing here in Smitty's room, yelling through a voice box that feels like it's bleeding, because of you. My emotions are a twisted mess, because you are fucking with his heart and it bleeds into mine. Your own emotions are so nasty right now that I want to throw up. You don't know me, yet you are judging me unfairly based on your own insecurities. You are hurting someone I love right now, and it makes me want to slap the shit out of you."

Smitty coughed a little, shocked at the ferocity coming off the angel in front of him. Mags was right, don't piss her off.

"You don't know what I'm feeling!" Jillian threw words at Airiella hoping they would stick.

"That is exactly what I do. Exactly why I was hired. It's why I am called an empath. Would you like a dictionary? I can tell you every single emotion that is in your body at any time. Do you need an example? How about this? Jealousy, though anyone with eyeballs could see that. Fear, anger, shame, selfishness, indignation. There are no positive emotions in you right now. Not even love. If you claim to love him, where the fuck is it?"

Smitty's heart broke a little bit. "Baby girl..." he started but she cut him off.

"I'm sorry Smitty, I'm not trying to hurt you. I'm trying to cut through the bullshit so I can focus my energy where it's needed, without worrying about you. I will fight for you the same way I will fight for any of the others."

He stood and walked over to her, kissing her on the forehead. "I know. That was just hard to hear."

"Of course, I love him! I'm here aren't I? Despite wanting to be," shouted Jillian, her anger growing at seeing Smitty give affection to someone other than her.

"That's not love. I'm too fucking tired to show you what love is. I've died twice in the past three days. I've had my body shattered, been told a lot of unsettling things, and I'm trying to help Jax. This shit with you, right now, is ridiculous. If you loved him like you say you do, you'd have listened to him. No matter how much you don't want to hear something, you do it anyway," Airiella ground out.

Smitty admired Airiella more than he could say, and his heart hurt at the thought of walking away from Jillian, but he'd do it in a heartbeat if he needed to. "Jillian, I don't know what has gotten in to you, Airiella is not your enemy. I've been nothing but honest with you about her. About the things we've been dealing with, and how she's helped me. Changed me. I've repeatedly told you my feelings for you haven't changed. Why are you acting like this?"

"Fear," Airiella answered for her.

Jillian snorted. "I'm not afraid of you."

"Yes, you are. You have no reason to be, yet you are. I've been bullied and abused by people far better at it than you are. There is nothing you can say that I haven't heard from somewhere else. Letting your fear control you has consequences you might not like so much. Are you willing to lose him because you are too foolish to actually suck it up and listen to him?" Airiella brutally asked.

"I'm not going to lose him," she argued.

"Yes Jillian, you will," Smitty broke in. "I don't want to be with someone who thinks acting like this is okay. It shows you have no trust in my words or me. I've given you no reason to act like this."

"You've given me every reason! You told me she changed you. Jax told me it wasn't a hook up. You wanted me to meet her, like you wanted my approval to have a fuck buddy," she cried.

"That's fear," Airiella said again. The anger leaving her body and she sagged. Smitty catching her before she fell.

"You aren't okay," he told her quietly.

She gave him a weak smile. "I'm tired. My energy isn't quite back up to normal yet." She fought back tears and gave Smitty a sad look. "I also have to have a hard conversation with Jax whenever he wakes up and I'm not looking forward to it."

Smitty felt the emotions she wasn't saying, and forgot all about Jillian. "Do you need me there?"

"Pretty sure Ronnie is going to be my shadow. If it doesn't work, I don't know what we can do. I can't lose him, Smitty. Neither can I be the one to put his life on the line." He wiped the few tears that escaped her eyes.

"It won't come to that, we'll figure it out. Will the connection from all of us help?" Smitty was open to anything.

"I don't know. My walls will be down, so you might have a rough night. I'm hoping that by doing it in the little carriage house back there it will be easier on you guys." She pointed between him and Jillian. "You've got to fix this though. I feel like I'm in a tug of war right now between all of you. That energy and Jax, Ronnie's protectiveness, this between you two, Aedan's skepticism, Mags wild emotions from her, um, stuff. Legends, myths, powers, spirits...it's just a lot."

"Um, hello? I'm still here," Jillian said bitingly.

"Jillian..." Smitty warned.

"I've got an idea, though if the result isn't what you want, I'm sorry. Remember this morning with Mags, or with you, Ronnie, and I?" Airiella whispered to him.

Smitty knew what she meant. She'd touch both of them and act as a magnifier for what they were feeling. He was ready to walk anyway if this was how she truly was, so if he didn't like the results there was nothing really lost. He shrugged. "Might as well."

Airiella grabbed his hand and walked over to Jillian and snatched hers up from where she was holding on to a blanket. Smitty immediately felt the connection flare to life, and instead of giving in to the hypnotic effects it usually had on him, he tried to channel Airiella and instead feel through all the emotions and see if there was anything there.

He felt all the things Airiella called out, though now he also felt wonder. He figured that was the effect of Jillian feeling something like Airiella's power for the first time. He gave it a minute to see if anything changed, and he felt things moving around. It gave him hope.

"What are you?" Jillian whispered.

"Exactly what I told you I was," Airiella retorted, dropping her hand. "If you had listened to him and let him explain, maybe you would understand that. I have nothing to gain by lying."

Smitty had let go of Airiella's hand when she had let go of Jillian's. He didn't think she would feel anything when she reached out to grab Airiella's hand again because there was no connection between them. Her face still showed wonder though and he gave Airiella a questioning look.

She smiled a half-smile at him. "Just calm."

Ah, it was a subtle display that benefited him, but

would be lost on Jillian he knew. He pulled her away from Jillian and hugged her tight. She slid her hands under his shirt and drew on the connection. "Love you, baby girl, I'll take it from here. Good luck. If you need anything let me know."

"Love you too, Smitty." Airiella turned back to Jillian, and in true Airiella fashion, "It was nice to meet you Jillian. I hope you understand I am not your enemy." Airiella gave a real smile and turned to leave.

Smitty saw Ronnie standing in the same spot in the hallway, a troubled look on his face. He was still worried about Airiella. Smitty was too, if he was honest. Her recovery was taking a lot longer than it had last time. He braced himself as he shut the door and turned back to Jillian.

"You ready to talk like an adult, or are we through?" Smitty put it simply.

"What is she?" Jillian asked again. "What just happened?"

"I'm not answering anything until you do. Are you going to act like an adult and have a normal conversation?"

"Yes. I'm sorry for acting like an ass. I'm not sure I like her, but she was right. It's fear."

"She's always right. Emotions don't lie. Neither does she. You and I will never work if you can't get past it. I'm not giving her up." Smitty was unbending in this.

Jillian sighed. "Can you at least see where I was coming from?"

"If I look at it from a third-party standpoint of someone that knows neither of us, maybe. You know me though, you know I've never given you a reason to doubt me, or not trust me. Yet, you still did both. That hurts, Jillian." Smitty wasn't giving an inch. He couldn't.

"Bitches be crazy?" she quipped. Smitty fought back a smile. That was more the Jillian he knew. "I really am sorry. I know I was being utterly hypocritical. I also really didn't think anything through when I saw Jax and just let my insecurities fly. I didn't think it would set him off."

"Jillian, we are *all* in love with her. Including Mags.

You attacked her verbally in front of someone fighting something we don't know a whole lot about, who also has hot button issues with abuse of any type. No sugar coating it, babe, that's what you did."

Shame lit her cheeks a healthy red. "I know. I owe her an apology. Jax too." Smitty nodded. "So are you going to tell me what she is? Or what that was that she did?"

"She didn't lie. She's an empath." Smitty hedged a little. Airiella had let a lot of stuff out of the bag and Smitty wasn't sure exactly what to come clean with. He'd been hoping she'd feel the magic of Airiella, and not question it. He should have known she was too logical for that.

"It's more than that. She died twice? Had her body shattered? The bruises were pretty gruesome around her throat, I feel bad she felt like she had to yell. Must have hurt."

"Yeah, it hurt her. Her admitting it, that was rare though." Smitty ran his hands through his hair.

"Well?" Jillian pushed.

Smitty knew he still loved Jillian, and with Airiella admitting the things she did, even if it was just in the heat of the moment, he believed that meant she saw something between them. He also thought her coming in to try and fix it said something as well. If she had any inkling that it wasn't a lasting relationship, Smitty didn't think she would have made as much effort as she did. He took the risk.

"She's an angel." The look of shock on Jillian's face was priceless.

Chapter Twelve

Ronnie was worried about Airiella. She hadn't been sleeping well, and her energy wasn't restored yet. She's shouldering quite a load, way too pale, and had circles under her eyes that were starting to look permanent, he listed off in his head.

Add in that he could now feel what she was feeling, and it felt like there was a homing beacon in her, his attention was split. He was a little pissed off that Jillian was acting the way she was, and to add insult to injury, she was the reason Jax was now passed out in bed once again.

Ronnie went to find Aedan and found him and Mags in one of the office's downstairs shopping online for baby furniture. Babies, the thought made him pause. What a miracle, especially happening now, in the middle of all this. It hit him then, stopping him mid-stride. Airiella did this for them. He didn't know how, but she gave them this.

He diverted himself and went to the garage to work out instead. He knew Airiella was in there. Maybe she felt strong enough to train some more. He threw open the door, heard her music playing, but didn't immediately see her. He felt her though. Tired, worried, stressed, a little like she was falling apart.

Ronnie stepped around one of the bags and saw her balled up on the floor, one glove off, one halfway on. Her eyes were scrunched closed, her hair a curly mass of tangles splayed all over the mat and her face. She loosely held her knees to her chest, the blood red leggings blending into the mat under her. Her gray shirt bunched up, but visible enough that Ronnie could see the words on the front declaring that not all who wander are lost.

That was a good word for it. Lost. He knew she was trying to lose herself in the music to ease whatever was happening in her mind to make her emotions go nuts. He didn't want to interrupt her and yet at the same time, she needed to know she wasn't in this alone.

With the grace of a stealthy cat he walked up to her, and settled down next to her, pulling her head on to his lap. She didn't resist him, and he felt some of her anxiety bleed away. He tugged on the one glove to get it off and check the wrapping she had done on her hand. He fixed it, then put the glove on her and got it fastened. He did the same with her other hand.

He sat her up next, checking the floor around him for the hair tie he knew she always had. Once he found it, he pulled her hair up in probably the worst pony tail ever, but it got her hair out of that beautiful face. She looked like a mess, granted, and he still thought she was beautiful.

He stood and held out his hands to her so he could pull her up. He put the pads on his hands and held them up, letting her take the lead and do what she felt like she needed to do. There weren't any words necessary. Ronnie had been in her shoes many times before, and just needed a release. His old coach would do this for him when he found Ronnie in the same state.

He didn't even correct her form this time. She just needed to punch and kick until the worry backed off her enough for her to function again. This was easy for him to give her. When he saw her starting to tremble, he knew she was at her limit and he slowed her down.

The music playlist he had for working out had

switched to the other playlist he had created for her. The one he made out of the songs she had that described how he felt for her. It had taken him a while to make it, he had looked up so many lyrics to see if they fit.

He pulled her down to the floor and settled her between his legs as he rested his back against the wall, his knees bent, feet on the floor as he caged her in. She wrapped her arms behind his calves and held his legs to her, her body in the same position as his. She leaned forward, away from him though, and he set his hands on either side of her waist.

Airiella rested her cheek on his knee and her breathing started to slow down. She still didn't lean back into him though, and he wanted her to. Instead, he reached around her to start pulling the gloves off and rewind the wraps for the next time she wanted to use them.

"These songs make me think of you," came the whispered words against his knee.

Ronnie's heart swelled with love. "It's a playlist of your songs that I made that describe how I feel about you."

She had been rubbing her cheek against his knee and stopped at his words. "You did that for me?"

Ronnie's throat thickened at her tone. "Come here angel," he said, his voice gruff.

She slowly turned until she was sitting sideways between his knees, her eyes searching his. They were shiny, and wide, dark with an unnamed emotion that he couldn't figure out. Her arm snaked out behind his back and she settled into his chest. "Can we just run away? You and me, hide away from everyone and everything. Just us. I might not be who is meant for you, but I'll take it. I'll take you. I promise, I'll love you with everything I have."

Ronnie was so caught off guard he didn't have anything to say for a few minutes. "Angel, nothing would make me happier. I know enough about you to know that you'd hate yourself for it though." Ronnie dipped his head down to kiss the end of her nose, saw she was crying, and held her tight.

"You made me a playlist." Her throaty voice was

muffled as she buried her face in his armpit.

"Smitty's idea, I can't take the credit for it. Him and Jax did one too. He wanted you to feel appreciated."

"Ronnie, you are the only person to see all the broken pieces of me as whole. The flaws, the pain, and love me anyway. Every time I break, you pick up a piece of me and put it back. Your fingerprints all over that piece, and you fill me with you. No matter how many times I keep falling, you are there picking me back up. You always seem to know what I need, and I find myself falling more and more in love with you each time."

"Is that so bad?" Ronnie's heart was beating a mad rhythm in his chest. Her words touched him deeply.

"No. It makes me sad though, because I really wish that it were as easy as that. Can I keep you for a little while?" Her plaintive tone stabbed right through him.

"As long as you want, angel. Forever, if that works out for all of us. I'm all yours. Did you ever consider that maybe you were meant for both Jax and me?" Ronnie would take that in a heartbeat. He didn't think he'd ever be able to walk away from her.

"All the time." She tightened her arms around him. "That thought is never far from my mind. And I wish for it daily."

Ronnie shifted, lowering his legs to the floor and turning her so she faced him. He lifted her ankles and put them around him, doing the same with his around her. "Then just go with it. In my heart, I know I am right where I am supposed to be. That's enough for me." He tucked the loose strands of hair that escaped the messy tie job he'd done with her hair behind her ears. "I don't need to worry about the future and who I am supposed to be with. Right here, right now, this is what matters."

"I need to have a heart-to-heart with Jax when he wakes us." She switched gears on him fast and he took a moment to feel her emotions out.

She was feeling vulnerable, and it scared her. "Hey, look at me. Angel, not my chest, look at my eyes." When she finally met his gaze, he continued. "You don't need to be afraid of that vulnerability you keep hiding from. It won't go away, and I happen to think it's amazing that I can make you feel like that."

"See? There you go seeing those pieces and picking them up." Her weak smile did something to his heart. She touched her fingers to his lips. "Kiss me, please."

She didn't need to ask again. Ronnie tumbled her down on to the mats and devoured her lips with a blind hunger that took over every fiber of his being. He felt like she had invaded every one of his cells, there was only her. The intoxicating scent that was uniquely her wrapping around him, bringing him bliss.

He pulled back, resting his forehead against hers, his breathing staggered. "You deserve better than to be taken on a gym mat in a garage, angel."

She rolled him over so she was straddling him. He was rock hard beneath her and damn near swallowed his tongue as she rolled her hips over him. Her eyes lit with passion. "Location doesn't matter to me," she swiveled against him again. "All that matters, is what's between us."

Ronnie pulled her down so she laid flat on top of him. "It matters to me right now, sweetheart. As much as I want to hear you screaming my name again, I also just want to hold you. I still just need to be close to you."

"Taklishim told me I wouldn't always be able to come back. Did you know that?" Her ear was resting over his heart, he was sure she could hear the crazy beats her statement made happen.

"Is he sure?" Fear started to pool in his belly.

"Can you find a spot for me to go hide at the beach for a day?" She ignored his question and changed the subject. "After I talk with Jax, I need a day. Back at home, there's this beach that's my favorite place to go when I need to re-center myself. I spent summers there with my grandparents on my dad's side, when I was a kid. It's where we spread my grandpa's ashes too. Right now, I need that place. I need the salt water, the sand, the roar of the waves."

"We can go somewhere, I'll take you. I don't think

you should be going anywhere alone though. Might be dangerous." Ronnie's heart broke a little at her sad sigh.

"Is there somewhere close by that's not overran with people?" She almost sounded afraid to hope.

"I'll find one," Ronnie promised her.

"Thank you for being you, Ronnie," she whispered into his chest. There wasn't anything he wouldn't do for her. They laid there soaking each other up.

Chapter Thirteen

Aedan and Mags were sitting down in the TV room when he heard Mags exclaim, "Shit. They know her name. Look!"

Mags thrust her tablet in his face. Their Facebook page blowing up with comments about Airiella and the live show. "Well, that will make things a little harder now. Hopefully she has her page set to private."

"We aren't doing a very good job at keeping her private," Mags pointed out as she scrolled through the comments. "At least she has public support. Damn media."

Smitty and Jillian walked in. Aedan noticed that things were a little tense between them. "Hey Jillian, nice to see you."

Mags mumbled some sort of greeting, too caught up in reading the comments. Smitty snorted, "I saw too. She might be noticed if we go out somewhere now."

"Are all you as firm believers in her as Smitty is?" Jillian interrupted.

Mags stiffened beside him and Aedan put a reassuring hand on her foot that was in his lap. "She's proven herself to all of us."

"Why? Because she can make you feel calm?" Jillian's tone was getting under Mags' skin and Aedan didn't want a blow up.

"I told her Airiella was an angel," Smitty admitted.

"I heard my name," came the sultry voice from behind him.

"Of course, you did," Jillian fired off. Aedan flinched at how fast Smitty stood and faced her.

"Are you really going to start this again, even after we talked?" Smitty was having none of it. Concerned, Aedan stood but Mags pulled him back down shaking her head at him.

"Jillian, what do I need to do to show you I am not what you think I am?" Airiella's voice was tired. Aedan looked her over, she still looked wiped out.

"Hey, Airiella," Aedan said, "Ronnie told me that you showed him how it felt to have an emotion pulled from him. Can you show me that?" Aedan ignored Jillian and Smitty. "I'm trying to understand what Jax is feeling and how to get through this."

"Aedan, she's still tired," Ronnie argued, his arm possessively around her.

"It's fine, Ronnie." She came in and sat down next to him. "You know how the connection feels, and you know how it feels when I share with you."

"Yes, a feeling floods through me when you share, and when our skin touches there's that tingle and the flow of it. It's the taking of it that I don't understand," Aedan explained.

"Smitty, do you want to know too?" she looked over at Smitty, a question in her eyes.

"It's not necessary, but if you want, go ahead." His voice was so gentle with her, Aedan kind of understood the jealousy that was rolling off Jillian.

Airiella sighed deeply. "The only way you will really understand what Jax feels is if I pull something that is deeply rooted inside you. I am going to do this slow, and I will be gentle. Remember though, that what Jax feels would be a thousand times worse in ways that you won't really ever understand."

Aedan nodded. "What are you going to take?"

"Love," she said sadly. "I'll put it back, but if you really want to understand why he keeps passing out when he's overwhelmed, I will have to pull what matters. I'm not saying that this energy in him matters to him, just that it's so much a part of him now, it's embedded in his soul. With you guys, your love for each other is that way. His causes an intense pain in him, I'm going to try not to do that to you guys."

Aedan watched as her eyes unfocused for a second and then he felt it. She was being gentle as she said, but it still hurt to have something that was such a good feeling taken away bit by bit. It really did feel like she was taking his soul apart. He started to shake. "Enough, I get it."

Smitty and Jillian sat there, eyes wide. Smitty had a wild look on his face, "Give it back, baby girl."

Aedan felt the warmth spread through him again replacing the cold empty feeling that had started to grow. "Sorry, it was the best I could do to show you all at once."

Smitty took two giant steps across the room and crushed Airiella in a hug. Aedan heard him whisper, "Never take what I feel for you from me again."

Mags had tears rolling down her face as she looked at Aedan. "You need to be nicer to Jax if what he feels is worse than that."

Aedan buried his face in his hands. "I'm sorry, Airiella."

Smitty had released her and glared at Aedan. "I know you haven't seen what Ronnie and I have, but you need to be able to at least take a leap of faith here." He swung around to Jillian. "You too."

"You take that stuff away from Jax that's been making him crazy, and it hurts him?" Jillian asked Airiella. She nodded in response. "Does it hurt you?" Airiella nodded again. "Does it hurt to pull good emotions?"

"You mean does it hurt me?" Airiella asked to clarify.

"Yes." Jillian sat forward a bit.

"Pulling good emotions from someone makes me feel evil. I don't think it harms me, but it doesn't sit right with me. Pulling things from people like anxiety, or depression, stuff along those lines, doesn't hurt me like the energy with Jax does, but it wears me out. I end up taking on those emotions until I can find a good spot to release them back out once it's purified. It's the same with giving someone from my own stores. It feels good to give good back, but it wears me out. If I give too much after I've taken on some negative ones then my mood gets affected and I can get depressed, or angry quickly."

"You do this all the time? Manipulate people's emotions?" the question Jillian asked with a tone that set all their teeth on edge.

Airiella met each of their eyes. "I got it. Relax." She focused her gaze on Jillian. "I don't manipulate emotions. I can't make someone feel something they don't already feel. Emotions don't lie, they each carry an energy vibration different from another. I can feel those vibrations and either pull it from them, or feed into it. I can't look at you and decide to make you love me. I can only give you love if you feel love. What that love is for, I don't know. Maybe the love I pulled from you was love you have for Smitty, maybe it was love for something else. I can only use the emotions present in a person."

"You made me feel calm earlier," Jillian argued.

"It was already in you. The jealousy was just trying to take over everything. All I did was feed my own calm energy into the tiny amount of calm you had. I only fed enough of it to stop you from railing against Smitty. To be perfectly honest Jillian, I don't give a fuck what you feel for me. You liking me doesn't matter to me. That's your business. You seem to not be understanding though, your actions have a reaction." Airiella gestured to Smitty. "Your actions are hurting him."

"How can you be an angel when you swear like that?" Jillian just didn't want to let go and Aedan felt just how exhausted Airiella was. He had the urge to shake Jillian until she shut up.

"My language is a descriptor, not an emotion. I'm not calling you names, nor do I have any negative intent against you. There is no reason for me to act that way, for the simple explanation of it would hurt Smitty. I don't have intent to hurt anyone." Airiella stood, Ronnie at her elbow.

Aedan's own emotions feeling raw, he stood and hugged Airiella. "Thank you for showing me. I'm working on it, I promise."

She nodded at him. "I know you are. I won't be around tonight, if Jax wakes up. It's time I pushed some issues, Degataga made it pretty clear to me."

"I understand, if you need us, we'll be here." Mags stood and hugged her too.

"I'll be with her," Ronnie added, earning a surprised look from Airiella. "I will be there, I'm a part of it too."

"Oh, hey, Airiella." She turned to look back at Aedan. "Media has put your name out there. Heads up."

Her shoulders slumped, making Aedan feel like an ass. "Don't worry Airy, Aedan will talk to the producers to make sure no one finds us here," Mags broke in, elbowing Aedan.

The corners of her lips turned into what Aedan thought was an attempt to smile, and she left, leaning on Ronnie. He looked back to Jillian, "If that's how you want to act, you can leave. Sorry, Smitty."

"Don't be sorry, I said the same thing." Smitty glared down at her.

"It's all just a little fantastical." Jillian defended herself.

"Sometimes you just need to have faith," Mags snapped, snuggling into Aedan's side. "That girl didn't ask for any of this to happen to her. Yet she's still here, taking care of all of us."

Aedan kissed Mags on the forehead remembering how it felt when Airiella pulled on the love he had for Mags. The cold empty feeling that stabbed at his heart. He was willing to take a leap of faith to not have to feel that again.

Jax woke up tired. And not alone. His mind flashed back and he remembered Airiella trying to calm him down after Jillian pissed him off. That wasn't Airiella behind him though. He rolled over and saw Ronnie, heard the gentle snores and decided to let him be.

He was ridiculously happy he hadn't left Jax alone. He still didn't feel right, even though he now had less of that energy in him, he still felt raw and vulnerable in a way he didn't like. He was still angry about the things Jillian had said, though he had control of it right now.

"How do you feel?" He jumped at the voice of the siren that he hadn't seen sitting right in front of him.

"Oddly, still tired," he admitted.

"I understand." She stood up. "Why don't you get up and meet me downstairs in a minute after you do whatever you need to do right now? We need to talk."

"Is this a breakup talk?" Jax tried to joke, but it fell flat.

She approached him slowly, her face sad, and she looked exhausted. "No, but it's pretty serious." She caressed his face with those silky soft fingers of hers and Jax's heart tripped. "Please?"

Her thumb rubbed along the circles that Jax knew were under his eyes. He wanted to say no, something told him he wasn't going to like it. The look on her face was so tender, her voice so seductive, her touch magic, he could no more deny her than he could breathe underwater. He simply swallowed and nodded.

She stepped around the bed and looked at Ronnie with such love on her face that he felt jealousy flare up again. "He looks so peaceful right now. Don't wake him. He needs the rest."

Jax scanned her face, seeing exhaustion all over it. "So do you," he answered, finding his voice. "Looks like constantly saving me makes you tired." Jax stood up and fought with himself. "I didn't mean that how it sounded," he tried to explain.

"I know, Jax." Her eyes shone with something and she walked back over to him, stood on her toes and kissed the corner of his mouth. His skin sparked like crazy and he wanted to pull her back as she turned to go. "I'll wait in the kitchen until you are ready to come down."

He dropped back on to the bed, jolting it enough to wake Ronnie. He swore under his breath. "Sorry, man. I didn't mean to wake you up."

"It's fine. Where's Airiella?" Ronnie yawned.

"She said she would wait for me in the kitchen until whenever I was ready to come down. Any idea what this is about?" Jax tried to pry information from him.

"It's her show, man. I'm just the support," Ronnie said cryptically. "See you down there."

Ronnie heaved himself from the bed and walked out, leaving Jax alone. He rubbed his hands over his face and decided to shower and change into some sweats. Might as well be comfortable. He didn't shave. For some reason, he loved the way his stubble felt when she touched his face.

He found them in the kitchen as promised. Ronnie forcing food on her. His stomach rumbled, though the thought of eating made him nauseous. She handed him a sports drink. "You need to stay hydrated Jax."

He didn't argue with her. Ronnie said nothing, but Jax saw he had one too. "What's up?"

"Let's go to the carriage house, we'll have some privacy there." Her voice was cautious.

"Okay." Jax felt on edge, nonetheless he followed her.

Chapter Fourteen

This was going to suck. I dreaded it. We were both so emotionally strung out and exhausted that I felt like we were walking a fine line. The carriage house was cold, but had a lovely living room with a big fireplace that I had Ronnie light. I stayed close to it trying to absorb some of the heat.

Jax paced around a little and drank some of the sports drink. "What gives?"

"I talked with Taklishim, Tama, and Degataga today. Learned some interesting things. Apparently, the number of times I can come back is limited. If pulling all this from you will kill you, we have to look at different approaches." I jumped in with both feet.

"What do you mean the number of times you can come back is limited?" Jax paused to watch me.

"I, uh, I die when I release that energy that I pull, and whatever force or abilities I have, I'm not really sure about that part since I'm not alive, it heals me and I come back. They told me that I was limited on that. They don't know more than that." I faltered a bit in my explanation.

"Saving me kills you." He said it as a statement.

"You come back healed for the most part." I nodded. "Now they are telling you that you might not come back?"

"That's what they think, but they don't know for sure. Same with not knowing if it will kill you if I pull what's left." I tried to keep my voice gentle but it shook. Ronnie was having a hard time keeping still, I knew he was feeling my emotions roll through me.

"That's fucked up." Jax resumed pacing. "Why are you here?" He looked over at Ronnie.

"Support, I told you," Ronnie's voice was tight.

"Who? Her? Or me?" Jax snarled. I felt that energy in him stir.

"Both." Ronnie kept it simple, but there was fire in his eyes.

"Jax." I pulled out the tin I grabbed from his room. "You need to take this. You have to start fighting for yourself. My energy is so low I can't keep fighting you to get you to fight for yourself."

"So don't," he yelled at me. "It's my fight."

"Jax," Ronnie warned. "She's right. How is it not her fight when she keeps running head first into danger to save your ass? Her life is literally on the line, and she fucking gives it up to save you."

Jax stumbled. He was fighting, my heart stuttered a fast rhythm. I stood up and went into the small kitchen to heat up water to mix the herbal mix in. He was going to drink this, even if it killed me. Ronnie watched my every move. Jax watched Ronnie. The energy in him notched up.

I stayed quiet, and when the water heated, I grabbed a mug from the cabinet and mixed it up. I had been in here earlier and checked the master bedroom, it had a nice king size bed and I made sure the sheets were clean. Here was where we would stay until he came through his dreamscape and was safely out the other side.

I set it on the table near him and went back to the couch. "Why do you think you can't do this?" I pushed him, curious to see what would happen.

"Maybe I just don't want to," he said snidely.

"You can say that, but I know it's a lie. I can feel it,

Jax. Same way I feel the fear." It was hard to keep the emotion out of my voice, but it still bled through.

"Just because you did it, doesn't mean I can." He tucked his hands in his armpits to hide the shaking. I'd already seen it though. "What if I'm not strong enough to get through it?" came the harsh whisper.

"What if you are?" I challenged him.

"Jax, just drink it," Ronnie told him, frustration boiling up. "It's not like we will leave you alone."

"You can't face it for me, you won't be in there," Jax yelled at Ronnie and I flinched, not expecting the volume.

Ronnie saw the flinch and mistook it for fear, his anger flying free. "Goddamn it Jax! All we want is to help you get through this shit! There're no ulterior motives here. She wants you to fight for yourself so the risk is less to you! It doesn't change anything for her at all. She still has to die again."

Spittle flying between them as they got in each other's faces. This escalated way too fast. The energy in Jax flared up, his dark eyes reflecting the flames of the fireplace giving life to the energy inside him. My own anger jumped to the surface. I paced around trying to get a grip on my anger but between Jax's emotions and Ronnie's reaction I couldn't.

"Help me," Jax pleaded, his eyes locking on mine. "Don't let this take me right now."

I suddenly saw a line between me and Jax like there was between me and the others. Confused because I hadn't made that connection with Jax yet, I touched it. I felt how fragile this line was, the energy from it frayed and unstable. He gasped as I ran my finger on it. Tears started building behind my eyes, I knew I couldn't help him this time.

"Please, I need you," Jax begged. "You are my anchor, my lifeline, my rock."

I lost the fight with the tears and they spilled from my eyes in silent tracks. "Jax, you don't seem to understand though! In order for an anchor to work, it has to drown. Every time you use it, it voluntarily drowns. Every rock that holds someone safe from being swept over the edge, gets worn down by the same storms or waves that chip away at it. What happens to that anchor when the storm is so strong it snaps the chain?" I choked on my tears. "It lies broken, useless and dead on the bottom of the sea with its last thoughts being of how it failed you and lost you to the same stormy sea it was trying to save you from."

I stabbed myself in the chest, "That's what is happening to me every time you fight me." I touched the visible line between us, feeling it vibrate through my body and igniting my blood in an unsteady pulse. "This line can break," I sobbed. I gestured between us, "This...is broken."

"I'm trying," he pleaded with me, his emotions battering me like a punching bag under Ronnie's fists. Every blow feeling like it will take me down. "We haven't even made the connection yet, how is there even a cord you can see between us?" Confusion rained down on him in the middle of the angst.

"You aren't trying!" I cried. "That's the problem! Sometimes you shouldn't use the anchor, sometimes you have to ride the storm out." I sagged to the floor Ronnie at my side in an instant. "The cord is there because the connection I have with you is the strongest. It's not permanent, you're right. Every time we do this, you keep breaking it. I can see all the frayed edges, feel the drain on both of us."

"I can't compete with that," Jax shouted angrily pointing at Ronnie ignoring the rest of that statement I made. Nothing sinking in to him, the energy slowly creeping to his brain.

"Why do you think you need to?" I croaked out. "My connection with him isn't the same as the one I have with you. There's no competition. My connection with each and every one of you is different. It feeds on what we bring each other. What Ronnie brings to my life is not the same as what you do. We all need each other. It's balance," I whispered, feeling utterly destroyed.

Ronnie picked me up and I shook my head slightly telling him no, and he set me down on the couch and covered me with a blanket. Jax stayed standing there, his chest heaving, then sank down on the floor, doubled over, his body violently shaking with cries and fear. As much as I hated it, I had to let him go through it. He had to prove it to himself. Maybe a little to me and Ronnie too. But if he had to go through it, I'd leave my walls down and go through it with him, I just couldn't take it from him this time. I wouldn't leave him to do it alone though.

"I know you remember me telling you I wish someone would save me," I said quietly. "What I didn't tell you is that I know you can't. I have to save myself. I don't know who I am anymore. I was thrust into this world, and I've been rolling with it as best as I can because I feel the need in all of you. Because I feel it, I can't ignore it. I don't want to be a savior. Since I came into your lives, each of you has been saving me, and I didn't even realize it. Not until now, seeing you like this. You all are helping me put myself back together. Let us help you."

I couldn't even touch him, as much as I longed to wrap my arms around him and just give him love, I couldn't. I was numb with cold, and pain was ripping me apart piece by piece. My nerves were as frayed and raw as that tenuous connection, growing worse with each cry that tore through him. I slid to my side and lay on the couch, burying my face in a pillow.

I could feel how much it hurt Ronnie to watch this, but he refused to leave me. His anger at Jax was palpable, but I knew underneath that anger simmered a deep hurt that grew from watching Jax suffer through this and not being able to help him. It wasn't easy on any of us, though Ronnie and I bore the brunt of it. I knew he was close by and I looked for him.

As he appeared behind the couch, he leaned over and roughly whispered, "What do you need angel?"

I held his hand, his steady connection with me soothing in a way I clung to right now. "Should I tell him I love him?" I faintly whispered back. I'd said the words to all of them before, Jax had never believed me though.

"He might need to hear it," he half-heartedly agreed. "I know when you tell me, everything else disappears for a moment and I can see a clear way back when things are bad. He doesn't think he's worthy of love, or that he deserves it." He scoffed, "Right now I don't think he does either."

"It's right now that he needs it more than ever," I said softly.

"Angel, you *are* love." He dropped a kiss on my forehead. "We all know it."

"I can't touch him, my walls are down—" Ronnie growled a little. "—but you can. It might help all of us if he feels like you don't hate him," I suggested gently.

"Why are your walls down?" he asked me roughly.

"Because I won't ever leave him alone, I'll face it with him. I just can't take it from him this time. He's got to prove it to himself."

"Angel." Ronnie's eyes shone with tears. "You are feeling the full effect of this? Is that why everything is so intense?"

I nodded weakly as more pain tore through me. Jax's battered soul suffering under the new onslaught this energy raged on him.

"Tell him then, I'll get down on the floor with him," he ground out, fighting back the need to argue with me. I saw it all over his face. I squeezed his hand gratefully.

Ronnie walked around the couch and sat down behind Jax who immediately stiffened and went to move away, but Ronnie used his giant arms and held him in a steel grip around his chest, holding him up. "I've got you man. We aren't leaving you alone. Goddamn it Jax, fight this shit. She's fucking got her walls down. What you feel, she is feeling." Ronnie's voice broke. "I'm feeling it too."

Jax started shaking more and I thought he was just going to completely break down, I could see the strain on his body, feel it on his soul and this darkness fought him hard for control, but he let Ronnie hold him. He rocked back and forth, a high-pitched keening sound ripping from between his lips. The light from the fireplace dancing over his contorting face.

I couldn't touch him, but I couldn't stay away either.

I slid off the sofa and crawled over to him, sitting out of reach but in front of him where he could see me. "Jax," I said through my tears, my voice soft, "look at me please."

His tortured eyes lifted to mine and held them, I could see every emotion he had wash through them as his tears still fell, pain lining every crease his face held, fear rolling off him in waves that were suffocating me. I wanted to grab his hand, instead, I sat on mine, so I wouldn't.

"Keep looking at me Jax. That's it, focus on me and my words. I'm not walking away. I'm not leaving you to face this alone. But I can't take this from you. Baby, you've *got* to fight it. I know you have it in you, I feel it inside my body. Believe in yourself, it's how you win. Trust yourself. You can do this. It has to start with you." My voice broke again.

I looked at Ronnie desperately and he mouthed, "Tell him." Ronnie leaned his head against Jax's showing his love in a way Jax would understand.

Jax still watched me, I pointed to the line between us, and caressed it gently, letting the cord absorb some of my love. "Jax, baby, I love you. Despite all this, not because of it. With or without that connection, my feelings for you don't change."

Jax deflated as the fight left his body, he reached up and grasped on to Ronnie's arm, holding on like his life depended on it, his tears now silent. I felt the hope bloom in him, while something eased in Ronnie. The tension slowly bled out of the room and I dragged myself over to the couch, leaving them on the floor with each other.

I pulled myself up and curled up in the blanket knowing that for the first time, Jax had just fought for himself and won. It was the small victories that mattered the most here. I hadn't lied to him either. I didn't love him out of pity, or because that was the way to kill off this darkness. I loved him despite that, I loved him for who I saw inside of him, and now he knew that.

I drifted off to sleep to the sound of the two best friends whispering to each other in solidarity, mending what had broken between them.

Ronnie was holding on so tight to Jax that his arm started to ache. Once he felt Jax stop fighting him, he eased up. He saw Airiella go back over to the couch and collapse on it. Pure exhaustion taking over her body.

"Jax, man, you see that? See how she dropped? She's not recovered yet. Please man, just drink that shit and let's do this." Ronnie pushed taking a chance.

"Why does she love me?" Jax had no fight in his voice at all.

"It's who she is." Ronnie let the awe he felt for her color his tone. "She sees something in you that she feels is valuable. We all do. You mean more to me than I know how to convey to you. Remember what I told you about what she goes through? If I could, I'd do it for you. I just want my brother back."

Jax made another keening sound. "Ronnie, so much of what this shit is inside me is because of how fucking awful I have been to you. Then and now. I can't possibly hate myself more than I already do. I'm terrified if I drink that, it's going to display it all in technicolor for me to relive and that energy will just take over because the guilt is so deep."

Ronnie didn't know how to respond to that. It shook him badly that he was the cause of this feeling in Jax, and at the same time, it gave him hope that he could change and come back from it. Jax recognized what it was.

Jax went on when Ronnie didn't respond. "This hate in me, it's so black, I don't even think her light can get through it. It's layer upon layer, all aimed at myself."

"Jax, why do you think I haven't forgiven you?" Ronnie went with the direct route.

"I don't know, why?" Jax muttered darkly.

"No, you misunderstood that. What makes you believe that I haven't already forgiven you?" Ronnie reworded it.

"Why would you have? I'm a selfish asshole. I don't deserve your forgiveness." Ronnie plainly saw just how deep this hate in Jax was.

"You can't tell me what I can and can't do, how I get to feel. My forgiveness is for me to decide who gets it. Not you. You *are* an asshole, but you aren't selfish. Not really." Ronnie worked on his words carefully. "Everyone does selfish shit. It doesn't mean they are selfish though."

"You want me to drink this, don't you?" Jax pointed to the mug Airiella had set down.

"You know I do." Ronnie pushed back the memories of Airiella drinking it. "You wanted to save her, remember? This is a start to that. Even if she says no one can save her."

Jax tapped Ronnie's arm that was still around him. "You can let me go now. I'm not going to freak out."

Ronnie dropped his arm and shook it out while Jax studied the sleeping Airiella. Jax scooted across the floor and got closer to her though he didn't make a move to touch her. Ronnie thought it was probably safe if he did now that he'd gotten over that initial battle.

"She told me she was madly in love with you, you know," Jax told Ronnie wistfully.

"Did you miss where she just told you she loved you?" Ronnie pointed out.

"No. I heard it. I don't understand it. I can't take her away from you Ronnie." Jax dropped his head down to lean his forehead on the couch near her arm. "Does she really love me like she loves you?"

"You've got to listen to her more. You wouldn't be taking her away from me. She needs us both. All of us really." Ronnie was tired of this argument. He picked up the mug and forced it into Jax's hands. "Drink it. I'm going to grab her, and we are going to go lay in the bed in there and stay with you while you see what you need to see."

That startled Jax. "Here?"

"She planned everything. She thought you'd want a little more privacy away from the others, so she got the room ready." Ronnie gestured to the room. "Go turn the light on so I don't trip over anything please."

Ronnie stood and gently slid his arms under his angel, lifting her and rolling her towards him. She was so tired she didn't even wake up, just shifted her arm so it was around his neck. God, he loved this woman. He brushed a kiss across her forehead and headed for the bedroom.

"Want her in the middle, or do you want me next to you?" Ronnie gave Jax a choice.

"If she's touching me, does it make it easier?" Jax questioned.

"I don't know. I'd assume it does, but I haven't done the drinking part of this. I was only there when she went through it." Ronnie was honest.

"Then keep her over there, you be in the middle. I guess if I'm going to do this, I need to do it on my own." Jax sounded sad.

"You aren't alone. You were somehow pulled into hers. My guess is the same will happen with her. Even if she doesn't, we are both still here. She fell asleep with her walls down. I have free access to her emotions right now. Whatever you feel, she will know." Ronnie settled her down on the edge of the bed and climbed over her, pulling her next to him.

Jax went to shut off the light and flipped on a lamp by the bed instead, angling the shade so it wasn't bright on them. "Can I ask you a question about the connection?"

"Sure," Ronnie agreed, his belly tightening as in her sleep Airiella slid a hand under his shirt, his skin alive where she touched him.

"What do you get from it?" Jax was curious.

"Life. She brought me life." Ronnie closed his eyes and let it fill him. "Everything is more vibrant. I can feel things I've never felt before. My moves have meaning. I'm not just going through the motions anymore. I'm more aware there is a higher purpose that we don't know."

"Is it the same as the others?"

"No, like she said, it's different for each person. I can't tell you how it will affect you, just that there is nothing like it. It was the most amazing thing I've ever felt." The moment would be forever etched in his mind, this angel forever in his heart.

"Am I going to be glued to her like you are now?"

Jax added as an afterthought.

"This is due to being with her when she released that energy. I watched her die, twice, Jax. Not really ready to let her out of my sight yet." Ronnie was weary, his mind was racing though. He grabbed his cell phone and sent a text to Smitty.

"Find a secluded beach somewhere for Airiella, she needs to go to one. Jax is going to drink the mix, we are here in the carriage house with him." He got a thumbs up emoji back.

"Bottoms up," Jax said quietly and slammed the liquid in a gulp and lay back on the bed next to Ronnie. "Thanks bro."

Ronnie watched Jax. "See you on the flip side. We'll get through this." Jax trembled. "I've got you, man. Relax, keep your mind open." The sudden sound of flapping wings had them both looking around.

Jax opened his eyes. He felt like he was asleep, but he also felt awake. He looked around him and he was just in the dark. Except the two eyes he saw that he figured had to be the most beautiful eyes he'd ever seen. Airiella's eyes glowed from a pure black raven. She was with him.

"You've seen all this before, and like you, I fear it will make you not love me." Jax felt stupid talking to a bird, but she was listening. She made a soft cawing sound and hopped over to him. His hand reached out tentatively and he ran a finger over the feathers. Soft and silky, like her hair. "I already hate myself, what if this makes me hate myself more?"

He stared into the eyes that stripped him so bare. He heard no words, but he knew what was being communicated to him. He had to see the bad in order to see what needed to be fixed. The raven brushed up against him again.

He was six, it was the first time he was spending

the night at Ronnie's. He was excited and scared. They got to watch a movie and eat pizza. He heard a man yelling and he got scared, wanted to go home. Ronnie told him it was okay, that it was normal. They camped out in the basement and Jax remembered hearing someone come down to check on them. When he peeked out of their makeshift tent, he saw Ronnie's mom, she was crying and it made Jax sad. He crawled out of the tent and went to sit in her lap, his mom always liked hugs when she cried.

The scene shifted again.

He was ten years old now, at Ronnie's house again working on a science project for school. This time Ronnie's mom had a cast on her arm. When Jax and Ronnie got the volcano they made to erupt, it got all over Ronnie's shirt and Jax saw all the bruises on his chest. He was old enough to understand something was wrong, but Ronnie never told him.

The raved cawed at Jax, her eyes telling him something, but guilt swamped his chest and tears filled his eyes. He should have done something sooner to save his friend from going through this.

Jax was a teenager now. They were graduating to high school the next year. Him, Winnie and Ronnie all ran track. It was their last meet of the year and Winnie had been pointing out the bruises that were on Ronnie's arms and legs. Ronnie was the best in the school at doing the hurdles. Every time he jumped his shorts moved, showing a long bruise on the outside of his thigh. When Winnie questioned it, Ronnie told her that it happened when he tripped over a hurdle. Jax had tried to get her to leave it alone, but she wouldn't. She told the coach that something was wrong and Ronnie ended up getting called into the principal's office.

Jax remembered the fight that had happened between Winnie and Ronnie after that. Jax had agreed with Winnie, but he knew Ronnie was sensitive about it. He had started drinking then. Sneaking a few beers from the fridge when his dad was too drunk to notice. It was at that time that Ronnie stopped having Jax over too.

Jax was a sophomore in high school now. Ronnie had been fighting with bullies for a few weeks, getting his ass kicked frequently. He was drinking heavily, and getting high as often as he could to avoid the situation at home. Jax had made a trip over there and seen Ronnie's mom all beat to hell. The rage that had taken over Jax when he saw her was absolute, and it all made sense to him then. The bruises all over Ronnie, the drugs, the drinking. Their new friend Art had made a few comments that had set Ronnie off. This was also when Jax learned that his family life was a lie. He'd had a brother a year younger than him that had lived two streets over. Jax had felt like his world had flipped upside down.

Jax went with Ronnie one weekend after school to a lake, decided to get high and drunk with him. Art had told them both they were stupid, and Jax didn't know what to do about his new brother yet. He'd started hanging out with them, but Jax kept him at an arm's length. Winnie came with so they didn't do something stupid, even though Jax didn't want her there. Ronnie had just started judo and was trying to show off his moves but Jax was too caught up in his own drama on top of being high and ended up starting a fight with Ronnie.

Ronnie ended up leaving and the guilt had eaten at Jax. He started fooling around with Winnie. Something they'd been doing more and more lately. Neither of them had been ready to go all the way, but the guilt had taken over and Jax pushed until Winnie relented and they both lost their virginity.

Shame slammed into Jax as he watched it. She had only given in to try and make him feel better. Jax had so badly wanted their first time to be special. Instead they ended up on top of a dirty picnic table and Jax being so high he didn't care.

Jax was a junior now, closer with Art and his brother Aedan than he had been. Ronnie was still in a downward spiral that no one could get him out of. He'd made Jax promise not to say anything about the abuse he was going through.

Ronnie showed up to school so beaten he could hardly walk. Jax had been terrified that Ronnie's dad was going to kill him, and he knew he should tell someone, but every time Ronnie saw him, he made him promise not to. Art hadn't made that promise though. When Art, who they'd started called Smitty now, asked Jax if Ronnie was being abused, Jax hedged enough without breaking his promise to Ronnie that Smitty took matters into his own hands and told a counselor.

Ronnie assumed it had been Jax and refused to speak to him for a couple of weeks. Smitty finally told him that it had been him, not Jax that had told. Ronnie forgave him, and due to the intervention of the school and police, his dad had been arrested.

Jax had wished he had broken that promise a lot sooner than what had happened. Ronnie had endured so much more than he had needed to. Jax had never forgiven himself for that. The raven cawed next to him.

Jax was fighting with Winnie. Neither of them had felt close anymore, the love they both had thought was forever faded into a friendship. He knew Ronnie had feelings for Winnie. He wasn't blind. He refused to let go though. Being with Winnie was all he knew. He was scared to be alone. It didn't bother him that they weren't attracted to each other. Ronnie was a better choice for Winnie than he was anyway. Well, he would be if he would quit drinking and getting high.

Maybe that was the reason Jax didn't want to let

go. She'd made it clear to him they were no longer together. Jax figured when she stormed out she was headed to Ronnie's so he called there, just to talk to Ronnie. He felt petty and childish, and he knew it was wrong. He'd get over it soon.

He hung up when she got there. He almost didn't answer when she called him either. Guilt got the better of him and he did. She was more pissed than he had ever heard her. Then he heard it all. The screams of twisting metal on the impact, the screams of pain she made, the shattering glass, the sound of her phone being tossed around in the car, then the deadly silence.

He called 911 and reported the accident saying he had the line open to her phone. He gave them the route she was on. He called Ronnie, who left to come get him. He sat there listening until he no longer heard the medics trying to get her out of the car. He saw her broken body in the hospital, and it crushed him. Emotions tore through him so fast he couldn't even name them. He lost his mind when he heard her tell them no surgery. He heard himself cursing at her, and watched as the only person he'd ever loved like that, die.

Jax stood there in shame, watching the scene play out. His chest was heaving, breathing was hard for him right then. He felt the tears build and well up, but he refused to let them fall. This was on him. He deserved this pain. The raven cawed loudly at him, flapping her wings in an angry rush. Jax wrongly assumed the raven was judging him the same way he judged himself. He didn't even flinch when she pecked at his hand with her sharp beak.

Scene after scene of all the wrongs Jax made played out, and he hated himself more and more. Each time the raven got madder and madder at him. How was he supposed to fix this? How could he move past all these wrongs he caused others?

Glowing. Wherever he was now, it was bright. He still heard the raven, but is was so bright that his eyes felt like they were burning. "Jax," the siren voice that haunted him spoke. "Open your eyes."

He opened his eyes and fell to his knees. She was in front of him, but it wasn't her. It was Airiella, but so much more. She had wings. She was a majestic angel floating in front of him. The pure white light so warm and filled with love he didn't deserve to look at her.

"Jax, look at me," she demanded, her husky voice sinking into his soul. "No one is blameless."

"You are." He looked at the swirling smoke of the ground below him.

"No, I'm not."

"I know what you went through, I saw it. There's no blame for you in that, these were choices I made out of pettiness and insecurities," he said, his tone harsh.

He felt her hand on his face, forcing his chin up. He saw the little girl at one of the first investigations they had done. He saw the bruises on her scrawny arms and the sinister look in the step-fathers face. He knew. He contacted the authorities after the show. He later learned that the step-father was arrested.

Next, he saw a gangly teenager that reminded him so much of Ronnie at that age. He was strung out on drugs, his escape from the nightmare that was his life. He arranged treatment for the kid behind the scenes.

It changed and now he was looking at the young mother holding her infant, the bruises under her eyes telling Jax what he was afraid to see. She flinched every time one of them spoke. A captive in her home to verbal abuse. She deserved a chance. Jax contacted a women's shelter nearby and convinced someone to come look in on her. He found out a couple months later they helped her relocate.

"You ask yourself why you deserve love. Are those not enough examples? Mistakes from the past are just chances to learn and grow. Do you think the man that helped save people with no recognition didn't learn? Those are actions of someone acting out of the goodness of their heart."

"It's guilt," Jax argued. "I acted out of guilt."

"You must forgive yourself, Jax. The events of your past were not something you could control. Yes, you made foolish choices at times, everyone does. The actions of others are not your burden to carry. You didn't strike Ronnie. You didn't abuse his mother. You didn't run a stop sign and crash into someone's car."

"I could have spoken to someone about Ronnie earlier, saved him from years of abuse," Jax cried. His best friends' injuries flashing through his mind.

"At some point, you will realize that things happen when they are supposed to. Nothing you did caused any of that to happen. The guilt you feel is not your own. It's empathy. You've created a monster inside you that you think is you. It's not. It's all the emotions that you felt and didn't understand, collected in one spot. You never learned what to do with those emotions. It's not your fault."

"Tell me what to do." Jax closed his eyes, willing the tears to dry up.

"Forgive yourself. Talk to the people you think you've wronged. Tell them how you feel, open yourself to love. Listen to them when they tell you they don't blame you, that it isn't your fault. Let go of the hurt."

"Saying that is easy, doing it is another thing entirely." Jax's voice was flat.

"Nothing worth having is ever easy." Her words spoke of her own journey. "Jax, love is both a gift and a burden. There will always be bad with the good. Your past doesn't define you, it only helps shape who you are now."

He looked up at her and gasped in shock. Her wings were as black as the raven. "Your wings," he whispered.

"Life is a balance of dark and light. I am no different. If my darkness can lift me, yours can do the same. You are worth your own effort. It's a painful lesson, albeit a necessary one. It took you guys for me to see that I was worthy of the love freely given. I can't expect others to love me if I don't love myself. It's the same for you."

"I'm weak," Jax declared. "I'm not like you."

"*Kindness isn't weakness. Neither is love. Love is why you drank that. Your love for Ronnie. Let that love guide you, mend the pieces. Build yourself up. Forgive yourself, ask for forgiveness from others.*"

The light started to dim and she was gone. The raven watching him carefully. He stroked a finger across it's feathers again, then it flew away. Jax had his work cut out for him.

Chapter Fifteen

I bolted awake, sitting straight up trying to twist to look at my back. I'd fucking had wings! Big, beautiful black wings. Clearly, they weren't there now or Ronnie would have a much different look on his face other than the concern he was currently sporting.

"Angel? Everything okay?" He rubbed small circles on my back and looked over at Jax.

"I had wings." I gave him a wide-eyed look.

"Um, what?" he asked confused.

"In Jax's dream thing. I had wings. They were huge. Pure black." I looked over at Jax. "How is he?"

"You tell me, were you in there with him the whole time?" Ronnie searched my face for clues.

"I was. He's harboring a lot of hate in him," I told him, my voice carefully even.

"Jax? He doesn't hate." Ronnie scoffed a little and looked at his friends face closely. "He cried pretty hard for a while there."

"He does hate, Ronnie. He hates himself. He blames himself for everything." I hoped he listened to what I told him. "Do you have any idea how much he loves you?"

Ronnie's face softened. "He's my brother."

"It's the love he has for you that has kept him going all this time. He's trying to make up for all the things he feels he did wrong." Sadness gripped me.

"What do you mean? Other than the Winnie thing, he didn't do anything wrong. Even the Winnie thing can be chalked up to youth and pettiness." Ronnie frowned.

"He needs to bring it up with you. I'm sorry. I want to tell you, but if he does, it will be a huge step for him. I don't know if he would tell you how much he hates himself or not, that's why I gave you that little insight. And the love thing." I lay back down resting my head on Ronnie's arm trying to fight a giant yawn.

"Why are you awake?" Ronnie ran his thumb across my cheek.

"The wing thing was weird. I don't want to be awake. I don't think I've ever been this tired before," I admitted.

"Go back to sleep, angel. We all need it." He leaned his head towards me and brushed a soft kiss across my lips.

"Should I move between you?" I yawned again. Ronnie started stroking my hair and my brain went fuzzy.

"No, he didn't want you to make it easier for him. I gave him the choice."

I nodded, or at least I think I did, I don't remember, I fell asleep.

Smitty had spent hours talking with Jillian. He didn't want to walk away from her, though he had decided he would if she didn't come around. He didn't need her to be friends with Airiella, he did need Jillian to respect her and treat her civilly though.

It had taken him a while to fall asleep, but when he did, the sight that greeted him was enough to send his pulse racing. Airiella in full angel form. Glowing that light that was so uniquely her and with the most gorgeous, downy looking black wings. She was talking to someone, her hands clasped in front of her hanging loosely, her face an expression of heartbreaking love.

He woke up fast. What did that mean? Was she okay? He fumbled around for his phone and sent a frantic text to Ronnie. *"Is my baby girl okay?"*

"Yeah, she just went back to sleep. Jax is through now, too. Why?" Ronnie texted back.

"I just saw her in angel form when I was sleeping. Woke me right up," Smitty typed.

"She did say she had wings when she woke up. She was twisting around trying to look at her back," Ronnie replied.

"You didn't see it?" That confused Smitty since she had made the connection with Ronnie.

"No, I was awake watching over these two," Ronnie answered.

"Scared the hell out of me. I thought she had died or something," Smitty admitted.

"She's okay, I think. The circles under her eyes are worse. Did you find a beach spot?" Ronnie wrote back.

Smitty dug around in his phone for the map coordinates he'd saved and attached it to a text. *"I found this. Need to take SUV, and we have a small walk to get there."*

"Looks good. It's secluded?" Ronnie texted back.

"Asked a surfer friend. He said that place was perfect, no one's ever there except when big waves come in, and even then, it's only a couple of people. None expected tomorrow," Smitty replied.

"Then I'm taking her there tomorrow. It was her request. She said she needs to re-center."

"Can I join?" Smitty was hesitant to ask.

"It's her call to make. I'm just trying to help her recover. She hasn't bounced back like she did last time," Ronnie pointed out.

"I've noticed an extra strain on her," Smitty replied. *"I'll talk to her tomorrow before you leave. Putting Jillian on a plane back home in the morning."*

"You done?" Ronnie bluntly asked.

"I hope not. She needs to get over whatever this is. Besides, we still have shoots coming up and need to prepare."

"See you in the AM," Ronnie signed off.

Smitty plugged his phone back in and crossed his arms under his head. He was trying to process the sight of Airiella with wings. She had been breathtakingly beautiful with them, and he still didn't know what it meant.

"Everything okay?" Jillian asked softly, running her hand over his stomach.

"Yeah, just a dream. And I checked in with Ronnie to see how Jax was," Smitty told her, feeling a touch guilty about the lie though not wanting to argue anymore.

"Is he okay?" she actually sounded concerned.

"Ronnie said he was. Time will tell." Smitty found himself saying a little prayer that this put Jax on the right track to fixing this.

Jillian molded herself to Smitty's side, resting her head on his arm. "I don't hate her."

"You sure had everyone fooled on that one." Smitty tried to keep his tone under control.

"I hated the thought of losing you, not her really. She makes me feel defensive," Jillian tried to explain.

"You were never in danger of losing me, not until you started acting like that." Smitty held himself back from hugging her. She needed to make more of an effort this time.

"I understand that now. I also see how much she cares for everyone here, not just you. There's a tension between her and Jax that is noticeable when you are near them." She spoke softly and he could hear the curiosity in her voice.

"I'm only going to say this once more, because I'm tired of saying it. I don't need you to be her best friend, you don't even have to like her. You do need to respect her, and the fact that she is now a part of my life. If you can't act civilly towards her, this will never work. I understand your insecurities and if me having sex with her bothers you, then you need to speak up." Smitty was tired of it.

"I can't complain about the sex unless I am willing to stop that myself. You were right in that being a double standard. I'm being honest in saying that I need more than one sexual partner. I don't think that will ever change. The fact that you were willing to discuss not having sex with her, does a lot to allay my fears. I promise you I will make an effort to behave better towards her. Just, please know that logic doesn't match up with anything you've said she is and I'm having a hard time wrapping my head around that," Jillian conceded.

"Believe me, I am well aware she defies all logic. If I hadn't been present for the things I'd told you, I would have a hard time believing it myself." Smitty dared to hope that this would work out. "You'll really try? Stop this nasty attitude that's popped up?"

"Yes, I'll do better than try. Ronnie's certainly a smitten kitten," she said slyly.

"They are pretty close," Smitty agreed. "We are all in love with her, Jillian. Every single one of us. From her cussing, dirty mind, fiery temper to the way she freely gives of herself and her love to anyone that needs it. She provides us with the pieces we never knew we were missing."

"I think seeing the way Aedan felt was the biggest eye opener for me," Jillian spoke gently.

"Aedan?" Smitty was taken aback.

"He's always been a little more distant than the rest of you, firmly rooted in science and fact. His face when she did her little demonstration for him was pure shock and awe," Jillian said.

"He loves her," Smitty reassured Jillian. "He panicked when she was in that house the same way the Ronnie and I did. Mags will always be his number one, but he loves Airiella too."

"I know. I don't really think she's awful. She has a certain draw to her, I'll admit that. Does she always look so worn out?"

"No, that's a direct result of all the stuff that's happened over the past week. It's got all of us concerned. She told Ronnie to find her a beach to go to, she said it helps her re-center. She connects with nature in a different way than most of us do, so maybe it will work," Smitty hoped.

"I can stay another day. We can go with. I'll behave. I haven't been to the beach in a long time, it could be fun," Jillian tried to persuade him.

"It's up to her. Ronnie won't let her go alone, so he's taking her. I asked to go," Smitty admitted. "I also told Ronnie I was putting you on a plane in the morning."

"Give me a chance to make things right," she pleaded, trailing her hand down his belly.

"Don't manipulate me with sex, Jilly. I already said it's her call to make." Smitty stilled her hand.

"I'm not trying to manipulate you, I want you," she said bluntly.

Smitty gave in, and rolled over her. "How much?"

Jillian wriggled under him, then pushed him back over. "Let me show you."

Smitty let her show him, she worked his body like a master artist with a vision, attention to every detail. Feeling better about this, they drifted off to sleep.

Chapter Sixteen

Mags stepped under the shower head and rinsed her hair. "Aedan, did you have a dream last night about Airy?" Mags called from the shower.

She saw him walk in the bathroom and took a moment to appreciate his glorious nakedness. "If you keep looking at me like that, I'm going to be in that shower with you in one second flat and be buried in you the next second." Aedan growled.

She giggled. "Come get me then, because I'm not going to stop looking."

True to his word, Mags found herself pressed up against the shower wall with Aedan buried in her deep. She rode him hard, her body needing his and the passion reaching a frenzied level fast. "Mmmm," Aedan moaned into her neck. "I love you Mags." She felt every pulse of his cock as he emptied in to her.

Coming down off her own orgasm she smiled, "Love you too, baby." She let Aedan clean her up and as they rinsed off, "So you never answered me, did you have a dream about Airy?"

"I didn't answer because you gave me a look that

sent the blood rushing to another part of my body and you weren't complaining about it," he teased. "Yes, I did. Does that mean I talked in my sleep or did you have one too?"

"I had one too. She was floating, talking to someone, and had enormous black wings. She looked so sad," Mags remembered.

"You just described my dream." Aedan gave her a weird look. "Is this the connection thing?"

"Maybe? I don't know," Mags said. "Should we be concerned?"

"Probably not, or one of the guys would have woken us up. Ronnie for sure would have brought the house down around us if something had happened to her," Aedan mused.

"Well let's see what this day holds for us," Mags said, swatting Aedan on the ass as she walked by him on her way to the closet looking for clothes.

Jax woke up slowly, like he was surfacing from deep underwater. Ronnie was facing Jax, on his side, his arm on Jax's shoulder, and still fast asleep. Behind him was Airiella, not asleep, sitting propped up, her knees to her chest, watching Jax.

Angel eyes locked gazes with him. His breathing hitched as he remembered she stayed with him, open to him the entire night. Desire licked at his body as he sunk into those glowing amber eyes. He said the first thing that came into his head, "Do you forgive me?"

The words startled both of them, though Jax knew he needed to know if she was angry with him. For anything. He'd been an ass so many times. Her eyes shimmered and Jax's heart tripped as she moved, gently climbing over Ronnie and settling herself in front of him.

Jax watched Ronnie's arm snake around her and pull her to his chest. She pushed her hair out of the way so Ronnie didn't breathe it in and Jax rolled to his side to face her, one arm under his head as he used that hand to wind her hair around his fingers.

"Of course, I forgive you," was her quiet whisper. Her fingers and palm sliding across the stubble on his cheek, his face becoming electric. He was absolutely addicted to the feel of her hand on his face.

He was still tired, his body feeling sluggish and drained. Until she touched him. He tipped his face to hers and lightly brushed her lips with his own. That was all he planned to do. Then she moaned at the contact and he couldn't stop. He sucked her bottom lip into his mouth and nibbled at it. She tasted intoxicating.

He slid his tongue between her lips, exploring every bit of that delectable mouth. His hand wove through her hair pulling her head to him, holding her captive. She gave just as good as she got, nipping back at his lips, her tongue dancing an erotic dance with his own. It was perfect.

Life flooded through his veins, her enticing smells wrapping around his senses, his body flushed with the spark only she brought him. "How do you do this to me?" he said against her lips.

She took his hand and placed it over her heart, her pulse was racing beneath his palm. "You do it to me, too," she said with a smile. He could swear he felt a piece of his soul mend itself back together in that moment.

"This isn't weird for you?" he asked curiously, gesturing at the intimate hold Ronnie had on her and the kiss Jax had just shared with her.

"Not even a little. I have the two greatest loves of my life on either side of me. Nothing has ever felt more right." Her tone was genuine and filled with warmth.

"Say that again, angel," came a muffled and sleepy response from Ronnie.

"I have the two greatest loves of my life on either side of me. Nothing has ever felt more right," she repeated. Jax heard Ronnie's contented sigh and watched in fascination as Ronnie's hand moved over to that hip that Jax wanted to sink his teeth into.

"Do you mean that?" Jax suddenly felt insecure. He figured asking was better than assuming she hadn't.

"With all of my heart. Give it time, Jax. She stroked the back of his hand that she still held over her heart.

"You had wings, in my dream," he remembered, leaving his hand right where it was.

"Yeah, that woke me up fast." She laughed quietly. "I woke up and tried to see my own back to see if they were still there."

"She did," Ronnie backed her up. "Scared the hell out of me, I had no idea what she was doing."

"Am I supposed to feel this tired?" Jax asked suddenly.

"I did," she told him.

"You still look tired." Jax finally moved his hand to swipe his fingertips under her eyes. "These are starting to look like bruises."

"Exactly what every girl wants to hear in the morning from a sexy man," she muttered. Ronnie laughed behind her.

"He's not wrong, angel. He just had bigger balls than I did to say it," Ronnie said gently. "I have a beach spot to take you to. It's about an hour's drive from here. Weather shows clear for the day, so we'll go."

Jax watched her face transform to a look of relief. "The beach?" He watched her face as he listened to her story about the beach back home and the way the ocean made her feel. "Can I join you?"

There was only a moment's hesitation before slowly nodded. "Just know that I'll need to be alone for a while. As long as I can have space, I don't care if people are there."

"Smitty wanted to come too. I told him it was your call, that we would talk to him this morning," Ronnie added, sitting up.

Jax hated to break the contact he had with her, though he did, sitting up too. "I'll give you space, but is it okay if I keep you in eye sight?"

She smiled and hugged him. It hit him hard, he was completely in love with her. "Of course." She looked at her watch. "It's still pretty early. Do either of you know if that pool out there is heated?" She pointed to the back yard.

"It is," Jax answered. "It's not warm outside though."

"It doesn't need to be." She stood. "Give me a couple hours before we leave."

Jax and Ronnie followed her out of the house and stopped when she dipped her fingers in the pool. She seemed satisfied and they followed her in the house. "I'm going to go shower and get some breakfast," Jax told Ronnie as she walked up the stairs.

"Well, it appears she's going to swim," Ronnie answered in amazement. "Um, there's a small walk to get to the beach, so bring appropriate shoes."

Jax nodded and they walked up the stairs, Airiella already on her way back down, wearing one of Ronnie's shirts and carrying a towel. "Go watch over her, I can see you don't want her to be alone. Rather, out of sight," Jax amended. "I'm fine."

Ronnie gave him a salute and raced off after Airiella. Jax felt a little lighter today, though he knew it was going to be tough going for him for a while. She had faith in him though, and that gave him strength. He stripped his clothes off and glanced out the window to the pool.

He was in time to catch her make a perfect dive into the pool, never breaking the surface until she was halfway back across from where she started. Jax had to force himself away from the window and climb in the shower.

Ronnie slowed his pace as the pool came in his sight line. She'd dropped her towel on one of the chairs, and it was like she didn't even notice the cool air surrounding her. She poised on the edge of the pool and dove right in like she was going home.

Her every movement was the definition of grace, she moved like she was one with the water. Ronnie was spellbound by the strength and fluid motion her body had as it sliced through the water. He could feel the joy coming from her and a sense of rightness. It was very clear that she was a skilled swimmer.

His thoughts flashed to the scar on her shoulder he'd seen and he wondered if that was why she hadn't mentioned swimming. Had she? He couldn't remember now. He rolled his pant legs up and sat on the edge of the pool, letting the warm water lap at his legs. He knew how to swim, but it wasn't one of the things he was good at.

He watched the ease and precision of her strokes, not with envy but admiration. She held her pace and kept form the entire time she was in motion. She was in her element here. It was like being in the boxing ring for him. She swam for about thirty minutes straight without stopping, varying her strokes on each lap, the transition seamless. She made it look easy.

He stood as he saw her slowing down, swimming a few laps skimming the bottom of the pool, her lung capacity amazing. Ronnie stripped to his boxers and lowered himself in the water. He wanted to be a part of this with her. It might have been selfish of him; he couldn't stay away though.

I knew Ronnie was there. I felt him come up and it didn't surprise me. It didn't bother me either. He let me be. The water flowing around my skin a comforting feeling to me as much as he was. The chlorine smell was as normal to me as oxygen.

In the water swimming, was one of the few places in my life I felt truly at ease and completely confident in myself. The connection I had with Ronnie was a close second, so him being here felt just as natural to me.

My shoulders were bothering me a lot more than normal since the nightmare of the live show and following events. I didn't push myself as hard as I could have, though I kept pace for fifty laps and then slowed down with a couple of underwater laps, letting my legs do the work. God, I missed swimming.

I surfaced at the shallower end of the pool and

pulled my hair from the tie I had it in, letting it flow free. I sunk back below the surface letting my hair float around my face as I sat on the bottom for a minute letting all the air out of my lungs so I stayed down.

When I popped back up, Ronnie was in front of me, his smile a sensuous one that had me on fire instantly. He advanced towards me until my back was against the side of the pool, his hands braced on the edge on either side of me, trapping me. This man drove me wild without even trying. God, he was incredibly fucking sexy.

He slid his knees between mine and lowered his face, capturing my mouth in a searing kiss while holding his body from touching mine. My senses flooded with nothing but this man, the water around us alive with our connection, amplifying everything. There was no outside world, there was just Ronnie, claiming my soul with a single kiss.

"Fuck, angel," he rasped as he tried to control his breathing. "You undo me like nothing else ever has. You taste like pure sin. Your body moves like it was made for me." He kissed up my neck over my jaw. "I thought you were beautiful before, but here, in the water, it was like I was seeing you for the first time. More beautiful and angelic than anything has the right to be."

My eyes were riveted on his, as he rained kisses down over my face. "Seeing you under the water just sitting there, your hair floating around your face, I saw the siren Jax see's in you."

I suddenly was aware that my hands were not on this living, breathing, steaming hot sex god standing in front of me. I slid them around his waist to his back, trying to pull him to me. His words making me burn with need so hot I was surprised the water wasn't boiling around us.

"Ronnie, please," I gasped, biting his shoulder as he leaned forward, his chest lightly pushing into me.

"You are incredible in the water, you know that?" he groaned as my hands slid under his boxers to dig my nails into his perfect ass. "I thought seeing you and Jax kiss earlier was sexy as hell, that doesn't even come close to how you are here. Why is that?"

"I'm not insecure in the water." My honest words surprised me.

"Fuck, you need to be in the water all the time," he growled as he gave in and settled his body against mine. He was magic. Our skin touching in that water damn near made me come. His rock-hard cock nestled right up against my most sensitive places, the buoyancy of the water making it even more erotic.

"Don't move, oh fuck. Ronnie, just stay just like that for a minute," I said, my voice husky and raspy with the feelings he brought out, my nerves teetering on an edge so pleasurable I didn't want it to stop.

"Why angel?" he growled into my ear. He shifted closer, and I felt it creeping up on me. That delicious release he brought to me.

"Oh.... god... Ronnie..." I groaned loud, my body starting to shudder. "Fuck... it feels.... so good..." I came in a rush, biting my lip as I drowned in his eyes.

A moan ripped through him as he crushed himself to me, his lips back on mine, his tongue stroking the fire even hotter. "Shit, angel, I love you so much," he said as he ground his hips into mine. "This, right now, isn't fucking," his hot whisper in my ear pushing me right back to the edge. "This is making love and I don't give a fuck who sees us."

I clung to him desperately as I wrapped my legs around him, every bit of that cock pressed between us. My hands desperately trying to free it from his boxers as he pushed aside my swimsuit and rubbed his finger against me, my hips bucking into him. I got him free and stroked him with my hand a few times until he stopped me.

"I want to be in you when I come, angel," he said and he guided himself to me and slid in. I'd never get tired of the feel of him inside me. His fingers worked magic as he slid in and out slowly, wringing cries of ecstasy that he swallowed from my lips as he tipped me closer and closer to another orgasm.

"Please, Ronnie," I begged, needing that release, the

connection a live wire between us, my legs anchored around his hips.

He switched his angle just slightly and brought my hips down hard, his cock hitting that spot inside that sent me flying over the edge, the climax blasting through me. The pleasure so intense that my voice was a silent scream, as I clenched around him tight, his hips thrusting at a mad pace as he jumped with me over the edge.

A gust of wind tore through the yard as we came, neither of us even noticing through the high our bodies brought us. We clung together, shaking through the aftershocks, his body still sealed to mine. He gave me another kiss that sent pleasure coursing through my veins again. I traced his tattoos with my finger, I didn't want to stop touching him.

"I may have to take up swimming now," he said with a smile, then kissed me again.

"Any more of that and I might drown." I dragged my fingers back up putting my hand around his neck.

"You in the water might be the most beautiful thing I've ever seen." He rested his forehead on mine, his gaze boring straight through to my soul.

"I'd have to argue that you hold that title." My hands splayed across that magnificent chest.

"Call it a tie then?" he chuckled.

"Deal." I nibbled at his jaw. Unhooking my legs, I slid back down him. "Let's go clean up." I held one hand out to him, while I used the other to hide his cock back in his boxers. I didn't want to share that view yet. "There's an ocean calling my name."

"Will you teach me to swim like that?" he asked me, his face serious.

"You don't know how to swim?" Our little pool adventure seemed a lot more dangerous now.

"Oh, I know how," he said and held my hand as we climbed out. "Not like that, though."

"Like what?" I had no idea what he was talking about.

"Like you are part of the water," he said and tugged

me closer. "Why didn't I know you could move like that?"

"I can only move like that in the water," I answered, wrapping the towel around me as he put his clothes back on. "Maybe on it too, I don't know. Rafting comes pretty easily to me."

"We can go kayaking," he suggested.

"No, you can." I shot him a look. "The thought of being trapped or held in on the water freaks me out. Plus, fish scare me."

He burst out laughing. "You move like that in water and fish scare you? You are as natural in it as they are!"

"I don't have gills or scales and am not slimy." I shuddered. "Yes, fish terrify me. Fish and reptiles. I used to be scared of birds too, but the raven has eased that a bit."

"The more I learn about you, the harder I fall," he said and tucked me under his arm as we walked back to the house.

"Ditto, Heracles." I kissed his chest.

Aedan blushed and looked away as Ronnie and Airiella walked back in the back door to find all of them staring at them. Aedan cleared his throat, but no words would come out. The look on Ronnie's face told him that he knew they'd all been watching.

Aedan blushed, "Um, you are good in the water." Realizing how that sounded, he coughed and looked down as Mags broke out in mad giggles.

Airiella's face flushed red. "Thank you? I don't know how to respond to that."

Jillian broke the uncomfortable silence, speaking what they all were thinking. "Fuck, that was hot."

Aedan refused to look, but he knew Smitty and Jax were just as hard as he was by the way they were standing. Only, Jillian and Jax didn't know what it felt like to feel the power of an orgasm with her. Aedan sat quickly in a kitchen chair pulling Mags on his lap to hide his arousal from the others.

Mags, of course found it hilarious. "Airy, you are like a goddess when you swim. That confidence looks amazing on you. And the sex with Ronnie, well, now you don't have to tell me details." Mags smiled at the look on her face.

"Mags, stop," Aedan whispered into her ear.

"She's not lying," Jillian added. "You're a natural in the water. The rest was just hot as hell."

Smitty looked like he was going to choke on his tongue. Jax, well he didn't know what was going through Jax's mind, but he figured a change of subject was a good thing. "Ronnie said you wanted to go to the beach. Do you mind if we tag along?"

Airiella shifted uncomfortably. "I don't mind. I told Ronnie that, but I will ask that you give me space. It's a healing thing for me, being at the ocean. I can feel that I need to be there. Also, I typically stay there until after sunset, not sure if you want to stay that long or not. If not, we can always take separate vehicles."

Mags jumped in, "You can have all the space you want, sweetie. I'll keep these overgrown apes away from you."

"Um, okay then. Maybe we should pack food and stuff?" Airiella looked nervous, and Aedan couldn't figure out why.

"If you don't want us to go, we won't go," Aedan broke in gently.

"It's fine. I, uh, I just need to go de-chlorinate," she stuttered, her face still pink.

Aedan got it, it was them seeing her and Ronnie. "She's embarrassed," he whispered to Mags.

"I'll take care of packing up some food. You go shower, don't worry about anything." Mags jumped up and gave Airiella a hug. Aedan knew she was whispering something naughty in her ear by the sudden new flush of color.

Airiella practically ran out of the room. "What did you say?" Aedan pulled her over to him.

"That maybe we should have another session with

her." Mags kissed him on the nose.

"Jesus, Mags," Aedan growled. He'd been thinking the same thing.

Jax trailed after an amused Ronnie and scarlet red Airiella back upstairs. He was horny beyond belief. Never did he once think that he would get turned on watching Ronnie have sex with someone he was in love with. Not ever a thought like that, once. Yet, here he was walking down the hall hard as steel.

They went into their own rooms, which made Jax absurdly happy for some reason. He used the connecting door and invaded Ronnie's space. Ronnie was stripping off his wet clothes and Jax noticed the nail marks on his back.

He gritted his teeth as his cock jumped. "Nice show."

"You liked that?" Ronnie grinned, not the least bit embarrassed.

"I'll admit to some voyeurism." Jax couldn't stop his own grin. "I don't fault you one bit. The way she looked in the water had me wanting to vault out my window."

"I gotta shower, chlorine makes my skin itch, I really don't want itchy balls," Ronnie said over his shoulder. "You can talk to me in the bathroom."

"You sure you don't mind all of us crashing this beach party?" Jax asked as he followed Ronnie in.

"It's not my call, and even if it was, no, I wouldn't mind. It's not like people can't wander off on their own," Ronnie called out over the noise of the water.

"Just checking, I don't want to intrude. That little show looked pretty intense," Jax added as a side thought.

"It was. First time I've ever said the words making love to a woman." Ronnie's tone was warm.

"That real for you?" Insecurity took hold of Jax, it must have shown in his tone because Ronnie stuck his lathered-up head out of the curtain to look at him.

"It is. Imagine, if you can, that you can understand

how she feels for me, and now think about what she has said to you, that she feels even stronger for you. What does that tell you?"

Jax realized he was being stupid, especially after seeing them together and not being turned off by it. "That I should take swimming lessons?"

Ronnie guffawed. "Indeed, you should. I asked her to teach me."

Jax laughed along with Ronnie. "You might have an additional person in your class now."

Ronnie peeked out the curtain again, studying Jax's face. "Interesting. This is something we should discuss further."

Jax paused before heading out. "Yeah, um, I'm going to go grab some extra clothes to bring with. See you downstairs."

Jax went back into his room and pulled out a bag he had stuffed in the closet. A skirt he had seen when he went to get replacement clothes for Airiella. It made him think of her the minute he saw it. He pulled it out of the bag and crossed the hall.

He tapped lightly on the door, but she didn't answer so he poked his head in, the smell of the jasmine lotion he had gotten her settling on his senses was as potent as what he witnessed between her and Ronnie.

She peeked around the corner of the door, steam wafting out of the bathroom. "Hey, Jax." She smiled and pulled the door open. Jax immediately put his hands in front of his crotch to hide his erection.

"Hey. Uh, sorry, didn't mean to intrude." He felt like a horny teenager.

"You aren't." She walked over to him and stood on her toes to kiss him. "You looked like you needed that."

He pulled her back to him, her scent heady and he sunk into her lips. "Definitely needed that," he said, his voice sounding desperate.

"I never would have figured that," she gestured at the skirt, "was your style."

Jax grinned. "I need swimming lessons," he blurted

out.

She paused and looked back at him. "Fuck," she said under her breath, but Jax caught it. She was back in front of him in two steps. "We could arrange some private tutoring," she all but purred, her hand slipping under his shirt and up his chest.

Visceral need tore through him so violently he shook from the force of it. "Oh god, I'm going to drown," he muttered, forcing himself to take a step back. "I want you so goddamn bad it hurts."

She had an unreadable look on her face. "But?"

"Not yet. Not like this. I want you to know what it means for me when we do, because I'm pretty sure there will be no going back for me." Jax's voice got rough and he thought he'd made a mess of things.

"I understand. I'm not sure I'm ready for you yet either." She gave him a look that made him want to take back everything he just said. "Don't stop kissing me, though." Those angel eyes held him captive, leaving him no doubt she wanted him too.

"When I saw this, I immediately thought of you." Jax thrust the skirt out to her, talking fast.

"I love it. Thank you." She brushed a kiss over his cheek. "I'm glad you are coming with us."

She pulled the towel off her head and those dark wet locks fell down her back in a tangle of curls and waves. "I'm, uh, I'm going to go grab a few things. See you downstairs." He backed out of her room before his body took over and he buried himself in her. Then he stepped back in. "Wait."

She turned back to look at him as she set her backpack on the bed. "Something else?"

Jax fisted his hands, "Can I see you?"

Confusion passed over her face, "I'm not following."

Jax crossed the room, gently closing the door behind him. "I want to see all of you."

She flushed, that beautiful bronze skin taking on a pink glow. "I, uh, I'm shy like that."

Jax reached his hand out and with a flick of his

fingers the towel around her dropped, a guttural groan spilled from him and his eyes closed, her curves seared into his mind. Jax sunk down to his knees. "When we were talking this morning, and Ronnie moved his hand to your hip, all I kept thinking about was how fucking sexy that hip was and I wanted to sink my teeth into. Brace yourself, siren." He leaned forward, the scent of her arousal making him crazy, but that hip was right there in front of him.

The curve so enticing he kissed it first, then ran his tongue over it. At the sound of her quickening breathing, he nipped lightly first, then bit down just enough to leave little indentations on her skin. He grabbed the towel and stood back up, wrapping it around her. "Don't be shy with me. You have the body of a goddess, soft, sweet, curves and valleys, it's fucking perfection. If I don't leave now, I won't leave."

He kissed her again, a bruising kiss that left those luscious lips swollen and her big angel eyes filled with desire.

Chapter Seventeen

Smitty decided he would drive. Thankfully, the SUV they had seated seven, and they all piled their bags into the back, Jillian sitting up front with him. Mags and Aedan in the row behind them, with Ronnie, Airiella and Jax in the last row.

She was sandwiched between the two, but appeared to be leaning on Jax a little. The swimming had put a little life in her eyes, or the session after with Ronnie, he wasn't sure which. Exhaustion still lined her face though, and her normally tan skin color was so much more pale than normal.

Every one of them had expressed concern for her, surprisingly, even Jillian. After watching her and Ronnie in the pool, Jillian's attitude had seemed to completely flip around. She had even gone far enough to suggest a threesome between them, and Smitty had swiftly knocked that one down. For some reason, he didn't want Jillian to be a part of what he shared with Airiella. It was theirs.

They had at the minimum, an hour's drive if they hit no traffic. He glanced back in the rearview mirror again and saw that Jax had shifted so he was more turned to her and she was slumped over into him, his arm around her and her eyes closed, her legs must have been in Ronnie's lap.

He caught Ronnie's eye and mouthed, "Is she okay?" Ronnie nodded back, then pointed to her ears. Smitty couldn't figure out what he was trying to say, then he moved her hair and saw ear buds. Oh. She was shutting them out already, or she was just that tired.

He saw Mags look back at Airiella and nudged Aedan and motioned for him to stay quiet. Smitty got it, she was asleep. Smitty glanced back at Jax and saw his eyes were closed too, and he looked more relaxed than he had ever seen him before. She was good for him. Hell, she was good for all of them.

Ronnie still looked concerned, and his arms were moving so he guessed that he was rubbing her legs. Smitty focused back on the road, he hoped this little trip is what she needed to regain some of her strength back.

He thought back to the vision of her in wings, the heartbreaking look of love on her face. He thought about the story of her life and marveled that she could be the way she was after all of it. He heard wings flapping and his eyes flew around the inside of the SUV looking for the raven. It didn't look like anyone else heard it though.

I was comfortable, warm and didn't want to move. I knew I was on Jax, there was no mistaking the feel of him for anyone else. I also knew I was on Ronnie. The music played for my ears only, the songs Ronnie had put together for me. The vibrations of the road had changed though, and that's what woke me up.

I sat up. Jax kept his arm around me like he didn't want me to move. That was fine. I didn't want to move either. I wanted to see where we were though. On a dirt road, not a well maintained one either, judging by the way the SUV was bouncing around.

Long grass or weeds were all around us, and we

were in the middle of hills. Steep rocky inclines on either side with this narrow dirt road cutting a path through it. A shiver of fear tore through me at the thought that the tall grass might hide snakes and I'd have to walk through it.

"What's the matter, siren?" Jax tightened his arm around me and spoke directly into my ear, his voice mixing with the music.

I pulled out the ear bud next to him, "Are there snakes in that grass?"

At the look of terror on his face I assumed he was afraid of them too. "I hope not."

Ronnie rested his hand on my thigh. "No, angel, not at this time of year. You both are safe from them," he chuckled.

"I think that if we saw one, you'd be carrying both Jax and me, so you'd better be right," I fired off. Mags and Aedan trying to hide their laughter in front of me.

The sky was clear, no sign of clouds. The temperature on the dashboard that I could see read 63 degrees. That was about normal for me. It was still morning too, so it could warm up more. I hoped that it would because after all the sexual tension this morning with Jax, I'd forgotten to bring a coat.

I wore the skirt Jax had gotten me. It was a gauzy material, like a gypsy skirt. Bright colors in a patchwork pattern with knitting between them. Red, orange, yellow, green and that aqua blue, the color of Smitty's eyes. Vibrant, it made me think of life. I had been smart enough to wear a pair of my capri leggings underneath so I could wade around in the water and not get the skirt wet. I had one yellow shirt that matched the color in the skirt so I wore that too.

I also had my hiking boots on because Ronnie had told me we'd have to walk a little bit. I packed an extra set of dry clothes, a flashlight and a pair of flip flops I could wear on the beach. Anticipation was bubbling inside me and I reached across Jax to open the window a bit.

He pulled me on to his lap and like a dog, I stuck my head out the window, his chest rumbling with laughter behind me. There it was, the scent of the ocean, faint, but it was close. And that air was not warm. I closed the window and went to sit back in my seat.

Jax locked his arms around me, "Stay there, please," he said softly into my ear. "I love how this feels."

If I was honest, I did too. I just leaned back against him, his body heat chasing away the chill of the morning air. Not too much longer and we came to the end of where the vehicle could go, and there was maybe enough space for 2 cars to fit there. We were the only ones though. Perfect.

Jax opened the door and helped me out after Aedan and Mags got out, and Ronnie was in the back handing out bags. "Angel, your pack is awfully light."

"Yeah, I uh, forgot my coat. Not a big deal, I don't get cold easily," I tried to deflect. Ronnie wasn't having it though. He started to argue with me when Jax interrupted.

"I have an extra sweatshirt, we're good," Jax told him, grabbing his pack.

"I brought a few blankets too," Mags added.

Ronnie smiled knowing he was beat. "They saved you a lecture," he said with a laugh.

I stood on my toes and whispered in his ear, "Maybe you should spank me later," and darted away before he could grab me.

"I have no idea what she just said, but the look on your face is priceless." Jax laughed and took a picture of Ronnie with his phone.

I pulled my pack on and tightened my laces on my boots. The call of the ocean was strong now and I let it pull me. I popped my ear buds back in and left them standing there laughing at each other. The narrow little trail went up for a little way, then dropped down to the beach.

The view bowled me over. Dramatic rocky cliffs to my right gave way to a beach filled with large rocks that met the shoreline, kissed by the breaking surf. To my left was another cliff, but this one all sandy dirt, opening up to miles of beach spreading out to the left. The blue sky meeting the white-capped blue of the ocean.

Didn't have the same feel as the one at home, but it

was still the ocean. The salty air filled my lungs and the roar of the breaking waves filled my soul. I made my way down and found a premade firepit with some large washed up trees as makeshift benches. I pulled off my hiking boots and socks and put on the flip flops, setting my dry clothes on top of the shoes so they didn't get dirty.

As the rest came down the trail, I looked at them all and felt love. The beach was already working its magic on me. I dropped my walls and felt them all out. Every one of them had a variety of negative emotions and I needed them gone, so I took a deep breath and faced them all as they started placing their bags around the fire pit.

"One last thing before I wander. Aedan, I know you struggle with understanding this, but in order for me to get the benefits I need from being here, I need to have my walls down. That means that everything that you are feeling is going to keep battering at me, leaving me exactly where I'm at now. Will it be okay with each of you if I take those negative emotions away?"

Ronnie practically leapt forward at me. "Angel..."

"Not that particular one from Jax, just the others," I clarified.

"Only the negative one?" Aedan looked at me strangely.

"Yes, the insecurities, concern, fear, worry, anger, frustration, stress, those that harm you. I will just take them on and release them out when I wander off to have my own space," I said lightly.

Smitty swallowed. "Why?"

"It's not going to hurt me, Smitty. It will help all of us. You'll have a carefree day, and I won't be feeling those things coming from you." I focused my energy inward on to the connection I shared with them all. I heard Mags gasp and opened my eyes.

Now visible was the connections I had with each of them, except Jillian. I pointed to the glowing threads. "This allows you to feel what I'm feeling, each of you touch yours, my walls are down, and you'll better understand what I mean."

"How did you do this?" Smitty asked in wonder.

"No idea, I just knew I could," I answered him as plainly as I could. I felt each one of them touch it, the echo of their own emotions rolling back at them. Aedan was the first to capitulate, Jax the last.

"What if I hurt you?" he stepped next to me.

"I'm not going to pull that energy from you right now. It wouldn't benefit either of us. You need to heal as much as I do. Without these other things weighing you down, you'll have a better chance at that." I touched the frayed thread between us that looked a little stronger today. "I'll give you what you need, Jax, always."

His eyes held worry, but he agreed. The only one I didn't do anything with was Jillian. She had to be separate. As a group I pulled all the negative into me, taking it on, letting it weigh me down like a heavy gravity on my soul. Then I picked up the thread of love that was strong in each of them and I pushed as much love as they could hold back into them.

I gave them a weak smile at the expressions on their faces and let the connections fade from sight. "Jillian, will you come with me for a minute please?"

She gave me a startled look, though she nodded her head. Smitty looked like he wanted to argue and Ronnie stepped over to him, a smile lighting that beautiful face. "She's fine, she knows what she is doing."

Jillian followed me towards the surf. "I didn't feel you do anything," she started.

"I haven't done yours yet, I don't have a connection with you." I turned to look at her, and exhaustion pulled at me. "I know you don't trust me or like me, that's fine with me. Please allow me to pull those insecurities from you so that you can have a nice day here. I don't want anything to taint the group emotion wise. You have nothing to fear from me."

"I know that now. Please accept my apology for my behavior. I do mean it, and if possible, I would like to have a second chance."

"Deal. Can I pull it from you?" She nodded and I

plucked out the bad stuff swirling around in her and pulled it away, taking on more. "I'm going to replace what I took with the emotion you are feeling from being here in this place. I call it calm; you can call it whatever it is you are feeling, okay?" She nodded again. Her face was already lighter without the crappy emotions in her. I pushed the calm feel from me into her.

"That's amazing." I stiffened as she threw her arms around me and hugged me.

"Smiling looks good on you," I told her. "Please let the others know I need space now."

"Of course." She took off running back to the group.

I headed directly for the water, stopping just short of the tide line, digging my feet into the sand and connecting to the earth. I shut the music off and tucked the earbuds and iPod into the pocket of my backpack. Right now, I needed just the earth music.

There was a slight breeze to the air coming from the north, chilling my skin, my hair floating across my vision and off to the side, the gauzy skirt pressed against my right leg flying out away from my left. The sound of the waves filling my ears with the power of nature, the water very the essence of life.

I stepped out of the skirt, folding it and putting it in my backpack to keep it dry. I hadn't been to an ocean since all this started, and the heaviness of all the emotions I just pulled was begging to be released. The diminished capacity I had at the moment letting me know it was time.

I stepped into the receding water, the sand sucking my feet down with the tide's ebb and flow. The healing energy that only the ocean can bring me soaked into my feet and I let it go. The sun shone down on my back, the salt water swirling around my feet, and now the grateful tears that fell easing the heavy feeling that had been holding me down. "Thank you," I whispered to the wind.

Ronnie and Jax followed the path of Airiella, keeping their distance while maintaining sight of her. The weight of their combined emotions he had felt in her was staggering. Filled with the love she freely gave them all, he felt lighter than he had in a while without the other stuff eating away at it.

They were both mesmerized at the sight of her standing there, the vibrant color of her clothes molded to her curves on one side and flowing with the breeze on the other. Her dark hair glowing a coppery red in the sunlight, the long tresses perfectly suspended in the air.

Jax said softly, "Can you see them?"

"See what? I see Airiella." Ronnie was transfixed by the sight of her like that.

"Her wings, I can see their outline." Jax's finger traced a pattern in the air in front of him.

Ronnie looked closer, following the lines Jax drew, and he felt the air rush out of him as he saw them. "Ghost wings," Ronnie exclaimed. "They look like they should be on a ghost."

"Or an angel." Jax gave him a sideways look. "Is it just me or is it almost physically painful to not go to her?"

"It's not just you." It had been like that from the start when he was around her. It bothered him to not touch her. She was taking off the skirt and putting it in her backpack, he noticed her body moved more fluidly here as well, like when she was in the water. Not the same amount of grace, but she moved with a feeling of complete peace.

She stepped into the water and Ronnie heard Jax's breath catch in the same moment that his did. Her head was slightly tilted back as if she were looking at something in the sky, her arms loose by her side. That's not what stole the air from them though. It suddenly became completely still, no movement in the air, no sound, and in front of her Ronnie saw a swirling mass of air like a mini tornado. Even more astounding was the air had a color to it. Dark like a storm cloud and it was pulling the color right out of her body.

"Is this real?" Jax's words sounded muffled and far

away, and a feeling of deep contentment settled over Ronnie.

"Holy shit," Ronnie breathed. "That was all those emotions from us leaving her."

Ronnie looked back to the others and saw they were all staring at Airiella. He desperately wished that releasing the energy from Jax was as easy as that. The unpleasant thought of just how bad that energy must be to do what it does to her struck him like a sucker punch.

She started to walk again and Ronnie followed, keeping his distance, Jax silently following Ronnie. Neither one aware that the sound had now come back into the air. "Can I talk to you?"

Jax broke the spell Ronnie had fallen under. "Of course." Ronnie looked over at him, seeing more of the guy he used to be.

"I learned that one of the ways I need to heal is to forgive myself." Jax looked uncomfortable. Ronnie put his hand on Jax's shoulder. "There's no one on earth closer to me than you, well maybe her now, but you know what I mean. Since we were kids, it's always been you and me."

Ronnie wasn't sure where this was headed and he could see that Jax was struggling with the words. "Always."

"For so long now, I have hated myself with such dark thoughts because of what you went through. I should have stopped it, should have done better or more to protect you, to protect your mom who was as close to me as my own. I saw it, I heard it, and I did nothing. I watched as he destroyed you, every bruise made me hate myself more and more. Every time you were drunk or high was another nail in my coffin of being someone who you couldn't rely on."

Of all the things Jax could have said, that was the farthest from what Ronnie expected. He tripped over his feet in the sand, Jax steadying him before he could fall. "What?"

Ronnie faced him, the broken pieces of Jax visible now that Ronnie knew what to look for. "I'm so sorry, Ronnie," Jax cried. "I wanted to save you and I didn't know how."

Ronnie hated talking about his past. Jax was the only one who really knew most of it. He'd made Jax promise not to tell. "We were kids. Jax, nothing that happened to me was your fault." Ronnie's lungs felt like they were being squeezed. He couldn't breathe.

"In my eyes, I should have done more. I was terrified every day that you wouldn't show up, that you'd be gone, that I would lose you." Jax's eyes shone with total honesty and a pain Ronnie didn't want to see. "I was afraid that if I broke your promise, you'd never talk to me again. It was only years later that I learned that having you never talk to me again would have been better than seeing what you went through."

He had no air. The past beatings from his father flying through his head, the echoes of the blows landing silently on his skin, his mom's empty eyes. "Ronnie, look at me." His skin tingled. He knew that voice. He couldn't breathe, his vision was darkening. "Ronnie, baby, please." He shifted his eyes.

She was in front of him, her hands on his face. Love, he felt love, the darkness pulled away by the angel that was constantly saving them. Shaking he looked at Jax. "Why? Why would you assume blame for something someone else did? Jax, why didn't you fucking say something?"

He wasn't aware that Airiella had walked back away from them. She was right to, this was between him and Jax and was most likely what was at the root of that shit that grew in him. They'd been just kids when it had started. Young kids, neither of them knew about violence from a parent. She'd warned him about this possibility last night.

"I couldn't, you didn't want to talk about it. Ever. Then later, you were so angry, so violent that it just grew in me." Jax paced in the sand. "I felt selfish for not talking to you about it because I didn't want to lose the friendship. I never broke the promise, Ronnie. I never told. I made Smitty guess, and he told. It made me feel even guiltier and by then I hated myself so deeply, that everything that hurt you made me feel worse. I didn't understand what being an empath was, I never knew that the feelings that your mom, your father and you felt resonated in me. I didn't know those were feelings you were having. I couldn't separate them from my own."

Ronnie pulled Jax down to sit on a log, he felt like his legs were going to buckle, and he couldn't look Jax in the eye and see the pain that had broken him reflected there. "Jax, there wasn't one day in my life that I blamed you for anything that had to do with that. It's not even a thought that crossed my mind. Why would it? I was ashamed that it was happening, I was scared he'd hit you too."

"I know you've never blamed me for any of it. But I did. God, I feel like I'm in a twelve-step program right now. I needed to tell you, I guess, to free this from inside. I'm not trying to burden you with it, I don't want you to carry it. I want us to heal. You and me. From all the other stupid shit I did to you with Winnie, with leaning on you all these years, letting you carry me. I can't try and fix that shit unless you know why it all built."

Ronnie understood with a startling clarity now. Knowing what he knew about empath's, about energy from all this research he had done because of Airiella, he got how this could have manifested and become so dark and powerful. Hate was strong. Thanks to Airiella, he knew love was stronger.

"Jax, back at home, when we fought, I forgave you then for the shit with Winnie when you talked it out with me. It might still make me mad at times, but I don't hold a grudge against you or hate you for it. We were both young and dumb. All three of us are equally to blame for where we found ourselves with that. As for my childhood, you are right. I don't like talking about it. I didn't then and I don't now. It hurts, and for sure left physical, mental and emotional scars, but it's over. Even if you had said something to someone back when we were young, it could have made it worse. You don't have anything to ask for forgiveness for. If you need to hear it though in order to forgive yourself, I forgive you."

"Watching you go through that shaped so much for

me. When I hit you, I fucking broke inside. I don't know how to forgive myself for that, much less anything else." Jax's breathing was rough, though he was holding it together reasonably well. "I wanted you to beat me to death."

"That *was* a low point in our friendship. I also know it wasn't you," Ronnie said slowly.

"Why are you letting me off so easily on this?" Jax was serious.

"You are far harder on yourself than I could ever be. The truth is, I don't blame you. Yeah, the punch was low, and it hurt. I saw red. What held me back from retaliating though is I won't let myself be like him. I knew it wasn't you, and hitting you wasn't going to make me feel better. He won't ever have a part in my life anymore, not through my actions, or any other way. Jax, your friendship got me through those years. I knew I had a safe place with you. I stayed because of my mom. We've always had a different relationship than others, we've always been able to talk about our feelings without feeling awkward and share our lives. I've always known how much you love me, even if it's words we don't really say often. Actions show it."

"When Airiella joined us and I saw how you reacted to her, I wanted to hate her. Actually, I think that part of me did hate her. Those feelings made me so insecure and jealous of how much you wanted to be around her, I thought I was losing you again. I can't say I won't be an asshole any more, but I am aware of my reactions now and am trying to control my them." Jax leaned forward and cupped some sand and let it fall through his fingers.

"When she chose Smitty over me, I had a hard time controlling my reactions," Ronnie told him. "I was insanely jealous. From the start I wanted her. The fucking second she walked in the room, my heart was gone. I was drawn to her like a magnet. I didn't get it. After she pulled that energy from you the first time and told Smitty she needed him and for me to stay with you, I still didn't get it. In my eyes, she kept choosing Smitty. When I saw how he looked afterwards, my views started to change a little bit. He wouldn't talk about it, I felt shut out by one of my best friends. I saw how you were reacting to her, and how Aedan pretended like he knew what was going on. There was a constant in that though, that first week. You, Jax. I had hope for the first time I was going to get you back, and I knew that this woman was the way it would happen."

"Once I learned she slept with Smitty I had hope you would walk away from her. I never saw her treat you differently though. She looked at you like you were the best piece of chocolate on earth," Jax said, a far off look on his face.

"It was after Smitty talked to me, well, he blew his top really, fucking lost his shit on me, that I started to understand we were in the presence of something that was bigger than us and the petty bullshit we called our lives. I need to be around her, touching her, protecting her. It's a feeling I can't lose. There was one point where she told me that you and I were her strongest connections and it scared her. I swear, I almost lost my mind thinking she was afraid of me. Then I focused on you, she had told me the connection she felt with you was the strongest. I told myself that I would back off, you needed her far more than I did."

"Ronnie..." Jax started.

"No, chill Jax. Let me finish. It's been one traumatic event after another, and it always comes back to us as a group. We get through it together. When she told you that the anchor has to drown to save you, it hit me hard too. She's been saving us since the first day she walked into our lives. There's no shortage of love in her. It took me a bit to understand that. When I did, I realized that even if you are her strongest connection, even if you are supposed to be in her future, so am I. All of us are. I stopped backing off. Her feelings for any of us never changed, no matter what we did. That love didn't go away. Every heart attack she's given me by running head first into mortal danger, to every sarcastic reply, to every tear she's let loose; that love has never changed. Steady, reassuring and there. It took root in me, it's a part of me, the same way you are a part of me. I know how freaked out you are about being with the same person I am with, but consider this, maybe it's supposed to be that way. I was never worried about sharing her with you. It's you, there's no one closer to me. It doesn't feel wrong."

"I'll never forget her words, Ronnie. None of them. The ones I will remember the most though is when she told me she wished someone would save her once." Jax closed his eyes. "One of the biggest gut punches I've ever gotten from words. You're right, it does weird me out a little, mostly because of the Winnie thing, and that's something I need to get over on my own. When I saw you guys in the pool this morning, it didn't bother me. It was fucking hot."

Ronnie chuckled, "Just wait until you are on the receiving end of it."

"I'm scared, Ronnie. I'm terrified I'm going to hurt her. I'm afraid to let her love me, I'm even more afraid to admit that I love her."

"Just go with it. Whether you are afraid to let her love you or not, she still loves you. Three times since you have met her, she has died for you. Four if you count the energy she pulled from Winnie before she even met any of us. The hate you have inside you is no comparison to the strength of the love she gives. You want to save her? Give her the love right back. She said as much. She's trying to heal her past just like you are." Ronnie shook his head. "Hearing the few details she's shared with me tore me right open. I understand why she feels the way she does, the only way I can fight that is to love her. I'm always touching her, telling her she's beautiful, strong, amazing, it's those little things that are healing her. Just like it's doing with you. Every time she touches you, whether you know it or not, a little piece of the Jax I used to know comes back."

"She doesn't believe anyone could really love her." Jax's tone broke. "God, Ronnie. The things one of the guys of her past said that I saw sent me into a blind rage, and I was trapped there. He beat her with golf clubs."

Ronnie flinched. "She hasn't shared that story yet. I don't know if I want to hear that one."

Jax gulped, "The rape, when you guys pulled me

out..."

"Don't. Not here, not now. She needs to rebuild her strength here. Let her tell us those details when she is ready." Ronnie didn't want to hear it. He would listen if she needed to tell him, to clear it away, and he was just as sure it would kill a part of him.

"Here, she's kind of like she was in the water." Jax changed the subject. Ronnie nodded, his eyes following her form as she got farther away from them. "There's a difference here."

"She connects to nature." Ronnie stood. "She's too far away, let's move."

Jax followed him. "It's not only Smitty that's different now, you are too." Jax observed him.

"We all are, Jax. She's changed all of us." Ronnie threw his arm around Jax's shoulders. "Just keep the lines of communication open. Even if it's only with me, or her, or both of us. Hell, any of us. Healing will come from letting go of that hate, replacing it with love." Ronnie hoped something had gotten through to Jax today, as much as it had hurt dredging up his past, he'd do it all over again if it brought him back.

Chapter Eighteen

Smitty was huddled over the fire pit. "What the fuck is that?" came the exclamation from Jillian. Smitty looked up from piling wood in the fire pit.

"What?" he didn't know what she was looking at.

"Holy shit," came Aedan's startled cry.

His eyes were drawn to Airiella who was now standing in the water and had a cyclone thing in front of her. He bolted to his feet, amazement washing over him as a feeling of peace settled. "Oh my God," he said as understanding came to him.

"It's the release of our emotions," Mags said quietly standing next to him.

"Fuck, I wish the one I had seen had been like that," Smitty swore.

His gazed moved over to Jax and Ronnie who were huddled together, talking. He only sat back down when she started moving again. Working on piling the wood up just right to get a good strong fire going.

"She's actually pretty cool," Jillian stated sitting next to him. "I'm over my tantrum now, sorry about that. I apologized to her too. I'll apologize to Jax when they get back."

Smitty looked over at her, the smile he loved to see planted on her face. "That makes me happy to hear."

"She seems more relaxed here than she does at the house," came the next comment.

"She was like that when we were at her place too," Aedan commented. "Well, when she took us to the mountain anyway."

"Nature is how she feeds her soul," Mags told them all. "What? You couldn't figure that out?"

"How do you know that?" Smitty was curious.

"Besides it being obvious? She told me. Her energy gets restored in nature, the bad gets taken out and purified and the earth energy that's clean fills her back up. She said she can pull from the earth anywhere she feels it, but that in nature she feels restored. There are no emotions out there, just pure life. Nothing battling her for space or time."

"Huh," Smitty mused. "I should have realized that."

"Didn't you feel it when the negative energy just left her?" Mags seemed shocked.

"I felt a feeling of peace," Aedan admitted.

"Me too," Smitty added. He paused, looking at Jillian before going on, not really sure if he should say it or not, "I just figured I felt it because I was watching her. Typically, when I touch her, I feel the same way."

"Crazy! I felt that too when she put her hand on my arm!" Jillian exclaimed. Smitty breathed a sigh of relief she didn't flip out.

"So, uh, did anyone else see the outline of wings when she was standing there?" Aedan's tone was hesitant. Smitty almost laughed.

Mags to the rescue, "Duh. Took you this long to figure it out?"

Smitty wondered if he should start the fire now. He checked his watch, no, it was too early and would probably warm up a bit. He held out his hand to Jillian, "Let's go explore that way over by the rocks."

He wanted to keep the space Airiella needed to do whatever she needed to do. As he stood, he saw her running over to Ronnie who was now on the ground. "Go." Jillian pushed him, but he held his ground.

"She needs space. I don't know what's happening but I know she won't let anything happen to any of us. She's got this." Smitty sounded a lot surer than he felt. He forced himself to move away from her, his brain protesting at the distance. "Come on."

Those two were going to kill me with the emotions flying between them. I knew it was necessary and that Jax was making an effort, he had totally caught Ronnie off guard though. The panic and fear that slammed into me sent me flying when I saw Ronnie stumble. I'd never felt that from him before.

I didn't want to pull it, but I had to. Ronnie was in full panic mode and not breathing. I pushed love back at them both and when Ronnie was under control slipped away again. Salt water definitely helps, I realized as I stepped back into the water.

I wandered farther away from them while they weren't looking. Not that distance was going to change the way I felt about either of them, it gave me a sense of space though. I lost myself in thoughts, not even really paying attention to the thoughts themselves, just soaking up the salty air.

Whoever had made that saying about salt water curing everything was a genius. Sweat, tears and the ocean. The sun felt warm on my skin in between the breezes and the sand between my toes even better. The water rolling over my feet was the best though.

The immensity of the oceans never failed to astound and amaze me with their mysteries, power and ability to give life and destroy it. I waded out farther, the water up around my knees now. It was cold, the push and pull of the water making me sway with it. It was freeing being around the ocean.

It had always been that way for me. I missed my

beach, the memories it held for me, the moody skies and always fun tide pools. Rippled sand drifts and drift wood scattered all over from the crazy waves depositing its treasures on the beach. The water stretching endlessly to the horizon, sparking my imagination about far off places and sailing into the sunset. No, this place wasn't the same, the calming and soothing effect were just as helpful though.

I splashed around, having fun kicking water up and watching it sparkle in the sunlight. Slowly I was coming back to myself. I was still exhausted, though now I could feel it was a feeling of not enough sleep, and not this heavy weight of expectation laying on me. Expectation only I put on myself, and the magic of the ocean washed away.

I felt childlike and spur of the moment flung my arms out to the side and spun in circles in the water, only stopping when I felt myself begin to tip over. I didn't want my dry clothes to get wet. I looked back and saw that I could no longer even see where the fire pit was at. I glanced at my watch and saw I had walked 3 miles.

Jax and Ronnie were still following me, though they were feeling much better now, and my heart soared. Progress! I knew Jax had it in him. And Ronnie, he was a dream. He made this happen for me. I turned toward the guys and headed towards them. I still needed space, but I also needed to feel them for a minute.

They kept their word though and the closer I moved to them, the more they moved. I paused. Hmmm. I'd frozen them in place before, I wonder if I could do it again. I felt around the earth energy, letting it speak to me, feel out my intentions and followed the energy source to them. I felt their weight pressing into the sand and I asked the energy to hold them there.

I had no idea if it worked or not, so I started moving towards them again. I didn't see them moving. It worked! Elation flew through me. I shrugged off one of the straps of my backpack and jogged to them. I dropped the pack and asked the earth to let them go. Jax moved first.

I launched myself at him and he caught me, stumbling backwards, a look of utter shock on his face. I laughed and rained kisses down on his face until I got a crooked smile and his eyes lit up. I let go and launched at Ronnie, who was now expecting it.

"Angel, you scared the hell out of me when I saw you running. You need to kiss me and make it better." He grinned.

I planted a big wet kiss on him and slid back down. "Sorry. Well not really. I was so happy to feel things settle between you I couldn't help it. Also, I just needed to feel you both for a moment." I grabbed the waistband of Ronnie's pants and tugged him closer to Jax so I could hug them both at the same time. "You guys had me worried."

Jax buried his face in my hair. "You smell like sunshine."

"How'd you do the freezing thing us to again?" Ronnie asked, sliding his hand up my shirt to skim my back.

"I asked the earth to hold you there."

"You asked the earth?" Ronnie looked confused.

"I always feel the energy of the earth, wherever I am. In nature though it's so much stronger for me, I can connect to it. That's the first time I've ever tried that, I'm kinda surprised it worked." I grinned excitedly.

Ronnie was still feeling up and down my back. Jax was doing the same, but over my shirt instead of under it like Ronnie was doing. I liked their hands on me, I wasn't about to question it. Especially with Jax. "You look completely different right now than you did when he got here." Jax searched my face.

"Is that good or bad?" I wasn't sure where he was going with this.

"Definitely good," Ronnie jumped in. "You still look tired, but that fire in you is back."

"Is that what you meant, or is Ronnie jumping in so you don't say something you think will upset me?" I gave Jax a look.

He cracked up laughing. "That is so true it's funny. It's what I meant this time. I probably wouldn't have said fire, that's a little too soon for me. I would have said life."

"The sound of you laughing is beautiful." He captivated me. I pulled his head down and kissed him, showing him exactly how I felt. When his grip tightened on me and his breathing became staggered, I let go.

"Hey, what about my laugh?" Ronnie poked me in the side.

"The sound of your silence is more beautiful right now," I shot back at him.

Jax starting laughing so hard he clutched his sides. Ronnie grinned at me, "Nicely played. You get points for that one."

"Okay, I'm going back to my alone time. I just needed to satisfy a craving I had for you two." I stepped back to Jax wrapping my arms around him in a tight hug. I loved that he did it back. "Whatever you are doing, keep doing it. It's working," I whispered in his ear.

I turned to Ronnie and hugged him the same way. He hugged me back lifting me off the ground and spinning me in a circle. "Thank you for this," I whispered in his ear.

He put me down and I put my pack back on. "I'm heading back the way we came." I took off back towards the water. I still needed that fix. Only now, I put the music back on.

Mags stared down the beach. Airy had wandered far enough off to be out of sight. It made Mags uncomfortable because Airy looked so done in. She sat with Aedan in front of the fire pit looking out to the ocean. Smitty had found a good location that was for sure.

They were alone here. "Let's go walk." Mags pushed her shoulder into Aedan. "We never just do simple things like that anymore."

"Sure, why not? We're here for the whole day. No electronics, no people to help us if something goes haywire." Aedan had a tone.

"Is that what's wrong with you? You're worried something is going to happen?" Mags stood, put her hands on her hips and glared down at him.

"Wouldn't you be? Look how much bad shit has already happened?" Aedan hung his head under her glare.

"Look at the good that's happened," Mags challenged him.

"God, I'm an ass. I'm sorry Mags. My brain is having a hard time processing everything." He stood and held out his arm. "Come on, let's go get our feet wet."

Mags looked hard at him as they walked. She saw signs of the strain he was putting himself under to try and make sense of everything. "Next week will be 6 weeks." She put his hand on her belly. "What if they are both girls?"

Aedan groaned. "If they are both girls, I'm moving in with Jax."

Mags laughed, "If they are boys, I'm moving to Washington to live with Airy."

"What? Boys are so much easier than girls," Aedan stated.

"I'm not sure I can survive the penis is my new toy stage. Though I also don't think I'd survive the period stage either." Mags threw her head back and laughed. "We're screwed either way."

"That's what got us here is getting screwed," Aedan said snarkily.

Mags shoved him as they got close to the water and he stumbled, splashing around before getting his footing. She saw that evil spark in his eye and started running. He chased, splashing and kicking as much water as he could at her.

She was soaked, and didn't even care. "I'm going to make some sand art." Mags tried to catch her breath. She was bent over, her hands on her knees as Aedan walked up.

"Oh yeah?" Mags nodded and headed back towards their packs.

"I need that Tupperware I packed though, so eat some cantaloupe," she called back to him.

She started scouring around and found a few sticks that could help her draw in the sand, and she cut apart a water bottle to use too. She hadn't drawn in a while. It was something that Jax and her had in common, they were both talented artists. Mags was better with sketching out a design and molding clay to life, Jax was bringing those sketches to life on paper.

She gathered up the things she had collected while Aedan ate the fruit and set them down on a nice clear part of sand, close to the water, but not close enough to get washed away for a while. She headed back to the fire pit.

She had found a good stick for Aedan to use for his part. "Go find me long pieces of brown grass, get them wet and wind them around this stick and put it in the sun to dry." She picked up the Tupperware and headed back out to start her little project.

Jax watched Airiella closely. She was taking her time getting back. He'd seen her put her ear buds back in, so he knew she was listening to music now. She'd completely caught them off guard with her little stunt and Jax had loved it. He hadn't felt this free in years.

He felt better after talking with Ronnie too. He jammed his hands in his pockets as they walked. There was something to be said for this solitude out here and no other interference except nature. He was used to city life, noise, constant interruptions with the occasional break of watching TV.

He got a different kind of break out here. The silence stretching between Ronnie and him was natural and comfortable, two people who were used to the other being around. None of the tension Jax had made himself believe was there. He didn't know if it was being here, because they talked, or because of Airiella. It could be all of the above, he didn't care, he was happy.

Airiella had stopped now, dropped her pack and was sitting on the ground the surf tickling her toes. She had her arms wrapped around her legs and her face turned to the sun, her hair waving with the breeze, catching the sunlight making it look fiery. The bright yellow of the shirt a great contrast to the sand and sky. Jax pulled out his phone and took a couple of pictures. He wanted to remember her like this when things got rough.

Ronnie had done the same thing. "Her ear buds are out. Go sit with her for a while. I'll head back and see what the others are up to," Jax told him with a nudge.

Ronnie shrugged, "She wanted space, I can give her that. I'll sit back here. If she wants company, she will come to me."

"You mind if I head back? I think I need to spend a little time with Aedan. Try and prove to him I'm doing better," Jax spoke quietly.

"Go, I'm good. As long as I can see her, I'll be fine."

Jax gave him a fist bump and continued back. He didn't know what he could say to make Aedan come around, or if he would even try. He did want to reassure Aedan that he was doing better and going to make an effort.

He looked back once, and caught his siren at a different angle, the sun in a different position and his breath was taken away. The salt water spray that the breeze caught had her captured perfectly with the position the sun was in. He kneeled down on the ground and pulled out his phone, zoomed in a little and took another picture. He made a few snap decisions in his mind and looked at the picture he had gotten. It was perfect.

The closer he got back to where they started, he saw Mags doing something out in the sand and Aedan trailing behind her trying to help. He didn't see Smitty or Jillian, which was fine with him, he still wasn't very happy with her.

As he approached, he realized Mags was doing a sand sculpture. "Holy fucking hell, Mags, that's incredible," he breathed as he came up behind her.

"Jax! I could totally use your artistic skills right now." Mags jumped up and hugged him.

"I'm in." Jax didn't hesitate. "But first look at this." Jax pulled out his phone and showed her the picture he had gotten.

"Oh my God! Jax, this is pure art right here. Can

you print me a copy of this?" Mags held her fingers above the screen of the phone.

"I was planning on printing you, Ronnie, and Smitty one, and one for her so she can see what I do." Jax smiled. "Don't tell them though, it's going to be a gift."

Mags looked closely at his face. "Today has been good for you." She hugged him. "Now help me. I'm not good on the detail work."

"That's a lie, you're great at it, but I have a vision. Do you have a long pointy stick?" Jax looked around.

"I do! I think we are on the same page!" Mags squealed and raced over to a pile of stuff she had collected. "Let me tell you."

Aedan scoured around the beach for the list Mags had given him of what she needed, and Jax got to work on making this vision they shared come to life.

Chapter Nineteen

The more time I was alone out here, the sharper things came into focus in my head. I was starting to see patterns where I hadn't before, clues to actions and maybe a more defined path for me to follow to get Jax through this. The council's words filled in pieces now that my head was not as cluttered.

I still missed my beach, though I kept sending up silent thank you's to the universe for this one. I let my gratitude flow from me into the earth and back, a steady stream of pure and clean energy washing in and out of me. I hadn't asked for any of this to be dumped on me, and I still wasn't sure who I was after it all. I did know that I wasn't able to walk away from them, or this. I was in love with them all, as crazy as that was, and as hard as it was to believe.

It was past lunch time now and I was sure the guys were hungry. I looked back and only saw Ronnie. I felt a pang of sadness that Jax had gone, but I let it wash away. I couldn't push progress on him, he had to make it on his own.

I stood up and grabbed the strap of my pack and headed to where Ronnie sat in the sand propped up by a log. His smile lit my heart and he held an arm out for me to snuggle in next to him as I sat down. He was warm, I hadn't realized how chilled my skin had gotten sitting in the water.

I tucked my feet up under his leg and curled into him. I'd been hesitant to say they could all come, and now I am glad that they did. Ronnie had kept the space I'd asked for, and they all had left me alone. It felt natural to have him and Jax here with me, the only worry earlier when they had been talking.

"You *do* smell like sunshine, angel." Ronnie kissed the top of my head. "You have your own smell too, which already reminded me of the ocean and jasmine. Now it's sunshine, ocean and jasmine."

"You aren't bored, are you?" I tried to suppress a shiver that ran through me.

"No. Are you cold?" concern laced his words.

"A little, but sitting here with you is taking the chill away."

"You've been in the water for hours. I'm not surprised. You are even sun kissed now." He tilted my face back to look at me. "Gorgeous." He kissed me, parting my lips gently as he tasted me. "You even taste like sunshine."

"Well that warmed me up even more." I held him close. "Jax okay?"

"Yeah, he went back to spend a little time with Aedan. Coming out here was a fantastic idea you had, angel. He came clean with me about a few things, and I understand better why what happened has happened. He made me face a demon of my own, which you saved me from, thanks, by the way."

I slid my hand up his shirt and put it over his heart, "Your childhood?"

He put his hand over mine. "Yes. I thought I'd moved on from it, but hearing him talk about it hit that panic button that used to surface a lot back then."

"We all have scars. I think you can expect that to happen every once in a while. Triggers lessen over time; they are still there though. I've got a ton of them," I admitted.

"He talked a little bit about some of the things he had seen when he was stuck in your dream healing thing. Some of the stuff you haven't told me yet, and how it related to his own triggers and his feelings about me. It was hard to hear, angel. Not just the stuff about you, but about myself and him." Ronnie tilted my head up to look at him again. "Are you going to talk about the freaking out when people touch you thing?"

I kissed his chin, this stubble he had was sexy as hell. I loved touching it. "I'm not hiding anything from you Ronnie, if you have questions you can ask me. I'll tell you whatever you need to know. Especially if you think it will help you, or him."

"Nature suits you." His deep green eyes held mine.

"Can I run some things by you? My head is a bit clearer now and things are starting to fall into place more. You might be able to help me fill in missing pieces, or together we can maybe put more in place," I wondered aloud.

"You don't even have to ask. Let's have it." He ran his hand up and down my arm, spreading warmth.

I pulled out a bottle of water and granola bar from my pack and split it with him. "In that house, that guy that came after me, he was a spirit? Right?"

"That's what Degataga and Taklishim said, yes," Ronnie's voice rumbled.

"We know that energy in Jax is intelligent, and if it's based off emotions, that makes sense to me. Because our emotions can be influenced by the environment that we are in. That guy took plays right out of my past. The past that Jax saw, that he associated with you, and attacked me in the same ways. That spirit either got in Jax's head, or was communicating with that energy in him," I surmised.

Ronnie stiffened. "What do you mean?"

"Most of Jax's dreamscape had to do with you, and your shared past with him. Jax saw scenes from my first serious relationship, the one that was very physically abusive. He had to watch mine play out, the same way he had to watch yours," I tried to explain.

"I'm with you on that part." Ronnie's voice had an interesting edge to it.

"If this isn't comfortable for you to talk about, we don't have to." I still had my hand under his shirt and I stroked his chest.

"It's not that, well it's partially that. What makes me uncomfortable is that guy using your past, Jax's feelings about mine and acting it out to trigger him to hurt you." He shifted to look me in the eyes. "The thought of you going through anything I went through, which yes, I know you did, it hurts me. I had this conversation with Jax too. He saw it, I didn't, and I told him that it was hard for me to hear, but that I would listen to it anyway because it will help you. I can't really control my bodies reactions, I'm trying though."

I understood. Seeing the child version of Ronnie with those bruises had torn me up. "Okay, well, thankfully there were no golf clubs around, so I didn't have to relive that part. The choking though, was something that happened a little too often, and some of those parts were in that dreamscape. As well as the shoving me into a wall and slamming my head into the ground, and kicking me."

"Since those things were most likely in the forefront of his mind, it makes sense that you think there was some sort of communication or ability to see that information," Ronnie put together, trying to skim over the abuse parts.

"If that guy could see in Jax's head, he would have known those were triggers. Or likewise, if he had been communicating with that energy in some way. Triggering those emotions in Jax frees that energy to feed and grow, giving it power to take over. I'm leaning more towards it being able to see in Jax's head, or that energy giving it access to Jax's head rather than it communicating though," I laid it out for Ronnie.

"Why is that?" he asked me, frowning.

"If the energy had been communicating with that guy, I'd think the spirit would have known that the energy wasn't able to be controlled in the way it thought it would be." I wasn't entirely sure on this part. This was where I needed input.

"Maybe. We know the energy has only bad intent. If it's as intelligent as the council thinks it is, it could have been communicating and lying to the guy. We know it's afraid of your lightning. It might have been that since you were underground in a basement, it thought it was safe from that, and could use Jax to kill the guy, then you. The house burning down and you pulling it didn't play into its plans," Ronnie played devil's advocate.

"You have a point. Really either scenario is a distinct possibility, both are scary," I added.

"It also could have been a bit of both. You are a bit of a wild card. I don't think that the energy or the spirit was able to predict or influence your actions." Ronnie pulled me over to sit between his legs and rest against his chest.

"Out of everything Jax saw, that guy chose the easiest ones to try to use against me. That spirit could have easily gone for rape and several triggers would have went off in my head making me completely useless. One or the other didn't display a huge amount of intelligence on that part. Thankfully." I shivered again.

Ronnie held me tighter. "To help Jax then, we need to find a way to teach him to block his mind like you do?"

I nodded, "Yes. Triggers will still render walls useless, and those are a lot harder to lessen. I should be able to teach him to keep *me* out though. If he can keep me out, he can keep the energy out. That shit can't get through my walls."

"You are a way more powerful empath than Jax is, though," Ronnie said cautiously.

"That doesn't have much to do with the walls. That's just practice. I could teach you the same thing and I wouldn't be able to tell when you were irritated with me." My tone was light.

"I don't want to hide anything from you, angel, I don't need walls," he said and his voice was gruff.

"The other part that came to me." I went on, ignoring his tone, "is the way it affected me this time. Since we know it's intelligent and it changes, the last time I pulled it, it must have altered the way it attaches to him. Therefore, it's strength is different."

"You'll have to explain that one to me more since I don't know what it does inside you, I just saw the other part." Ronnie couldn't avoid the tremors that ran through him, so he just wrapped himself tighter around her to remind his body she was here.

"The first time I pulled it from Winnie, I had time to go very slowly and followed the threads to where it rooted inside her and I untangled them gently before pulling it. There was no threat of violence out there and I had time. The threat came afterwards. I was able to release that small bit I pulled from her relatively easy. What I didn't know is that it affected the land and the animals with its taint. Winnie had to come tell me. I went back and pulled the energy from the animals it had affected and from where it stained the earth. Imagine an oil spill, it was like that. The energy had been able to grow in that time and I pulled a lot more. That's when the danger for me started. It made me sick, it fought me, and I thought I was possessed." I recalled the memory for him.

"It has the ability to poison the land and animals then?" Ronnie sounded horrified.

"It does. That's why I had to find a different way to release it. I couldn't do that to the earth or those poor animals. I'd found an open Catholic church and told the priest what I needed to, in order for him to bless me. I really had no idea what it was, just that is was poisonous. He was seeing the pain it caused me, and how sick it was making me. I don't know what made him decide that drinking the holy water was the best way, but it worked. It was horrific though. Winnie said I died. I just remember the pain, and the poor priests face when I came to. He was the first person that told me I was different. I think he called me touched. The thing was, though, I was back awake in a couple hours. I was battered and in pain, but I was able to drive home and sleep."

"You were alone?" Ronnie's hand was a little too tight, so I pulled on it to get him to ease up.

"Technically, yes. Winnie was with me," I said gently.

"The first time was a couple hours until you woke up. It was longer when Smitty was there," Ronnie thought out loud.

"A day and a half, wasn't it? I can't say I remember, because I was out." The blunt words made him flinch.

"Yeah, it was right around that," Ronnie confirmed, tightly.

"I pulled from Dr. Stone though, and from Jax at the same time. I wasn't gentle with either of them because the situation was escalating fast. It also hurt that time to pull it because it fought me. It was like it knew I was going to destroy it." I remembered that part very well.

"You dropped fast," Ronnie remembered. "You told Smitty you'd need him to come with you and help, you told me to contain Jax."

"Yep. It was almost like I could feel its intentions. Once it was in me though, it fought like hell to get through my walls. My organs felt bruised. Kind of like, since it couldn't get through my walls, it was going to hurt whatever it could. I don't know how it did it, but bones broke and it felt like my skin had peeled back and all my nerves were exposed." I shuddered. "I remember hearing screams but I thought at the time that it was something else, I didn't know they were mine. Father Roarke was pretty shaken up when I saw him next."

"Smitty was a shell of a man," Ronnie commented. "He wouldn't leave your room at all."

He'd told me that. "Then with you, that time..."

"Wait, what about the guy in the park, and the thing that happened out in the woods with Tama?" Ronnie backtracked.

"The guy in the park I didn't pull at first because of how many people were around, I tackled him, trying to distract him with energy bursts through the earth. I needed to get that kid away from him. From what I understand is I bled on him when he cut me. They think my blood healed him. I had to pull it after, and I did it without thinking. I'm not sure I was aware that what I was pulling was that energy. At least not until I got back to the hotel and felt sick. His blood also tainted me somehow. The thing, person, whatever it was that came at us in the woods, lightning got it. I felt it, the energy, but Tama knocked me down before I could do anything."

"They did say something about being careful of your blood. That it could be the reason the spirits want to hurt you so bad," Ronnie commented.

"Maybe. So, the last time, with you, when I pulled down there, it was another situation where I didn't have time. I knew the second I latched on to it though, that it was going to hurt Jax. I did it anyway because I knew that if Jax killed that guy, it would push him over the edge. It fought me from when I first latched on to it. The entire time I pulled, it fought me. When it was in me, the pain was a hundred times worse than it was with Smitty. My head was filled with vile images and thoughts. I think it's trying to get me to release it out right away so it can go back or affect someone else. I don't know. It was desperate to take me over. It took longer to wake up and it's taken this long for me to even have a clear thought about it."

"Basically, the pattern you are seeing is it's getting stronger and worse each time." Ronnie's tone was flat.

"Essentially, though it feels like I'm missing something important. It's desperate because it's weakened now. Jax, if he starts fighting for himself, has a damn good chance of keeping it from growing." That was my instinct at least.

"I want to circle back to triggers. You told me you weren't afraid when I touched you. Are you afraid to let others touch you?" Ronnie shifted me so he could see my face. The look on his own unreadable.

"Yes,"I said as my vulnerability surfaced.

"Even Smitty, Aedan, and Mags? Jax, I get." Ronnie tried to drill deeper.

"Honestly, yes. I had to keep reminding myself that they aren't going to hurt me. Jax, the fear came from what I feel for him, not so much his touch. You, I had zero fear of your touch, but was terrified of what I feel for you, too." I had to tell myself to be honest because my instinct was to hide from those truths. I couldn't though, or I wouldn't heal.

"Is it because of that relationship, that first one?" he was hesitant to ask and his eyes were guarded.

"No. Well, maybe partially. I think it stems more from the rape." I looked down when I said it, shame crawling through me. I should have known he would feel that and not let it go.

He pushed my head back up to look at him. "Eyes on me, angel. Tell me about it." The hesitation was back, colored with fear, but his voice was still firm.

I involuntarily tensed up and he rubbed his hands on my back in response. "Which time?"

Definitely an edge to his tone this time, "The one that Jax saw."

I flashed back on it. Raw. Still raw. "Ronnie..." My breathing grew ragged and my eyes dropped.

"Look at me, sweetheart. Feel me," he said as he tipped my chin back up. "You are safe, I've got you. You want to get past this, you have to let it go. Feel my heart," he put my hand on his chest again. "You are safe, you are loved."

I can do this, I told myself.

Chapter Twenty

Ronnie knew this was going to kill him. What he felt through their connection was so potent he felt like there was a category five storm building inside him. He never once had even considered that touch would be hard for her. She was so free with her consoling them, or soothing them. He guessed the difference was the touching was her choice. It wasn't her choice coming from someone else.

He had her caged between his legs, his hands on her, hoping like hell that she was getting at least some comfort from him. Her chest was heaving with breaths and her body held a slight tremor among the tension. Her eyes were wide and shimmered with pooled tears that he knew she didn't want to let go.

It was rocking him straight to his core. She needed to let it out, and he figured here was the best place she could do it and restore balance easily. He leaned forward and brushed a kiss across her lips. "Nothing you can say will make me change how I feel," he reassured her.

She blinked rapidly, trying to clear the tears. "It started with a scam call at work. Some guy with a middle eastern accent asking for someone that doesn't work there. That happened for several days, weeks actually. The number on caller ID changing each time he called. It escalated from there and he figured out my name and started asking for me. I'm the only one in that office, but he didn't know that. If someone else answered, he got verbally abusive with them. The owner had me file a police report, block the numbers, file complaints with the FCC, everything." She leaned back against his leg a little, her body language telling him she needed the contact so he slid his hands under her shirt like she did to him. Her flinch made him want to cry.

"Soon he escalated it to trying to figure out my last name and threatening to show up at my work. I had friends that worked for the phone company try and trace the calls. They had me give their number to this guy saying it was mine. He went nuts. He'd call the office over a hundred times each day. It was so ridiculous that they told me to not even answer the phone anymore if I didn't recognize the number. They finally changed the office number, which for a business isn't all that easy."

"He stalked you first then?" God, she'd been through too much.

"Yeah, apparently. Michael seemed to think it was funny and kept making jokes about it. It was starting to be reminiscent of when my ex-husbands son was stalking me. I couldn't go places without feeling watched. I was constantly looking over my shoulder. Only this time, I didn't know who to watch for. I had no idea who this person was. With the number changed and unpublished the calls stopped, but the feelings of being watched hadn't."

She'd become cold and tense under his hands, so he stroked his fingers across her flesh trying to warm it. "He showed up. I didn't know it, though. There are other businesses in my building, there was no way for me to know he didn't belong there. He followed me home." She swallowed hard.

"You're safe. I love you, angel," Ronnie whispered.

A few tears fell, and she didn't even notice. Her eyes

weren't even seeing anything real anymore. "He hit me outside my apartment I shared with Michael. He drugged me and threw me in the back of a pickup truck and covered me with a tarp. I remember thumping against the truck bed and it jarring my bones, the smell of the dirty tarp. I had been tied; my brain stuck on fear. I can't tell you how many times I wished I had just gotten to my feet and jumped out of the truck. He drove somewhere out to the woods, I had no way of knowing which direction we had gone."

Ronnie tensed at the tone she had. It was flat, devoid of emotion, which told him she hadn't even come close to dealing with this. She sounded almost robotic, removed from the situation. It was scaring him, because she was so full of life and love, and right now, there was nothing.

"My head was throbbing, bleeding, my ears had been ringing. I didn't know where I was. He grabbed me by my ankles and literally dragged me out of the bed of the truck. I hit the ground hard and he laughed. The sound of his laughter was chilling, and I swore I knew he was going to kill me. I tried to fight back, flinging myself around, kicking, hitting when he untied my hands. It was like he didn't feel any of it. I remember all the words he said in my dreams, though when I try to think about it now, they don't come. He was taunting me, telling me the sick stuff he had planned."

Ronnie felt like he was on a speeding train going over a bridge that had collapsed. "He tied my wrists to tree trunks. Hit me over and over, choked me, kicked me. He put his knees on my legs so I couldn't move them. I don't know how many times I blacked out. One of the times I woke back up, he was kneeling on my ribs, I heard them break, couldn't breathe, and he was trying to stuff his dick in my mouth. I bit him, and it got worse. He was talking in some foreign language, alternating it with cussing at me in English, calling me a dirty whore, cunt, any cuss word possible. He raped me first, then he did it again with a tree branch."

Ronnie felt the tears fall from his eyes, hot and

silent; she was as still as a statue. He hated every second of this, and he knew she needed to break that wall of emotions to let it go. He didn't know how to reach her right now either. She wasn't here. She was firmly locked in that memory, and the words kept coming.

"I felt every tear of my skin. I wanted to die. I wished for death. The pain was overwhelming and the emotions rolling over me were so disgusting and black I felt stained. He raped me again while choking me. Twisted my arms up and flipped me over and raped me anally. I shouldn't have lived. The amount of damage he caused should have killed me, I shouldn't be here." More tears were falling now. "Hikers found me. I didn't know how long I'd been there. I remember the horror in their voices as they looked at me. I heard them throwing up. I felt their revulsion."

Ronnie couldn't take it anymore. He knew what she was thinking. He understood that she thought it was because of her they felt this, not the actions that left her that way. He wanted to crush her in a hug, but instead he pulled her gently against him. He tipped her face so she was facing him, cupping her cheeks until her eyes focused on him. He couldn't stop the tears that shook him, falling from his eyes in a stream.

"It doesn't change the way I feel about you," Ronnie choked out. "If it's possible, I love you more." She broke then. All the terror and pain, the humiliation and anger, guilt and shame came boiling out in those hot tears that fell on his chest. He rocked her, crying just as hard and held her tight, saying over and over, "I love you."

Smitty and Jillian had been gathering driftwood to burn in the firepit when he was crushed by a wall of emotions that literally made him fall over and start shaking. He knew in an instant that it was Airiella and he staggered to his feet.

"Smitty, what's wrong?" Jillian sounded like she

was miles away.

"Airiella," he croaked as he made his way to Mags and Aedan who were trying to pick themselves up off the ground.

Jax was utterly still, his face pale. "She's okay. She's remembering, she's healing."

"What the fuck?" Smitty snarled. "Are you sure? How do you know?"

"That's how it felt when I talked to Ronnie," Jax quietly answered.

"What the hell is she remembering?" Aedan asked, his fear and anger rising.

Smitty had a sick feeling in the pit of his stomach. He and Jax answered at the same time. "The rape."

Mags sat back down hard on the ground, Aedan trying to catch her. "We need to get to her now," she cried.

"No, let her be." It struck Smitty as odd that Jax was suddenly the voice of reason.

"Why?" Smitty asked carefully.

"I saw it. I watched it, remember? I know how she feels. More people will make it harder for her to let go of this," he answered warily. "Believe me, I want to run to her like crazy right now. Just, be here for her when she gets back."

"You know how she feels?" Smitty needed clarification.

"What you just felt is what I felt after I drank that stuff and watched my shit all over again. It's what I felt talking to Ronnie, airing things out. It's the same feelings in me, that if I give into them, takes over me and turns me into an evil lunatic." Jax shuddered.

Smitty understood then. "Ronnie's with her, right?" Damn, Ronnie was going to be a mess.

"He is. I trust him to take care of her, you should too." Jax bent back over to finish the work he and Mags had started.

Smitty walked uneasily over to Jax. "That's what that shit in you feels like?"

"That's how it starts, then it builds from there." The

truth shone from his eyes.

"Jax, I had no idea. That's a heavy weight, bro." Smitty felt compassion welling up in him.

Out of the corner of his eye he caught Aedan staggering wildly towards the water and throw up. Mags had tears pouring down her face and held up her hand to Smitty. "I've got him."

"How do you do it? It's literally made Aedan sick, I'm not far behind him." Smitty fought back against the nausea.

"In case you haven't noticed these past years, I haven't exactly been fighting it like you guys are right now. I'm starting to. I'm tired of this burden. Hopefully she can get this one out of her."

Smitty felt the tears burn his eyes and he blinked them away. Jax was right. All they could do was be there for her to soothe her when she came back. The emotions rolling through him, through that connection was intense in a way he couldn't even describe. The only way he came close was trying to explain the feelings and things he saw when she drank the holy water.

Chapter Twenty-One

I don't know how long I cried. Ronnie never let me go though. That was the first time I had ever let those emotions surface like that, or told the whole story. I'd stuffed them down since it happened. Telling it had hurt. Seeing how it affected Ronnie was even worse. He'd tried to control his emotions so it didn't make it worse, but he wasn't a robot. No matter how plainly I tried to tell it, if you loved someone, hearing it was going to hurt.

He gave me a safe place to get that out. He sat through it with me. I could never honestly doubt the way that man felt for me after that. When the last tear fell, he didn't run away. He still held me, he still loved me. "Thank you," I murmured into his neck.

"You trusted me enough to share that with me, that's all the thanks I need," he told me brokenly.

The raven landed on the log he was leaning us against. She cawed softly at me, and I opened my mind to her, feeling closer to this bird than ever. She gave me visions of the others reaction to my emotions. I understood what she was telling me. I needed to pull them and release it all back out now.

I reached down into the earth again, letting it feel me and understand my intentions. I held the picture my raven sent me in my mind and shared it with the earth, asking it to direct me to them. Seconds later I felt them all, found their emotions and pulled all that bad from them that they picked up through me. I left no trace of it in them and took it all back on. I pulled from Ronnie too, and in the next second pushed pure love back at them to fill the void.

"Angel," Ronnie gasped. "I'll gladly carry that for you."

"I know, but it's not for either of us to carry anymore." I extricated myself from him and stood, stretching slowly. "Let's go get rid of it." I held my hand out to him and he took it, standing with me. He grabbed my backpack, slinging it over his shoulder as we made our way back to the water.

I didn't let go of his hand, though I stood in front of him, our hands stretched between us as I let my feet sink into the sand and water again. I asked to be cleaned of this burden and watched in amazement as a tiny little wind storm formed in front of my eyes and pulled it all out of me. A dark little funnel cloud, spinning as it pulled at the salt water beneath it, cleaning the energy that it released out.

"That's new," I quietly said. "Thank you."

I stepped back towards Ronnie so we weren't stretched apart, though I kept my feet in the tide. I walked back towards where the others were, holding his hand. "You felt no fear when I touched you the first time? After that?" came Ronnie's soft question.

"Not once."

"I'm not sure I'd ever let anyone touch me again," he admitted.

"I didn't at first. Sometimes I pick up on things in others that make me not want anything around me. I still can't tolerate crowds well either. Panic creeps in." He rubbed his thumb over my wrist.

I stopped, tugging at him and pulled him up to dry sand. I sat down and put my legs out in front of me. "See these marks?" I pointed to my lower shin on both legs, front and back. He nodded.

"Those bruises were so bad they stained my skin. Those were the doctor's words to me. That I was stained. Bullets would have done less damage than those words. She didn't mean it like I took it, but it stuck. I'll forever wear the marks of that day. I know that." I had never voiced those words before.

Ronnie made a slight choking sound as he put his hands on my legs. "They don't take away from your beauty."

"Because of you, I'll now hear those words every time I see them." I gave him a smile. "Now, I need to ask you something else."

"Anything," he promised.

"Will you help me overcome my fear of being trapped?" I said it fast before I could rethink it.

"Trapped?" I nodded at his question. "I don't understand."

"Um, intentionally restrain me in a sexual situation. Replace the memories with something else."

He started to tremble. "Angel, I don't know that I can do that."

"I freaked out internally when Jax caged my head in for a kiss, I don't want that. I'm not afraid of you. I just need to know if I can overcome the trigger of my hands or legs being trapped. Don't tie me up, that's too much. But you can trap my hands, pin my legs."

"If you freak out will you tell me?" Ronnie hedged.

"Oh, you'll know," I answered calmly, but even the thought of it sent my heart racing.

He coughed. "I'll do it. We'll get you through this." He didn't look entirely comfortable with it. "I don't even know how you can enjoy sex."

I needed him to laugh. I took his hands and pushed them into the marks on my legs. "They don't hurt anymore Ronnie. Sex is easy when you have a sex god to work with."

There it was, the smile I needed to see. "You are incredible."

"I can't decide if you are Heracles or Eros," I told

him standing.

"I'm a Greek god now?" he grinned at me.

I squeezed his biceps, "Pure Heracles." I kissed him, then kissed his fingers. "Eros."

He laughed. "I'll be whatever you want me to be."

We started walking back, the silence between us easy and relaxed. It took us about twenty minutes to see the rest of the group. As we got closer, they noticed us, and I saw Jax make a beeline towards me. The rest gathered in front of a mound of sand.

"If he felt those emotions, give him a minute, that would be hard for him to process," Ronnie said and let go of my hand stepping away as Jax broke into a run. Ronnie gave me a wink and headed towards the group.

I stood still, my walls down so they could all feel me as Jax barreled at me. He stopped inches away from me and swept me up into a hug, my feet coming right up off the ground. "You're okay," he breathed into my ear.

"I'm okay," I whispered back.

"You took it all back from us, why?" he put me down, his hands on my waist as he searched my face.

"It's the past, none of us need that shadow lurking. It happening here was the best place it could have happened." I ran my fingers over his lips.

"You've been crying." I nodded, I'm sure my eyes were red and puffy. "It's gone now?"

"I don't know if I'd say that, some things won't ever go away. But all the emotions I buried from it aren't bottled up in me anymore. It's a step in the right direction," I told him truthfully. "It was rough, I can't lie." He'd be on this same path, there was no use in hiding it.

"How did you get through that? It was pretty intense from where I was standing."

I winced. I knew he'd seen what happened. "I wasn't sure I would snap out of it. Inside it was like I was drowning, it had me trapped in it pretty securely. Not sure what it looked like from where Ronnie was sitting. He brought me through it. Somewhere in there I heard his voice telling me he loved me. That it didn't change the way he felt about me. He brought me back." I stroked his face. "Love still wins."

He held my gaze for a moment, so many things I wanted to just say to him on the tip of my tongue, it was his move though. "Mags made something for you, come see." He captured my hand and brought it to his lips, brushing a soft kiss across the back of it. Change of subject it was. "Close your eyes, I won't let you fall."

That got a smile out of me. I'd already fallen for him. I did as he asked though, and closed my eyes, letting him lead me to the rest of the group. "Go," I heard Jillian say. Then I felt Smitty pull me into a hug, Jax still holding on to my hand.

"Can I open my eyes yet?" I asked.

"No," Smitty whispered. "God, baby girl, that almost killed me. You better?"

"Not yet, but I will be. I still need a bit of time. Stop worrying." I kissed his cheek.

Then I felt Aedan and Mags sandwich me as Smitty moved away. "If you need to talk, I'm here." Mags kissed my cheek.

"I'm not ever going to ask, because something that made you feel that way isn't anything good," Aedan whispered. "I'm with her though, if you need extra ears, whether I want to hear it or not, they are yours."

Mags took my other hand and between her and Jax they moved me a little, from the position of the sun on my skin, I believed I was facing where the SUV was parked. "Not yet, Airy. I wanted you to see how you inspire us. Bring out so much good in us, show you using the talents that Jax and I were born with. So, we made this for you."

"Open your eyes, siren." Jax's breath tickled my ear.

I opened my eyes and spread out huge before me was a sand sculpture of me. In incredible detail. I had wings. Drawn feathers, stones for my eyes that were eerily similar in color to my own. My hair was curled grass that was displayed like it was blowing in the wind. The skirt I had been wearing that Jax gave me, sculpted and drawn in details I didn't know were possible in the sand. My body lifelike in the curves she'd made. It was stunning.

"Made from nature, just like you. Everyone helped, except Ronnie, who is a slacker. I'll give him a break this time because he was taking care of you. He only gets this one pass though." Mags elbowed him. "Do you like it?"

I loved it. Those words weren't enough though. I flung my arms around her neck and sobbed. The love of this group floored me. I'd never had someone do things like this for me before. "You have an amazing talent."

Mags wrapped me in her wild energy and hugged me back tight. "Jax did all that detail work you see. I sculpted. Smitty, Aedan and Jillian collected the rest of the stuff for us and curled the grass. She's not as beautiful as you, but I wanted you to see your own beauty."

I let her go and attached myself to Jax. "Thank you for this," I whispered.

"It will never be enough to show you, but I'm going to damn well do my best to help you see what we do." His voice was gravelly and I felt the emotions in him and the way he tried to sort through them.

"Guys, close your eyes for a minute please," I called over my shoulder. "Shameless PDA coming up."

"If it's anything like this morning, I'm watching," Jillian quipped.

I pulled Jax's head down to mine and said softly so only he could hear, "I'm going to help you see what I see in you, too." I sunk my heart into the kiss I gave him, I molded my body to his, hard meeting soft. I wrapped one hand behind his head, his hair wound around my fingers, my other hand grasping his back under his shirt.

He broke the kiss off, his eyes dark with need and his voice low and rough, "I think Mags is jealous of that kiss."

I chuckled against his lips, "She'll live. Right then, I needed you."

"Hearing you say that does something to me inside," he said, his voice low, only for me. "It feels pretty damn good."

"It's true. Thank you again, Jax. This is the most

beautiful thing anyone has ever made for me. You have a great talent."

Reluctantly, I let him go. None of them had closed their eyes, and they were all smiling. "Jax hasn't drawn in a long time. This is momentous," Smitty said.

Mags came back over. "You still need time, don't you?"

I nodded. "Processing it will take a little bit." I didn't want to admit that, but she saw it.

"Go do you, we'll be okay here," Mags promised.

Ronnie made a move to follow me until I held up my hand. "I'm just going to go sit over on that rock right there. I won't go any farther. Give me an hour to get my head right."

He nodded and gave me wink. "I'm sure Mags has a list of things for me to do to make up for not helping."

"You bet your sweet ass, I do," came Mags voice calling back.

"I'll be okay, Ronnie. If I'm not, you'll know and I won't be mad if you or anyone else comes over. I swear it," I told him gently. He nodded and I walked away from them once more. I felt bad, yet I needed space still. That little break down had cost me.

I climbed up on to a big flat rock that was perfect for laying on. It was warmed by the sun, and the way the beach was curved, the water was breaking over the smaller ones below it. I let myself lay back and relax to the sound of the waves.

Chapter Twenty-Two

I must have fallen asleep. I'd needed it, though what woke me was the feeling of not being alone. I expected Ronnie and instead found Jillian. I tried to control my facial expression and clearly failed at it by her snort.

"I know, I'm the last one you expected to see. I asked permission, though. Both watch dogs are close by." She gestured at Jax and Ronnie who were sitting side by side in front of the sand sculpture.

"I'm not afraid of you, Jillian. I'm just surprised to see you." I didn't put my walls up, or guard myself. There wasn't really a point, she wasn't an empath nor did she have a connection with me. My only tells would be my facial expressions, body language and tone of voice.

"I know. You're pretty effective at shutting me down anyway. I only told you that so you know that I cleared it with them before coming up here. They are protective as fuck when it comes to you." A look crossed her face that was too fast for me to catch. "It's weird to see Art like that. He's protective naturally, but he's reserved about it. Not when it comes to you. Whatever happened that had Aedan puking in the waves, damn near gave Art a heart attack."

"It wasn't intentional, I promise you." I couldn't

hold back the wince. "It hit them that hard?" At least I knew she wouldn't pull any punches with what she told me.

"No joke, all of them fell to the ground, except Jax. He looked like he'd been hit by a bullet train."

"I'm sorry—" I started to apologize.

"Don't be," she interrupted me and put her hand on my arm. "Did it help?"

"I think so. I'm not sure I'll really know until I'm back in a city and not in nature." It was the most honest way I could put that.

"If it helped, then never be sorry. You know when you called me out and you named all those emotions?" I nodded. "Do you know why they were there?"

"I assumed because I slept with Smitty," I laid it out there for her.

"Not really. Did you feel those same emotions today?" I wondered where she was headed with this.

"To a degree, not as intense as they were," I told her.

"This is why I'm here. How long ago was it?" Her sideways slide in conversation throwing me.

"How long was... Oh. Three and a half years." My emotions started rolling again and I saw Ronnie stand and Smitty headed our way. "Sorry, if they barge up here that wasn't my intention."

She looked back. "She's fine," she yelled at them. Halting their movements. She looked back at me. "It was ten years for me. I don't know your details, and we don't need to go into them. Judging by Jax's responses and expressions, it was bad. That's enough for me."

"Oh, Jillian," I understood her emotions and reactions now. "Does Smitty know?"

"No. He doesn't need to, I don't think. Sex with many people is how I heal that wound. He lets me do it, doesn't question it and doesn't judge me for it. He accepts that as how I am. It's enough for me. I was threatened because those insecurities it caused me came roaring to the surface the minute he told me. Those emotions, the fallout from that, is overwhelming. It's been ten years and I'm not over it. For three and half? You are doing pretty amazing all things considered."

"You should tell him," I said quietly. "He can handle it. It can help."

"Maybe," she admitted. "It's just how I am though. I see the changes in him, and I like them. He has a lot more empathy now than he did. He's showing emotion more. I know you aren't trying to take him away from me, and that's the other reason I'm here. I'm fine with what you all have going on. It doesn't bother me, and I know he brings something to your life the same way he does mine. It doesn't bother me to admit either, that he needs you, just as I know he needs me."

I took her hand in mine and held it. "Thank you for telling me that."

"Today, this morning, when you took that shit from me, this is the best I've felt in years. Ten years to be exact. I know I apologized this morning, but I'm doing it again. I'm very sorry for how I acted. And in the future, if you need someone safe to talk to about this that doesn't have a penis, that knows how you feel, I'm here." Jillian's face was glowing with sincerity.

Something broke free in me at her words, and those damn tears came again. "I can't tell you what that means to me." I hugged her, which stopped the guys movement again from my sudden emotions.

"They can help, and I'm sure they will. They won't ever understand though." Her voice held pain.

"The closest to understanding would be Ronnie. You're right though, he can't understand fully. He can only understand the violence part. Not the violation." I couldn't bring myself to say the word rape.

"It was violent?" she whispered.

"Extremely."

"Fuck. Mine too, but I wouldn't say extremely. He slapped me around a bit." Her words were haunted.

"Violence is violence. Don't downplay your trauma based on what you think of someone else's." I squeezed her hand. "Want me to pull that stuff that's simmering in you now?"

"No, thank you though for the offer. If you are going to suffer with it lingering, I'll do it with you. Sucks to be alone in that, yet at the same time, you wish no one else will ever have to feel that." Jillian wiped a tear from her eyes.

"That was worded perfectly." I looked back out at the water. "They are hovering. It's almost comical."

"Almost. The reason is valid, I was a bat shit crazy bitch to you. I apologized to Jax too. Not sure if he believed me or not, I was sincere in it though." A ghost of a smile lit her face. "Really, I just wanted you to know you have another option in me for this."

"I still think you should tell him." I glanced back. "It would help him understand your reaction better."

"That's true. Maybe down the road some." She shifted, getting ready to stand.

"My offer is open ended, if you need me to pull it because something triggers you, just tell me. I'll do whatever I need to in order to help." I hugged her again.

"Ditto. Now I'm going to head back down before one of them storms your little castle here. Chances are it will be Art to make sure I didn't say something mean." She gave me a crooked smile. "I was going to send him up anyway. It's killing him that he hasn't talked to you yet."

"Thanks Jillian."

She climbed easily down the rocks and jogged back to the guys. I saw Ronnie and Jax sit back down, apparently appeased. She pulled Smitty off to the side and talked to him. I knew he'd be up next.

Smitty clutched at Jillian. "What the hell did you say?" he whispered angrily.

"Chill, we were talking about what happened. It's an emotional subject, she's fine. If you must know, I offered to be an ear if she needed one that wasn't attached to a dick."

Gobsmacked, he looked at her. "Are you serious?"

"Yes, I'm serious, you ass." She smacked him in the arm. "I would never joke about that."

"Okay, sorry, jeez. You can't blame me for asking," his voice softened.

"No, I don't. I apologized again. I also told her I was fine with whatever you two have going on, so she knows where I stand. It's all okay honey, I promise. Her and I, we're good." Jillian stretched up and kissed him. "Now go, I know you need to go check on her."

Smitty watched her walk away back to the fire now burning in the pit. She flummoxed him sometimes. She wasn't wrong, he did need to see her. He looked over at Ronnie and Jax and caught Ronnie's eye, who waved him on. Ronnie knew. He bet Jax did too.

He was surprised to see Jax get up and walk back to towards the fire as he started to climb up the rocks. Airiella was there waiting for him, a soft smile on her face. His soul breathed a little easier at the sight.

"Hi handsome," she said and held out her hand.

He took it gladly, happy for the contact. "Hi, baby girl. You've had me worried. I've never felt anything like that before."

"If you get my emotions going you better expect to have another two men crowded up here," she warned.

"I'm more afraid of Mags, than I am them." He looked back at Ronnie. "Feeling a little better?"

"A little. I told Jillian I wouldn't really know until we got back and I'm bombarded with city life, not nature. It's the truth. Out here I can be okay, it's a little harder there."

"I understand that now. Ronnie told me not to touch you unless you initiated it. Is he being overprotective?" Smitty was so tense with wanting to hold her he felt like he was going to snap.

"Only a little. Things are a little fresh and raw right now, though I would welcome your touch. It's okay Smitty, you can come closer." She patted the rock directly next to her.

It was all the encouragement he needed. He slid

over and in one smooth motion he had her between his legs and was hugging her. "The only thing that stopped me from running to you earlier was Jax. He knew immediately what was happening. I should have guessed, or thought about it, I just reacted instead."

She rested her head on him. "He was right to stop you. I would have totally freaked out. I wasn't present Smitty. I was fully locked in that memory, back in that time and place. Any other people that would have been around would have broken me all the way. I don't want you to feel like you made that happen. No matter what you say, you would have felt guilty, and it didn't have anything to do with you."

"I love you, baby girl. My voice of reason wouldn't have gotten through?" He was curious.

"No. There is no reason in any of that. The only thing that penetrated that was the pure emotions Ronnie was putting off. Basically, his love broke through." I shivered and he held me tighter. "Otherwise, I think I'd still be stuck in it."

"Is he okay? I can't imagine that was easy for him. He's got a soft heart." Smitty glanced back at Ronnie.

"He's okay right now, after I pulled it all back from you guys. He was just as rough as I was for a bit." He could tell she was understating it.

She snuggled up to him and he loved every bit of it. "We're all with you. Whatever you need."

"I know, and it helps. It keeps pulling me back from the edge and putting my soul right back where it needs to be." She tipped her head backwards and kissed his jaw. "I love you too, by the way."

"Your arms are chilly, so are your legs," he told her as he ran his hands over her, like he was looking for signs of injury.

"The sun is starting to set, I'm okay though."

He wanted to argue with her and demand she go sit by the fire, but he didn't. He knew it was the wrong thing to say and she still looked like she needed to be right where she was. Instead he just rapidly ran his hands up and down her arms to generate heat.

"I'm okay," she promised. "Kiss me, please."

He did growl then. He'd been wanting to do that since she came up to them on the beach earlier. He gently tipped her chin towards him and tenderly kissed her. His mouth soft against hers, his tongue slow and easy. She groaned and he broke it off before he got carried away.

"That was perfect," she said and she smiled against his lips.

"I'll leave you be. I'm sure one of the others will be up next. They are all kind of antsy."

"I know they are, it's fine. Thank you, Smitty."

"One of these nights coming up, reserve for me." He stood and dropped a kiss on her head.

"Nothing would make me happier," she told him.

His heart felt a little lighter as he climbed down. He walked over and sat next to Ronnie.

"You going up there?" Smitty tilted his head at the rocks.

"No, not yet. I think Jax will go up. I'm going to stay with her tonight, still not ready to let her out of my sight yet." To Smitty, Ronnie sounded worn out.

"You doing okay?"

"Been better, I'm just taking my cues from her, trying to give what she needs. I'm tired. That was a fucking roller coaster ride from hell I never want to ride again. I wasn't sure I could get her back. Fucking brutal." The look in Ronnie's eyes told Smitty all he needed to know.

"Don't tell me details." Smitty was sure it would send him off the deep end.

"I won't. Go on back. I'm fine. This is peaceful here. It helps." Ronnie gave him a crooked smile.

Smitty stood, and with a pat on his back headed back to Jillian, passing Jax on the way who was carrying her pack. "Make her put something on," he told him as they passed.

Ronnie stared out at the waves. "Hey Ron, come up with me for a few." Jax appeared behind him.

"I thought you wanted alone time with her." Ronnie was surprised.

"I do, when the sun starts to actually set, come sit with us until then," Jax clarified.

Ronnie would take it. Any opportunity he could get. He followed Jax up the rocks, and they each settled on either side of her. She wound her arms through theirs linking them at the elbows.

"Did you sleep, angel?" Ronnie kissed her on the temple.

"A little. Jillian woke me up. I thought it was one of you."

"We told her not to wake you up if you were sleeping," Ronnie grumbled.

"She didn't. I woke up because I felt someone near me," she clarified.

Jax was fumbling with her pack. "Stand up please."

She didn't question him, she just stood. That's when Ronnie knew that she wasn't back yet. She was just going through the motions. He stayed seated but watched as Jax pulled out his sweatshirt and tugged it down over her. It fell to mid-thigh and swallowed her arms and hands. He held out her skirt and she stepped into it, letting him pull it up.

He had her sit back down and he wiped the salt and sand off her legs and feet, then put her socks on her and her hiking boots. Satisfied that she had layers on, he dropped back down by her side. "Smitty wanted you to have more on," he told her.

"I was getting cold, it's okay. Thank you, Jax." She leaned her head on his shoulder.

"You aren't okay yet," Ronnie stated.

"It comes and goes with the waves," was her answer. "Ebb and flow."

"You put your walls back up, didn't you?" Ronnie wished she would look at him, instead her eyes were focused out on the water somewhere.

"I did when you two came up," was the even toned answer.

"Why?" Jax asked.

"To keep the others away. I'm not ready for the whole of them yet. If they don't feel anything they won't come running."

Ronnie understood. "Should we leave?"

"No. You being here feels right." Her responses sounded wooden though. Her tone distant.

Ronnie knew something was off. She was stuck in another memory. "Angel, can I hold you?"

She stood up again and waited for Ronnie to move to where she had been sitting and then she sat back down between his legs like she had been sitting earlier. Her movements were mechanical though. Jax gave him a worried look and scooted closer so they all were touching.

"Want to tell us where you are right now?" Jax's voice was barely louder than the waves.

"I'm here," she reached for his hand and intertwined their fingers together.

Ronnie had his arms around her waist and rested his chin on her shoulder. "I don't know where you are angel, it's not here though."

"I'm here, just remembering." Her reply was so distant, her tone nothing like normal.

"Tell me what you are remembering," Jax said bravely. Ronnie knew it wasn't the rape, she wasn't shaking.

She didn't say anything for a few minutes and Ronnie started to wish for the shaking, at least that was emotion. This vacancy was disturbing him.

"You know when you yell into an empty space and you hear the echo?" Her voice felt small. "I'm scared because I don't know what the answer to that echo is. I feel like an echo that has no answer."

Ronnie had no idea what to say to that. His heart ached for her. "You are the answer to my echo," Jax said, his tone laced with love.

Ronnie silently applauded Jax's response, it was a good one, and it was true. She was the answer to all their echoes. He didn't move, just stayed wrapped around her hoping she'd find her way back. Instinctively, Ronnie knew he couldn't pull her from this one.

"My ex-husband was an alcoholic. Is. He *is* an alcoholic. I almost divorced him after the first year I was married because of it, and I did something I never thought I'd do. I laid down an ultimatum. He quit drinking, which I was happy about, though he changed. It took me a few years to understand that alcohol was a part of who he was as a person, and I forced change on him."

She was still using that flat tone, Ronnie didn't know where this was headed, and beside him Jax stiffened. He tried to remember the few things she'd said about her marriage. He was drawing a blank though. There was something about the step-son and stalking.

"I never wanted to be that person that makes someone change. It does something to you. There was an answering echo to that I never saw coming. His son was a problem child. He hated that his dad drank, so when he finally stopped, his son decided his dad was an asshole. I tried to intervene, to make his son feel loved, gave him a fresh new start and fought the schools tooth and nail for him."

Jax was starting to feel like he was vibrating. This must be something she had seen in her dream thing. That meant it wasn't good and something she needed to heal. It didn't sound like her marriage had been easy, but at least it wasn't filled with the gruesome violence of the rape.

"It's odd how you can look back after the fact and see the signs, the beginning of the end, that all roads lead to the same place. It hurts to believe that you weren't enough to change the outcome. That you weren't enough to calm the demons inside someone you loved. Is it possible for the echoes of time gone by to lie?"

She wasn't looking for answers. She was thinking out loud, waxing poetic. Jax hadn't said a word and Ronnie was a little worried by that. She still held his hand though, her thumb stroking absently along the side of his fingers.

"My ex used to tell me all the time he wanted to have a kid with me, he wanted a little girl with my hair and eyes." She trembled a bit then. "I used to wear a mask that I put on, figuratively speaking, that no one could see through. It showed the world that I didn't care if I had that child or not. Underneath though, I wanted that child. I wanted her to show me that life was a miracle and that I was enough to be her mother. I wanted her for him, so he could prove to himself that he could be a good father, that his son's drug addictions weren't his fault. Maybe I wanted that little life to give meaning to my own, maybe she was the hope for me, for all the wrong reasons. If I'd had that child, I wouldn't be here right now."

Ronnie's emotions took a wild swing. He was wrong, this was just as traumatic as earlier, in a very different way, however. She still showed no emotions, like she'd put that mask she was talking about on.

"I saw countless doctors over the years trying to have that child. Things with his son escalated to the point of us having to file a missing person report with the FBI. I remember feeling better when he wasn't in the house which made me feel guilty. He still deserved a chance in my eyes. After he turned eighteen, he showed back up. Now it wasn't just drugs, it was drugs, alcohol and guns," she said hollowly.

Jax was definitely vibrating. There had yet to be a change in Airiella's tone either. "That echo was answering. I didn't know it though. My ex started getting verbally abusive and controlling to a degree I didn't understand. The echoes of the verbal abuse, I heard. I tried to put a stop to that, I'd already been through it. He always apologized. It wore on me though. Every time I turned around, I was accused of cheating on him. I couldn't leave the house without him calling every five minutes to see where I was," she told them.

Airiella moved forward bringing her knees up to her chin, making Ronnie's arms loosen around her. She wrapped her free arm around her legs and still held on to

Jax, stroking with her thumb. Not even aware she was doing it.

"What is it about violence that attracts people so much?" She didn't expect an answer. "Verbal abuse is just restrained physical violence that leaves marks no one can ever see. Marks that landed directly on top of ones that were already there. Marks that don't go away very easily, if at all. Anyone I talked to became suspect, male or female. They were complicit in me having an affair with someone. I was a liar, a whore, a user, I manipulated people into thinking that I was a good person."

Ronnie leaned forward to secure his arms around her again, sliding his hands between her belly and her legs. "He had his son following me. I didn't know it at first. He used his friends' cars so I didn't know what to watch for. He started showing up at my job. Telling his dad that I was talking with tons of other men. Of course, I was, it was my job. That didn't matter though. To him, I refused to give him a baby because I was in love with someone else, and he was going to find out who."

Jax shifted closer to Ronnie, he wasn't sure if he was trying to get closer to Airiella or him, or if he needed both of them. Parts of this story mirrored his parents' marriage, and it made him uneasy. Jax knew about it and Ronnie assumed he was trying to lend his support to Ronnie.

"I finally caught on to what was happening when I went for a walk in my neighborhood to just get away and I was confronted in the middle of the street. I was a cheating, lying, whore who was on my way to see her lover. My ex stood there as his son held a gun to my head, screaming so wildly that spit was flying out of his mouth, his face red. I told him to shoot the whore then. I walked away, called my parents but they weren't home. When I made it back to the house, they were all gone but the kitchen table was covered in beer bottles. Empty beer bottles. At least three cases worth."

Jax leaned against Ronnie. "I packed a bag and left, went to my parents' house. He'd called my parents already.

Told them I was cheating on him, he had proof, and that I'd left and was probably with him right now. I found that out when they got home. My own parents believed the worst of me. I'd been there alone that whole time. I felt abandoned, so I went back home and moved into the extra room, keeping the door locked and slept with my gun."

There was a hint of sadness to her voice now. At least it was emotion. "The entire time I had been fighting with doctors because I didn't feel right. It took them six months to realize I had cancer. Six months of being told I was a lying, cheating whore by the person who took vows to love and cherish me. Six months of looking over my shoulder everywhere I went, expecting another gun to be shoved in my face. Or worse. All those echoes slamming back into me with an answer I didn't expect. I had cancer. My marriage was cancer. My body was cancer. My family thought I was an awful person."

Jax kissed her hand. "My ex tried to come off like a supportive spouse. I didn't believe him though. It was too late for that. He'd openly started drinking again, and his abuse spread from verbal to verbal and physical, though he kept the physical part to a minimum because I was seeing so many doctors at that point. He left town the weekend of my surgery, flew back in the day of. I spent that weekend alone. Trying to make peace with my life, hoping that I would make it through, trying to come to grips that I would never have a child of my own. Feeling the loss of that baby that would never be."

Ronnie felt the pain in her then. She kept her voice neutral, though the pain was making itself known loudly, bleeding out of her. "My best friend at the time, and my parents, were there for my surgery. I'll never forget being wheeled away wondering if I'd live. I still get nightmares about that. When I came out the surgery my ex was there for all of fifteen minutes before he left to go home because he was tired and he needed to sleep before he went to meet his friend for drinks. After a month I ended back up in the hospital with a surgical abscess and was being prepped for another surgery. My parents were there, though my mom acted like she hated me. He'd been filling her head with poison about me."

Ronnie saw her shoulders shake a little and he did tighten his hold on her then. So did Jax. "The stalking continued and after I was released, I filed for divorce. They put me on low dose chemo then and it became a struggle for me and I had to choose. Continue to fight him, or fight for my life. I moved out, had to tell my job that I was being stalked. Had to explain to the apartment complex that I filed for divorce, no matter what papers he showed up with he was not on my lease and had no right to be there. I felt completely alone. Then, I found out he'd been sleeping with my best friend. Since the drinking and the abuse started. The entire I time I had cancer they were both lying to me. I lost everything. My sense of being a female, I couldn't even do what my body was meant to do, give life. My marriage, gone. My best friend, gone."

She leaned back into Ronnie then and pulled Jax's hand close to her body. "Then Michael came and instead of dealing with everything, I did the same thing I did with the rape. I pushed it down, I didn't know how to deal with the fallout from all that. I was stuck in a cycle, and the echoes had all lost the answers. After I began seeing Michael, my ex would still reach out and pull one of my triggers, sending me spinning into a downfall. I failed him by not giving him the child he wanted. I failed him by filing for divorce. He just kept doing it, until, eventually, I became numb to it. Then earlier, when we were talking today, that echo surfaced again. It resonates with the rape. The fear of being around people, or trusting people, letting them in."

Ronnie couldn't stay silent anymore. "Yet here you are, fighting those fears on a daily basis, staring them in the face and telling them to fuck off. You are right here, letting us in, trusting us, loving us."

"Why do I feel so numb then?" she asked.

"You're processing," Jax leaned into us both.

"Take your walls down angel," Ronnie whispered into her ear. "We've got you."

He felt them come down, felt the swirling vortex of

her emotions that took the shape of a hurricane in his mind. He welcomed the feel of them instead of the blank canvas she had been and he could feel the way the separate events intertwined and intersected.

"I won't let it break me again," came her harsh whisper.

"Maybe it's in the breaking that the healing begins," Jax said. "I don't know that you ever let it break you the first time."

Ronnie was taken aback by the wisdom in Jax's words. She didn't respond, just sat completely still staring out at the now sinking sun. It could be that she would only break for Jax on this one. It was time for him to leave them.

"Angel, I'm going to go back and sit with the others. Stay here as long as you need." Ronnie stood up and bent over her. She tipped her head back, but didn't look at him. She just closed her eyes. He kissed her softly. "None of it will change how I feel about you. I don't find you lacking in any way."

He saw a single tear escape. He put his mouth against Jax's ear, "Take care of her." He turned to climb back down and looked up to see Jax move positions. He'd slid one of his legs under her bent knees and bent the other behind her in a back support. His chest was against her side.

Ronnie pulled out his phone and angled it just right to catch them with the sunset as a backdrop and took a picture. The resulting photo was a great one. He headed back to the fire burning bright and his friends. Reassuring them she was fine to try and ease their worries about the emotions they were all feeling swirling around them now.

Chapter Twenty-Three

Jax was in heaven and hell both. "It's been a hard day for you, siren," Jax said, empathy coloring his words.

"Yes, it has. I wouldn't change it though." He thought her voice sounded thick. He wanted her to cry, or scream or yell it out. Just let it go. He could feel how much she was trying to hold back.

"You know you need to let it go. I can handle it." His voice took on a rough edge.

She leaned into him a little bit, he pulled her closer, wanting more. "I get tired of the ugly. Tired of the mask, of being strong. It's nice to hear you tell me I don't have to be."

"You are still strong, even if you let it go. You don't stop being strong even if you feel like you are weak. I'm telling you that it's okay to not feel strong. It's okay to feel, even the ugly. Like you told me though, you've got to let it go."

"It's a little weird to have my own words used against me." She wrapped an arm around him and cuddled into his chest. He felt strong when she did that.

"Did you know I only feel like half a person until you touch me?" He pressed his lips to the top of her head and felt a tremor run through her. She leaned her head forward, resting her forehead against his bicep and felt the hot tears fall on his arm.

"You are so much more than that, Jax. So much more." Her voice broke.

"I believe it when I'm with you." He cradled her head with his arm. One of Jax's broken pieces fell into place in that moment.

She slid her free hand up the front of his shirt and held her palm over his heart and cried. Not the huge dam of emotions she had earlier that had thrown them all, this was gentler though still as powerful. It spoke of years of pain and torment, broken dreams and promises, of loss. All feelings he was intimate with himself. Each of those tears washing a little away, here and there.

"Look, little witch," he said into ear. She turned her head and looked at him. He chuckled, "Not at me. At the magic your witchy ways is making," he said as he nodded to the sunset.

She turned her head the other way and at the view in front of them he felt her emotions settle. The sky a brilliant fuchsia color next to the water, above that a tangerine color fading to gold the closer it was to the sun. The water shimmering as it flowed. It was a spectacular sunset and his heart was happy he was sharing it with her alone, in his arms.

"When I'm with you, that's what my heart feels like." He voiced the words he was afraid to.

She kissed the arm that still cradled her head. "I love you, Jax."

Every time she said those words to him something inside him shifted. He hoped she understood he felt the same way. He just couldn't say the words that came so easily to the others. He wanted to show her in all the ways he knew how, and he was trying. Fear beat him back sometimes and he felt inadequate.

There hadn't been a time yet when she was up against his body that he hadn't noticed how perfectly she fit him. She was the water that quenched his thirst, and at the same time, made him thirstier for more.

Today was the first time he'd seen the struggles she faced, how many of them matched his own feelings inside. He saw, touched, felt and tasted how she stood her ground while those struggles broke her. He felt her fear at facing it all, and she did it anyway. Like a hero.

He'd never been a nature person either, sure he loved a good photo and walk in the park, but he didn't think he'd ever done something like this before. Similar to how he felt about Airiella, this place had been magical for him. He understood her need for it, the safety it brought.

They sat there, wrapped around each other and watched the sunset. Before it was completely gone, he reached back in the pack he'd brought up and pulled out a Tupperware and sandwiches Mags had made him bring up. He'd promised to make her eat something.

He unwrapped one and handed it to her. She shifted sideways so they were sitting side by side now, watching the last of the sun sink below the horizon in an array of colors. She nibbled on the sandwich, eating it and not really eating it. Mags would kick his ass if she didn't finish it.

"Siren, you gotta eat that and save me from Mags," he pleaded with her.

She smiled weakly and finished it. She pulled her knees up to her chest and rested her arms on top of them again. Her chin on top of her arms and stared at the night sky. Her emotions settled more the longer she sat there and she started to feel relaxed again.

More than once he wanted to reach out and hold her again, touch her. Her body language said hands off though. Instead, he just watched her. He could feel the energy of the earth coursing through her, the moonlight glinting off her hair and her eyes. So still that she blended with the night.

"When you sit here at night like this, watching the world, the waves, you are so still that I have to look closely to see if you are still breathing. You're so perfect and at peace here. You are the very essence of life. The moon bathing you in mystical light like it was made only for you." Jax spoke softly, his voice only carrying to her ears.

She turned her head so her ear was resting on her arms as she looked at him now. Those eyes of her, starlight. "So beautiful." He longed to touch her. "It makes my heart ache and I don't know what to do it about it. You feel like all of life's mysteries wrapped into one breathtaking package that I want to keep unwrapping and never stop until I discover everything."

She took the choice from him and stood in a fluid motion holding her hand out to him. He took it like a starving dog being given a meaty bone and she pulled him up and into her. "Jax, you make me forget all the reasons I tell myself that I'm not ready for you."

"I don't understand how any of this is possible. How you make me feel the way I do. I've seen the look on Ronnie's face, even Smitty's, that happens when you walk away. That darkness in me loves to see you go. The look on their faces is like they are in physical pain. I know, because I feel it too." He ran his hands through his hair, her face tipped up, watching him.

"It drives me insane with how much I want you. You have no idea how many nights I've lain in bed wishing you were lying under me. I want to taste every inch of your body to see if it tastes as good as you smell. I want to hear your voice calling my name. That voice that makes me feel like I'm going to come every time you get that tone. So damn sexy, I want you more than I want air. It's a pain that rips me apart when I wonder what your fingers feel like on the rest of my body. I have dreams about the things I want to do to you." He was too near the edge for this conversation, his body thrumming with the need to be inside her.

"I want to give in every single day, sometimes every hour of every day. Then that damn darkness kicks in and tells me it's not real. That the feeling will only last until I have you, then you'll be done with me. It tells me that what I'm feeling and can't say out loud, is fake. That it's just lust, and it fills my head with pictures of you being taken by force and I want to be sick. It lies, tells me that you don't really love me like you say that you do, and I know damn well it's lie. I can *feel* it every time I look at you. It fights me about you. I know none of that is true, I know it so deep inside that there are times it's the only thing I have to hold on to."

He kissed her on the forehead. "Then there are days like today, where every time I see you, I look at you and I feel it in every cell in my body. It tells me that you're mine. I want it to be true so badly, I want to scream. Sometimes that scares me more, because, there still is that little doubt in my mind that maybe the darkness is right. These perfect feelings that are so consuming will go away after I give in and let my heart and soul lead me into you. I'm terrified to admit that you already own it all, and it won't let me. It won't let me admit it. And I'm so scared I'll hurt you."

He drew her into him, always the perfect fit. Her hands under his shirt again, her lips kissing his shirt in the spot his heart lay beneath it, wide open for her. "Kiss me," she urged him. "Kiss me like you've been wanting to."

A deep groan tore from his mouth as he took possession of hers, giving in to the need she so clearly saw in him. It wasn't a gentle or soft kiss, it was everything he was afraid to say, everything he was afraid to want, and pure primal need. He took and demanded in that kiss. She gave it freely.

When he pulled back, her eyes were dazed, her lips swollen and face flushed with desire. "God, always kiss me like that Jax, don't hold back," she said, that sexy siren voice of hers wrapping around him.

"It's taking everything in me to not lay you down right here and take you like I want to," he said, his words raw with need.

She didn't flinch away at his words. "Are you ready?"

"No," he growled in frustration. "My body thinks I am in case you haven't noticed."

"Oh, trust me, I noticed," she said and she gave him a wicked look. "Let me help you with it, at least without doing what we both want to do but are afraid to do."

His body visibly shuddered. "How?"

She slid her hands over his rigid cock. "With my hands."

"Are you afraid of me?" He gave her a soulful look.

"No. I'm afraid of my feelings for you, just like you are." Her voice rang true. She stroked him through his jeans again. "I won't give in to that energy though. The feelings I feel won't go away. You'll believe it too, in time."

He trembled under her hands. "What about you? That's not exactly fair to you," he said roughly, his hips arching into her touch.

"I get just as much out of this as you do," she said and she stroked again. "The rest will fall into place."

He gave in as her fingers slid below the waistband of his jeans, her fingertips barely skimming against his swollen head. The touch so electric he bit his tongue to keep from crying out. He undid his jeans freeing his cock as she wrapped those exquisite fingers around him.

When she licked her lips, her intent plain on her face, he pulled her face up for him to kiss instead. He knew if she put her mouth on him that there would be no holding back, he'd take her here. He let his tongue explore every inch of her mouth while she stroked him. Her hands working a magic his cock had never felt before. Every touch implanting itself in his memory.

He was unraveling fast, the sensations she brought to him flooding through his veins like a wildfire. He buried his hands in her hair trapping her lips against his she stroked with one hand, then used the other to cup his balls, her fingers sliding over the sensitive skin like silk. His body bowed under her hands and he came in wild spurts, his cries buried in her kiss as she stroked until he was completely empty.

He hadn't even been aware she captured it all with her other hand to keep them from getting messy until she dumped a bottle of water over her hand when she pulled away. Jax's knees were shaking he'd come so hard. She totally undid him in every way possible.

"How did you get anything from that?" His voice was hoarse.

"I got to be the one to make you lose control in the best way imaginable, in this time and place. To swallow your moans and taste your sweet lips, knowing it was me that did that to you. Jax, that was sexy as hell." The smile she gave him had the power to steal his breath.

He crushed her to him, his arms like a vice grip around her. That connection between them a little brighter and stronger now racing along inside him through every crack in his heart. Tracing a path over each of those pieces she put right back together just by being her.

Chapter Twenty-Four

The feel of Jax hot and hard in my hand was seared into my skin. His words beautifully expressing the emotions and fears present in his mind, whether he wanted to say them or not. "For the record," I pulled his head down to kiss him again before I whispered against his mouth, "I *am* yours."

The possessive growl that left his throat made her heart flutter. "Siren," his eyes dark and wild, "we better go back before I start making my fantasies about you come true."

I buttoned his jeans back up and slowly slid the zipper in place. "In time, Jax." I slid my arms around his shoulders and kissed along his jaw, the rough stubbled texture erotic on my lips. "Thank you for letting me do that for you."

"Fuck." He took another kiss, more demanding than the last and my toes curled in my boots. "It's me who needs to thank you." He kissed my nose, then forehead. "You saying that you are mine, did something to me inside."

"To me, too," I admitted.

"You are Ronnie's too, right?" He sounded worried.

"Yes." My voice was strong but inside I felt a tremor

of fear that he was still concerned with that.

"Good." Then he gave me one of those smiles of his that slammed the doors closed on any doubts about his feelings or mine. "I might tell myself that you are more mine than his when I get jealous."

"I may have been his before you, but I'll be yours last and always." My voice ultra-sultry.

He quietly swore under his breath and dug through my pack for the flashlight I stuck in there. "You're going to be the death of me." He found it and put my pack on his back. "Hold this while I climb down first." He handed me the flashlight.

I held it and lit the way for him, passing it back when he was down. He waited until I had swung my legs over and then pulled me down, his hands sliding up my ass and to my back, my shirt bunched up under my boobs as I slid down him.

"The feel of your hand around me and how you fit perfectly into my body is going to keep me awake for nights," he whispered huskily.

"Oh, Zeus, me too," I replied.

"Zeus?" He gave me a look that it was too dark to read correctly.

"Yeah, sometimes you are Zeus, sometimes Atlas. I love mythology." I wriggled against him trying to get him to put me down before I wrapped my legs around him.

"Um, trying to remember. I'm either king of all gods or one who carries the weight of the world on his back?" He had a wry smile on his face.

"Both. Right now, you are Zeus."

"Does that make you Hera?" He was trying so hard not to look flattered.

"If we were married, I guess that would be true. She's considered a queen though, I'm only a mere angel," I joked. I pulled him towards the others. "If we don't go back, I am 99% positive Mags is going to drag me back."

He pulled back spinning me around. "You might not be *a* queen, but you are *my* queen, my siren, my angel, my witch." His face so serious it took me a minute to understand how hard that was for him to say.

"That right there, is why you are Zeus." His words had a profound effect on my heart.

There was that smile again. "So, who is Ronnie?"

I gave him a sly look. "Heracles and Eros."

"Which one is Eros?"

"Um, god of sex," I mumbled.

Jax howled in laughter. "Okay, I'll give him that one based on the sounds you made. Who is Smitty?"

"Apollo. He's the god of music and knowledge. There's other stuff thrown in there but since he gave Ronnie the idea for a playlist of songs and he knows a lot of shit that seemed to suit him."

"You're right, it does. How about Aedan?" Jax was amused.

"Prometheus," I answered. He definitely didn't know that one going by the look on his face. "God of forethought and counsel that had to make mankind out of clay. He's always trying to lead and help shape the team."

"Fitting. So far so good. What about Mags?" We walked slowly back, he kept hold of my hand, swinging them between us.

"Mags is Hestia and Athena."

"Athena is the goddess of wisdom? I don't know Hestia."

"Athena is the goddess of wisdom, yes, also of war strategy. She's pretty fierce sometimes and plays her moves where they will be most effective. Hestia is goddess of hearth and home, family basically."

"Holy shit, you pegged her right. There should have been a goddess of nagging. That would have been the only one better."

"That kind of falls under the family one," I laughed. "Better behave or I'll tell her you said that."

"Zeus," he whispered, a smile on his face. "That means I made you, siren."

"That's probably truer than either of us could realize right now," I told him softly.

"How about this instead, we are remaking ourselves

and finding each other."

"Just don't forget to keep kissing me, Zeus," I reminded him.

"Did you eat?" came Mags' question from across the fire. "Jax you better have fed her!"

"I ate, I promise," I answered her with a chuckle.

"Good, or I was about to lay down an ass kicking." Mags came around and enveloped me in a hug. Quietly she said, "I felt another little wave go through, are you okay?"

"Stop worrying Mags, I just did what I needed to do and Jax was there to see me through it."

"For a second, I was worried he was the cause of it, but when Ronnie didn't go flying over there, I gave him the benefit of the doubt."

"Gee, thanks Mags," Jax said, sitting on the sand, his back resting against the log Ronnie was sitting on. He held out his hand to me and I went and sat between him and Ronnie. Jax threaded his fingers in my hair as he put an arm around my shoulder and Ronnie slid down next to me in the sand.

The heat of the fire felt good and the group around me was filled with smiles, laughter and fun stories. I caught Smitty's eyes over the flames and mouthed a thank you to him. My world had been re-centered today.

Ronnie sensed there was a new closeness between Jax and Airiella. He picked up on it as they came back. It made him smile to see it. Jax was far more relaxed than he'd ever been in the past twelve years. His angel looked not as empty and drained. Yeah there'd been some hard parts to the day for sure, they all got through it though. And they were all more balanced than when they had gotten here.

They made the hike in the dark back to the SUV. Smitty, having fun and scaring the hell out of Jillian on the way, by hiding then jumping out at her. Airiella cracked up laughing as Jillian chased Smitty back to the SUV.

Aedan drove back and he and Jax sat in the back with Airiella between them again. They had a flight out in three days for another shoot and Jillian was leaving as regularly scheduled the next day. When they got back and unloaded all the bags, each one climbing the stairs exhausted, they all hugged and kissed Airiella, even Jillian, Ronnie was surprised to see.

Jax and her whispered in each other's ears, then she took Ronnie's hand and led him to his room. He thought that she would leave him there and go to her own, but she went into his instead. "Is it okay if I stay with you tonight?"

"I'd been hoping you were going to say that. Otherwise I would have waited until you fell asleep and snuck into your room then," he admitted sheepishly.

"Nah, I still need you close," she told him.

"Are you not better?" Ronnie tipped her face to see her eyes better.

"I am. I just still need you."

"You won't ever hear me say that I'm tired of hearing that." He hugged her close.

"Thank you for today, it was amazing." She kissed him on the chin. "That sand angel was fantastic. Blew me away. I had no idea Jax and Mags were such talented artists."

"Jax is the one who drew all my ink for me," Ronnie told her casually. "He's the artist for his own too. He has a friend that does tattoos. Jax draws them, his friend inks them."

"Wow! So your incredible body is thanks to him?" She smirked.

Ronnie broke out laughing. "Oh angel, this piece of art was all me." He waved his hand over his body.

"I guess you both are pretty talented then," she winked.

Ronnie swatted her ass. "Go shower the sand off, you wicked angel. I don't want sandy sheets."

"What about you? You are just as dirty as me." She winked again.

"I'm far dirtier than you, baby," he growled into her

neck, biting gently.

The twinkle in her eyes had him stripping both of them down and getting them showered as quickly as possible. His promise to her ringing in his head. Could he do it? Could he try to trigger her fears to help erase them?

"You are thinking too much," she told him rinsing his hair. "Just do what feels right Ronnie."

Domination and control were things that came easy to him in the bedroom, though it wasn't his forte. He just liked to let the woman guide him in what worked for her. He wasn't a selfish lover, but he'd also never been invested in any of those women like he was with Airiella.

He also knew Jax loved the control aspect of it, but rarely indulged. Maybe that was why she felt she needed this. She'd come unglued if she thought Jax felt like he'd been forceful. Whatever her reason, he'd promised and he would deliver.

"Remember, you are in control of this. You say stop and I will," he said as he kissed her. She nodded, her eyes lit with a new glow. He wouldn't need to try hard if she kept looking at him like that. He had one moment of hesitation wondering if he'd get over making her flinch or asking to stop because he went too far.

"Stop overthinking Ronnie. I'm not afraid of you, I never have been," she reminded him.

He backed her, crowding her space until the back of her knees hit the bed and she fell back on it. He never let more than a couple inches between them. He used his size and strength, stretching out over her as he lifted her and literally tossed her back on the bed.

She was turned on. He crawled over her and sat on her legs, pinning them as she wanted. He watched her face carefully, saw a tiny flicker in her eyes that quickly gave way to heat as he ran his hands up her body, pinching her nipples harder than he ever would have before.

She let out a small cry that was pure pleasure. She tried to put her hands on him and he captured both, holding her wrists down at her sides, pressing them into the bed so she couldn't move. In his mind, he was telling himself to stop. Her body was saying something entirely different.

She writhed under him as he sucked her nipples, biting and nibbling, then licking to take away the sting. She didn't try to move her hands or her legs but he felt her fingers grasping the blankets below her.

He slid down her legs keeping them pinned as he licked down her belly, swirling his tongue around her belly button, then back up over her breasts to her collarbone. Biting and nipping everywhere, then soothing with kisses and licks.

There was fire in her eyes, heavy lidded and burning as she watched him, breathing hard, biting her lip. He dipped in for a kiss, pulling that lip from between her teeth and into his mouth. His kiss was aggressive and demanded surrender, which she wouldn't give him.

He called on every skill he had picked up to drive her to the brink and pull back before she tipped over. He was harder than he'd ever been, and felt like he was going to come just watching her reactions. He needed his hands for this next part.

"Angel, I'm going to slide your hands under that magnificent ass of yours. Keep them there, you are not allowed to move them, understand?" his voice was hoarse and thick with desire.

She nodded, unable to speak. He moved her hands then slid down her body again, keeping her legs trapped under his. He spread her open with his thumbs, using his hands to press down on her hips. The scent of her arousal was heady and she was wet and swollen, ready for his tongue.

He blew across that bundle of nerves first, her body trembling beneath him. One flick with his tongue and a strangled cry escaped her lips. Then another two licks, his thumbs keeping her spread and exposed as he blew again, then sucked that luscious bud in his mouth flattening his tongue against it as she tried to buck her hips.

He alternated between licks and flicking his tongue fast, sucking and blowing air across it. She went wild under him, keeping her hands under her ass as he kept bringing her right to the edge but not letting her cross it over and over until she was begging him.

He moved one of his hands to hold her open and dragged his fingers across the exposed skin getting them wet, then slid a finger inside her and curled it right into that spot that made her cry out his name. He fastened his lips over that swollen bud and flicked his tongue rapidly as he curled his finger inside her sending her crashing head first into an intense orgasm, a rasping cry wrung from her lips as her body shook under the onslaught of his tongue.

He didn't give her time to come down. He grabbed her hands and dropped his knees between hers, shoving her legs open and bringing his body up hers crushing his lips to hers, making her taste herself on his tongue and he held her hands in a tight grip above her head as he drove himself into her.

She was hot, tight and still in the grips of the last orgasm and she clenched around him, pushing against his arms that held hers, her mind so far gone she didn't even realize her legs were free. His mouth plundering hers as he rode her orgasm out barely hanging on to his control to keep from crashing into his own.

He slowed the pace before it was over too fast, then took her hard and slowed down before she came again. Doing the same, driving her up and down until they were both past the point of no return and he thrust deep, letting go of her arms as he came and she bucked up into him taking him even deeper gasping his name, the waves of the orgasm crashing over them both drowning them.

She was shaking uncontrollably and Ronnie started to panic thinking he took it too far, when she smiled at him, her face flushed and shining with the sweat that covered them both. He ran his hands over her arms checking to see if he bruised her and noticed she wasn't the only one shaking, he was too.

"If I'm going to die, I want it to be doing that. With you coming beneath me calling my name like you just did." He gasped trying to slow his breathing down.

She couldn't talk, she just nodded in agreement. He was still inside her and didn't want to move. She wasn't pushing him away so he laid there trying to keep his weight on his elbows and not crush her. "Did I hurt you?" he asked quietly.

She shook her head no. "That was fucking incredible," she breathed.

He chuckled, "I'm still a sex god then?"

"Oh yes, maybe the inventor of sex even. Jeez, I don't even think I could stand and we are now laying in a big wet spot."

He laughed quietly. "Thank God we still have your bedroom with a dry bed then." He pulled out and stood on his own shaky legs.

She saw the trembling and laughed. "Glad it's not just me."

Ronnie pulled her up and back into the bathroom. He cleaned them both off in the shower again and checked once more to make sure there were no marks. "Did it work?"

"Well there was not one thought in my head that was not you and what you were doing to me. I think the only time I had even a moment's hesitation was when you trapped my legs, and even then, it was a split second before it was gone," she told him taking the towel and drying him off. "Guess that just means we need to keep practicing."

"No arguments here." He took the towel back and dried her. "I think that was the most forceful I've ever been with anyone."

"You do it well." She walked back into his room and grabbed a clean shirt of his to put on. "Look at that wet spot! It's huge."

He grinned and pulled on a clean pair of shorts, then tugged her across the hall to her room. "Fresh and dry," he said as he pulled the covers down and slid in waiting for her to turn the light off and get in. She pulled the shirt off and got in.

She angled herself so she was half on top of him, her head resting almost on his stomach. "Does this bother you?" she asked.

"A beautiful naked woman on top of me that happens to be one I'm in love with? Silly question," he said as he pulled the blankets up as far as he could without covering her head.

"It's a comfort thing for me, feeling you breathe under me," she told him, but her voice was already fading.

He rested his arm across her back, amazed at how fast she fell asleep. She was normally a light sleeper and didn't sleep much. It caught him off guard. He made a mental note to be her pillow as often as she needed it as a cure for the insomnia she often had. He fell asleep smiling.

Chapter Twenty-Five

Aedan felt like the routine they had fallen into was an uneasy limbo. The past three months had been relatively uneventful, though he still felt like they were waiting for an axe to fall. Even Mags had commented on it.

They'd gotten some great evidence thanks to Airiella noting where energy felt off and using the walkie-talkies when something came up on her radar. Their ratings were up, social media was in love with her, though they hadn't figured out her purpose with the show and called her a mysterious consultant.

There'd been numerous requests for interviews with her that the producers had managed to evade. The past couple of weeks they'd been bringing up the idea of it though. Aedan didn't want to for her safety, and he'd avoided discussing it with her. People loved to be critics against things they didn't understand, and most wouldn't understand Airiella. *He* didn't understand Airiella.

Jax had been hiding in his room wherever they were at. He didn't know what he was up to, though he hadn't been angry since that day on the beach. Ronnie didn't know what he was up to either and kept reassuring them that Jax was fine.

Half the time Aedan felt like he was looking to borrow trouble by waiting for something to happen and the other half of him wanted to believe that things were okay. Mags was showing and he thought that had something to do with the way he was being overcautious about everything.

Airiella had been spending equal amounts of time with all of them and had been working with Jax on building walls in his head like she did to try and mask his emotions. She told them that he was getting better at it and that she thought he was making progress on his own healing. Aedan was afraid to ask for more details.

She'd been working with Ronnie in the pool after their workouts and each of them had joined her at one point or the other. They'd all improved their swimming skills, none held the grace she did, however. Her strength had improved in fighting and Ronnie said she could hold her own, yet none of them had really taken the initiative to test that.

He wanted to talk to Smitty and Ronnie about setting her up to test it, but they were so protective of her he didn't think it would go over well. There hadn't been a good time to ask them about it either. Their shoot schedule had been hectic and crazy.

Now that they had a week off, he'd been trying to figure out a way. She rotated through their rooms at night depending on who she needed, or rather, who needed her. Sometimes she spent the night alone, it wasn't often though.

She was cooking dinner for them tomorrow with help from Jax, for Mags' birthday, which meant she wanted him to grill because Jax was a master at that. Right now, she was out at the store with Mags getting the groceries they needed for it, so if he was going to bring this up with Ronnie, this would be the time to do it.

Smitty and Ronnie were currently in the office editing some of the footage from the last shoot, pulling out the parts where Airiella had broken in over the walkies and adding in some of the voice overs from Jax that explained the evidence they collected.

They didn't hear him come in they were so intent on what they were doing. Aedan felt like being a jerk and watched until he was sure their focus on the screen in front of them was complete, and then he jumped and yelled, his feet slamming into the floor the same time the yell burst from him.

Smitty fell straight out of his chair and Ronnie bolted straight up knocking his chair over. Aedan howled with laughter at their faces. Payback would suck, it was totally worth it though. Usually, it was Ronnie doing something like that, which made it even more perfect because they never would have suspected it.

"You are fucking lucky you weren't close enough to hit." Ronnie struggled not to laugh as Smitty got up off the floor.

"I can't believe you stole a page from this jack asses playbook," Smitty grumbled, righting the chairs.

Aedan tried to get his laughter under control. "I should have recorded that."

"You'll get yours," Ronnie promised, an evil grin spreading across his face.

"No doubt," Aedan managed to get out before another bout of laughter struck him.

"To what do we owe this random pleasure?" Smitty sat and looked at him.

Aedan sobered. "I wanted to talk to you about an idea I had." He looked at Ronnie.

"What?" Ronnie crossed his arms and leaned against the edge of the desk.

Aedan backed up a step closer to the doorway and checked to see if Jax was near. He knew Jax would never agree to this idea. "You had said that you felt that Airiella could hold her own if she needed to. We've never tested her reflexes and how she would react if caught off guard again. Her need was to not freeze up. Are you certain she wouldn't?"

Ronnie's eyes had taken on a cold glare and Smitty's

face became like stone. "You want one of us to attack her?" Ronnie stood straight up, his stance aggressive.

"Well, kind of. She's not afraid of any of us though and we can't really know how she would react because she knows we would never hurt her," Aedan started.

Smitty shot to his feet. "You want to have someone else attack her?"

Aedan had been right, they didn't like the idea. "Aren't we supposed to be helping her? Taklishim was the one who gave me the idea with something he said about doing things that we wouldn't normally do to help her get over this."

"If you think for one minute, I am going to let some stranger put his hands on her in any way that looks like an attack you are sorely mistaken," Ronnie snarled.

"Not like that, Ronnie. She would know it was happening, she just wouldn't know his style or his moves and be able to predict what he would do. You'd be there. Think of it more like a sparring match," Aedan argued.

Smitty relaxed. "That's not what you insinuated. If you had said that instead of the way you said it, he wouldn't be ready to beat your ass down right now."

Ronnie still wasn't convinced. "Who? You realize she told me details about things from her past, this doesn't sit well with me. I get where you are coming from. Though, if Jax hears this, he'll fucking flip."

"Wouldn't you feel better if you knew she wouldn't freeze?" Aedan rushed out, checking the hall to make sure Jax wasn't coming.

"You didn't answer with who? Who do you know here that you would trust with this?" Ronnie prodded.

"I was thinking of asking at a local boxing club for one of the coaches. Or a local women's shelter for one of the self-defense instructors."

"A stranger then. No." Ronnie didn't budge.

"It might be worth it, man," Smitty said, siding with Aedan. "Think of the confidence she would gain if she knew she wouldn't freeze up."

"Fuck. I hate this." Ronnie paced. "I know you are

right, but I hate it."

"Would you rather not be there?" Aedan asked.

Ronnie was immediately in his face and Aedan worked to not flinch at the anger there. "If you even think of doing this without me there you will not like the consequences."

"Bro, chill. Aedan wouldn't hurt her any more than we would." Smitty pulled him back. "You know that."

"The thought of someone throwing a punch at her makes that shit she told me come to the front of my mind and rage takes over." He started pacing again and Aedan understood where he was coming from.

"How about you come with me and we ask around together, so you meet them beforehand. That way when we talk to her about it, she knows you approve," Aedan suggested.

"Fine." Ronnie threw himself in the chair. His anger still close to the surface.

"I'll do a little research on places we can go, right now. We can go in the morning, that way I can let Mags sleep in for her birthday."

"I'll be tagging along as well," Smitty said plainly, his tone cautious. "I defer to Ronnie on the capabilities of the person, but if I don't like them, I get a veto."

That clearly settled Ronnie down, so Aedan didn't argue. He held the same thought as Smitty did. He wasn't looking to get her hurt, he just wanted to give her that peace of mind she wanted. He nodded at them and left them to finish their work while he looked up places they could check.

Winnie circled around the house looking for someone to talk to. Ronnie had finally taken his necklace off and she'd been able to have many long conversations with him over the past three months when Airiella wasn't with him. It had made her so happy. He talked through the abuse of his past with her and how

Jax had taken the blame on himself.

She had been certain that was what was happening back then, no amount of arguing would change it though. They'd resolved their feelings over what never happened between them and Ronnie had told her how he felt about Airy. His love for her was so beautiful.

Winnie told him about all the places she'd been trying to find a way to get through, for someone to see her and how many investigations she's butted in wanting a message to come across. They laughed about how she had been able to make things move and scared the hell out of a few people.

Winnie felt like she had a best friend back now. It was amazing. She still loved them all, and Ronnie told her over and over how much he still loved her and thought about her. She passed on information about Airy that she'd been able to pick up here and there and told him that she was assisting Taklishim, Tama and Onida with seeking out plans.

Jax hadn't taken his necklace off once since they'd redone it after the fire. He was also getting better about masking his feelings because there were times that Winnie couldn't really tell what was going on. He'd suddenly go dark on the emotion front.

The first time it had happened, they all had their necklaces on and Winnie thought he'd died and freaked out. He'd never been able to go dark like that before. Airiella had finally told her what was going on. He'd made great progress.

She could tell also that he had come a good distance in trying to heal himself. His emotions were starting to be more balanced and she could feel the love in him growing for her favorite angel. Winnie still thought they should make their connection permanent, she believed that it would help Airiella in the long run.

Now she was stuck. There had been some movement in the spirit realm regarding Airy, but they all had necklaces on and she hadn't seen Onida or Taklishim in a while. There'd been rumblings about one of the spirits coming through to try and get to either Airiella or Jax. They wouldn't be able to get to Airiella, but Jax was vulnerable still. She hadn't been able to narrow down a time frame on it either.

Jax finished wrapping up the gifts he had. It was Mags' birthday, but he had gifts for all of them. He'd healed up some of the wounds he'd been harboring for so long over these past months. He felt grateful that nothing had happened and had given him a little time to work on himself.

He'd been working hard at forgiving himself, and the progress he'd made was remarkable. He'd been able to let go of a few of things and got closer to some others. It was hard and incredibly painful work. The darkness in him also hadn't reared its ugly head in a while giving him a false sense of security.

Airiella was downstairs making a cake for Mags, and he got to help her with dinner. The need he had to be around her hadn't diminished, if anything it grew stronger the more he got to know her. He thought he was closer to being ready to make that connection with her, closer to admitting that he didn't believe the feelings would go away. And he really enjoyed growing their relationship the way they had been, slowly and getting to know each other better.

The smells coming from downstairs were mouthwatering and making him hungry. He could always go see if she needed help now, it would give him an excuse to be around her. He gathered up all the gifts and in a couple of trips had them all set in the TV room for later.

Cinnamon, he was smelling cinnamon. What was Mags' latest craving? His brain raced trying to remember. Apples. She'd had a thing for apples lately. Maybe Airiella was making a pie instead of a cake. He walked into the kitchen and halted in his tracks.

She had every surface in use and was running

around like a mad woman. "Hello siren, would you like help?" He couldn't help the huskiness of his tone, it was just the effect she had on him.

"Oh Jax! Yes please! I forgot how damn hard this cake was to make." She gave him a tired smile.

"It smells delicious, whatever this is," he gestured to the mess she had going.

"I usually make it for my family in the fall, but Mags wanted apple something, and this was all I could think of besides apple pie, and I've never made a pie before. Here, can you peel these apples and slice them up? Not super thin, but not thick either."

Easy enough. Jax sat down at the island and got to work. "Crazy to think that in a little over three months she will have babies. Plural. Poor woman." Jax was excited though. These kids were going to be spoiled like mad.

"She's a natural mom, I think. It's Aedan you should worry about. They aren't even born yet and he's a helicopter parent according to Mags." Airiella giggled, "He's going to be so wrapped around their fingers."

He started slicing the first apple as she put three cake tins in the oven and set the timer. "Is there a bowl to put these in?" he asked.

"Oh, put them in this bag, it's easier to coat them that way, then I'll dump them in the pan." She handed him a large zippered baggie.

She cleaned up the mess from the cake part and loaded the dishwasher, prepping for the last parts of the recipe while the cakes cooked. "Are you making a frosting too?"

"No, it's not a frosted cake. The cake part itself is a spice cake, that's why it smells like fall in here. Then you cook up the apples in the spices and sugar until they are tender and layer them over the layers of cake and top with a caramel sauce. That's what this mess here is for, the caramel," she said as she pointed to the stuff still out.

"You are making your own caramel?" Jax was impressed. She was going all out for this to make it special for Mags.

"Caramel is easy, just have to watch it closely so it doesn't burn. For me it's the apple part that's the hardest." She came over to him and hugged him from behind. "Thank you for helping me."

He swung around and captured her in one of those kisses she was always asking him for. It floored him how used to touching her he was now, no hesitation. It felt natural and easy. Not to mention that he loved the way she tasted when he kissed her. "Will you stay with me tonight?"

Her eyes were glazed over from the kiss, and she just nodded at him. He loved that he could do that to her with a kiss. He'd gotten used to her sleeping next to him, and even though they didn't take it farther than that yet, his body knew she was near and he slept great.

He finished up the apples while she measured out the spices for him to put in the bag and mix while she made the caramel. They worked like a well-oiled machine and soon she was pulling the cakes out to cool. She searched through the cupboards and found a round plate she could use to set it on.

This feeling right here and now, them working together in perfect harmony, he wanted this. He wanted it forever. She felt like home to him. It doesn't matter where they were at, it always felt like this with her.

She finished up the first layer and had him pour the caramel over it, then repeated with the process with the next two layers. It was a stunning cake, and damn it smelled good. He wiped the caramel pan clean with his fingers, smeared some on her lips and licked the rest off of his fingers before he bent down and kissed the caramel off her lips.

He led her outside to the bench in the garden where they'd had their first real conversation. "I have something for you. Well kind of for you." He suddenly felt nervous.

She gave him a curious look. "Kind of?"

"Um, yeah. I wasn't planning on showing you yet, but it felt right." Jax fidgeted. "It's something I started working on after we got back from that day on the beach. It took me about a month to get it right, then it's taken this long to get it on me." He pulled off his shirt and turned around.

I almost drooled. Jax shirtless, was enough of a gift. I'd seen him without a shirt before, but it was always dark. This was the first time I was seeing him in the bright light of day and I practically salivated. Inked men were hot. Inked Jax was a living, breathing, wet dream in front of me.

He was just as sculpted as Ronnie, though not as broad. Then he turned around. I gasped and my hands flew to my mouth. He had gotten black wings tattooed across each shoulder blade. The feathers ending right above the waist of his jeans. Intricate detail was inked into each black feather. It was an elaborate tattoo that took up almost his entire back. I traced the lines with my fingers, able to feel the spots where it was still healing.

"Jax, did you draw this?" I whispered.

"Straight from the memory of you in my dream when you had wings. Keep looking, you'll see more things pop out," he said quietly.

I leaned forward to kiss the middle of his back. As I moved backwards, I saw my name. Airiella was written in the way the feathers fell in the negative space on the left, and Raven was in the same on the right. Farther down on the left I saw the word Love in the negative space, and started looking in the right for what was there. I saw it, it said Wins.

"Love wins," I breathed. "You tattooed my wings on you. My name. Jax this is breathtakingly beautiful."

"It's in no way enough to tell you how woven into me you are, how much you've left a mark on me in ways that no one could ever understand but you. There is no one else I would ever do this for," he said and he turned to look at me.

"I love it. You are incredible and I love you," I said softly. "This is why you've been gone so much," it dawned on me.

He turned all the way around now and pointed to his lower left ab right above his hip. There he had a raven tattooed. For me. I threw myself at him. "You are a part of me forever, siren."

I clung to him. "I can't believe you did this. Jax this is the best gift."

"There's one more thing." He pulled away from me so I could see his face. "After the live show in September, I was hoping we'd all take a group camping trip. We'd be on your turf, and it's still about a month from Mags' due date. I've done a little research and up by where Tama, Onida and Taklishim live is a hike called Ozette Triangle. Or something like that. We can camp on the beach. What do you think?"

"I think it's perfect," I said immediately. "That's one of the hikes that has been on my list for a while now. You really want to go camping and hiking?"

"With you, yes. I was hoping to do it closer to your birthday week," he said with a sweet smile.

What do you know? That rabbit hole of falling in love with this man goes even deeper than it already was. "I'm blown away right now. I don't know what to say." I gazed into his eyes.

"I want to explore your home. The places that speak to you. I thought it would be a great way to wrap up the season and relax after all of it," he said, flustered.

"I love every last bit of it. You keep finding new ways to amaze me. Every time I think that I couldn't possibly love you more, you do something like this and I'm proven wrong." I moved closer to him and ran my hands over naked chest and around to the wings he now had on his back. "I haven't stopped falling, Jax. The more I learn about you, the deeper I go."

He gathered me to him and laid us on the bench, his body pressing into mine, causing that chain reaction of heat and electricity. "I'm almost ready. Not quite there yet, but don't think I can hold out too much longer."

He gave me another of those barely restrained passionate kisses that had me arching up into him. I trailed my fingers across his back. "You are a masterpiece, Jax."

He sat up reluctantly. "Let's go prep for dinner before I take this too far. Your skin on mine makes me lose reason."

I laughed, glad he was feeling the same way I was. It was so easy to lose my train of thought when he touched me. I felt sad when he put his shirt back on covering the art he made. "Have the others seen that?"

"No, just you. I'll show them later tonight." He held his hand out to me and pulled me up when I took it. "What are we making?"

"She wanted steak. I can season it and marinate it, but since I don't really eat it, I find it hard to cook."

"Easy enough, I know exactly how they all like their steaks done. What are we having with it?" We walked and talked easily now like we'd known each other for years.

"Pregnancy hormones said she wanted a pasta salad, green salad and scalloped potatoes," I laughed. "She had an entire list of food she wanted and I got it narrowed down to that."

"Good thing we'll be here a week to eat the leftovers," he pointed out.

"Only if she doesn't eat it all. She's got some hungry kiddos growing in that belly, Uncle Jax."

He beamed in pride. "I love hearing that." He pulled me into his side as we entered the kitchen. I was hopeless when it came to him.

Mags stretched and smiled. Adan let her sleep in while he was out with the guys doing something that he was being secretive about. She had her suspicions based on Ronnie's attitude yesterday when he confirmed the time before bed.

She found a vase of fresh flowers on the dresser and a card he left her. She hadn't really had much morning sickness yet, and she was thankful for that as she climbed in the tub using some of the bath salts she'd gotten from Airy.

So far, her birthday morning was great. She smelled the cake Airy was making for her and her stomach growled in response. These babies wanted food all the time. Jax had started making fun of her for it too, she was constantly eating. It amused Aedan and Jax both to no end.

She soaked in the tub for a while then got dressed and headed downstairs. Airy and Jax weren't in the kitchen, so she got to pig out unwatched. She saw the finished cake and had to restrain herself from cutting into yet. She'd never live that one down. Finished eating, she cleaned up her dishes.

She saw Airy and Jax in the garden from a window as she wandered about looking for something to amuse herself with. She hoped for another scene like her and Ronnie in the pool, but she didn't think that they had made the connection yet.

Jax was different around Airy. He was sweet in a way she had never seen, not even with Winnie. Airy had a way of getting to him. Jax and Winnie reminded her of the way Airy was with Ronnie. It was easy, relaxed and fun. Airy might bring out the sweet in him, but he brought out her fire. They were an excellent match and complemented each other in so many ways.

She hadn't heard Airiella mention Winnie in a while now that she thought about it. She remembered her talking about taking the necklace off and being able to talk to her. Mags pulled the necklace off and went back to her room.

"Winnie, are you around?" Mags felt silly calling out like that, she was alone though, no one heard her.

"Happy Birthday Mags!" Winnie appeared in front of her making her squeal.

"Damn Winnie! Give a girl some notice! How's my favorite ghost?"

"Been trying to get a message through to Ronnie, Airy or one of the council. Things are stirring on this side about Airy. I think something is in the works. By the way, I love the belly. You are going to look so cute waddling around." Mags felt a cool sensation over her skin as Winnie stroked her hand over the growing ball of babies.

"It's pretty amazing, Winnie. I still can't believe it's real until I try to wear a pair of jeans that no longer fits. Is that the message you are trying to get to one of them?"

"For now yes, I just wanted them to be aware and stay alert."

"Who do you want me to pass the message on to?" Mags pulled out her phone. "I'll text them so I don't forget. I never really believed pregnancy brain was real until now, and I can't remember why I walked into a room. Unless it's the kitchen, I know why I'm in there all the time."

"Tell Ronnie. Eat all you want; you've got babies to feed. Do you know the sex yet?" Winnie asked excitedly.

"Yes! A boy and a girl! I get one of each! It's so cool," Mags gushed.

"You are going to be such a great mom. Aedan is going to be such a huge pushover," Winnie laughed.

"You are so right about that! He likes to act like he's going to be strict and laying down the law, I know better. Hell, we all know better."

Mags finished the text and slid the phone back into her pocket as Winnie popped in and out. "What are they doing?"

"Who? Ronnie and the other guys? Or Airy and Jax?" Mags asked for clarification.

"Ronnie and the guys. I can feel Jax is here and with Airy. I can't be happier about how that is developing. Slower than I'd like, but it's solid." Winnie grinned.

"I was just watching them in the garden. He's so different around her. As for the others, Aedan was being secretive about it, but I think he is trying to find someone to test Airy's fighting skills. He's mentioned it a couple of times and Ronnie was all pissy with him last night. Come to think of it, Smitty was a little too." Mags looked thoughtful.

"I assume Jax doesn't know and that's why he is here and not with them," Winnie replied. "Jax wouldn't like that idea, I can guarantee it."

"I agree, he'd hate it. I understand Aedan's point of view the little he has talked about it. I can also understand why Ronnie was so worked up about it too, given her past.

Damned if you, damned if you don't kind of thing, I guess." Mags fluffed some pillows on the bed and sat down stuffing them behind her back.

Winnie sat cross legged at the end of the bed. "She's in a better place now. Nightmares have slowed down from things that triggered her when I first met her. Being around you all helps her, she has firm connections that aren't just one sided friendships now."

"It still baffles me how people treat her like that and she keeps giving them chances. She's making dinner tonight; did you know that?" Mags was already hungry again thinking about it.

"I'm sure it will be amazing. Ronnie said she's a good cook." Winnie looked jealous for a moment.

"She's a damn good cook! Though from when I was at dinner with her family, they all seem to be good cooks. Must be an Italian thing. Enough talk about food, I'm already hungry again and I just ate."

"Sorry Mags," Winnie frowned. "Are you feeling okay?"

"Yeah. I get these waves of tiredness that come over me at weird times. The doctor said it was normal. I'm starting to feel like all I do is eat and sleep. It's kind of frustrating. Hey! Why don't you come with me for a walk?" Mags sat up, enthusiasm lighting her face.

"Are you sure it's a good idea to go without your necklace? Especially after I just told you to stay alert?" Winnie asked skeptically.

"Killjoy. Fine. I'm going to sit here and read a book then. You can hang out with me if you want. I can turn the TV on so you have something to watch," Mags suggested.

"I've got nothing better to do, why not? Besides, it's your birthday. I'm honored you want to spend time with a killjoy ghost," Winnie joked.

"Don't trigger the crazy pregnant lady hormones, Winnie."

Mags flipped on the TV, picked the show Winnie wanted and grabbed her book. She got two paragraphs in and was asleep.

Smitty was going a little crazy. They'd been to four places now and no one struck Ronnie as good enough. Three of them Smitty had agreed with, the fourth would have been okay in his opinion. He deferred the fighting skills to Ronnie though. Not one of them had been able to get the drop on him in the ring.

There were two places left and the place they were at now, they were talking with a guy who was ex-military and an assistant manager. He'd boxed in the Navy too. Ronnie was doing a round with him in the ring, and Smitty watched in fascination at a move he hadn't seen before that took Ronnie down to one of his knees.

"What the fuck was that?" came Ronnie's shout.

"Krav Maga," the guy, his name was Matt, answered.

"Ronnie doesn't look happy," Smitty told Aedan.

"Nope. Slick move, seemed kind of underhanded though since they were supposed to be straight boxing," Aedan said.

"As long as he doesn't pull that shit with Airiella, he's got my vote," Smitty chuckled. "First time I've seen Ronnie go down in a long time."

"Care to make a bet?" Aedan glanced at Smitty out of the corner of his eye.

"Depends. On what?"

"If Ronnie drops again." Aedan smiled.

"Sure, but I'm not betting against him." Smitty grinned back.

"Fine. I bet you twenty bucks he drops once more." Aedan stuck out his hand. Smitty shook it and laughed.

"He's not going down. Now that he knows the guy isn't playing fair Ronnie won't hold back." Aedan narrowed his eyes. "Dude, how many times have you seen Ronnie fight and lose?"

"Okay, fine. That was a sucker bet, but it's still on," Aedan groused.

Smitty sat back and watched Ronnie clean the floor with Matt as predicted. Ronnie could read an opponent's moves like a book. It was like watching a violent ballet. Ronnie had the grace and skill in a ring that Airiella had in the pool. Aedan handed over the money and sulked.

Ronnie jumped out of the ring and took the guys number. "I've got one more to visit. I'll let you know either way. Thanks man."

Smitty handed Ronnie his hoodie and they left. "Well?"

"It's a possibility, I didn't like him throwing in guerrilla fighting though. He held his own against me up to a point. Let's see this last guy and then I'll decide." Ronnie stalked back to the car.

Smitty smiled at Aedan and they went to the last gym. The guy that Aedan had talked to was overweight, slow and old. Ronnie had decided before they got all the way in the building. "Fine, we'll use that guy Matt. Might as well go back and find out his schedule," Ronnie grumbled.

"Should have bet on that one," Aedan smarted off.

"You bet on me?" Ronnie asked.

"No, Aedan bet against you, I bet on you." Smitty laughed at Aedan's expression.

"Really bro? You bet against me?" Ronnie was incredulous.

"Smitty didn't give me a choice." Aedan mumbled.

They walked back in and talked to Matt, getting more information about upcoming availability. Matt's only stipulation was that they do it there at that gym. Ronnie didn't like that, but he agreed. Now the hard part, Smitty figured, was going to be telling the others.

I was so happy! Dinner was a hit! Mags was glowing with happiness and the moods of everyone were great. So much laughter and love of this new little family I had. These moments had become precious to me, even more so right now, celebrating Mags.

Smitty and Ronnie were on dish duty since Jax and I had cooked, Aedan was on Mags duty, so Jax and I just sat there relaxing for a bit. I loved that he smiled so much more now. He'd even put gel in his hair to style it for Mags, something the other's teased him about relentlessly through dinner. I just wanted to wind my fingers in it and mess up.

Smitty and Ronnie didn't have a whole lot to do because I cleaned as we cooked, and they came back out and sat at the table with us. Aedan had Mags' feet in his lap and was rubbing them while she shamelessly moaned in satisfaction.

"Get a room you two," Ronnie joked as he sat down next to me throwing his arm over my shoulders.

"You mean like you did in the pool?" Mags fired back.

"Bunch of voyeuristic pervs," Ronnie said with a smile.

Aedan cleared his throat, "Um, actually I have something I wanted to bring up with Airiella before the cake comes out so Mags can't throw it at me."

Oh no. Now what? I sat up straighter and Ronnie's arm tensed on my shoulders briefly before he rubbed my neck with his fingers. "It's okay, angel," he whispered in my ear.

Jax, on the other side of me, was at attention also. Smitty had his face shuttered which gave me a slight pause. I could usually read him. Mags was glaring, which meant she thought I wouldn't like whatever was about to happen.

"Out with it," I demanded.

"Smitty, Ronnie and I went out and talked with various people today to see if we could find someone to spar with you to test you on your defense skills that Ronnie has been working with you on. We found a guy that we think would work and he's free tomorrow and two days from now. What do you think?" Aedan blurted out quickly.

"You want her to fight a stranger?" Jax growled, sending the hair on the back of my neck to standing.

"I fought with him personally, today, to check his

style and skill set. He got me down once using an unconventional move," Ronnie said evenly. "I would be there for this, coaching her through it and to kick the ever loving shit out of him if he steps out of line."

Jax's face was stormy, mine was a little shocked. I guess I understood where Aedan was coming from, and I didn't disagree with him. I needed to know if I would freeze up the way I did in the basement, but the circumstances were different. I knew this was happening. Maybe I didn't know what moves he would come at me with, but I still knew it was coming.

"If you think it's best, and Ronnie agrees, I'll do it," I said carefully.

"I hear hesitation, baby girl." Smitty sat forward. "Tell me."

"I'm sure Ronnie has already thought of this." I paused, "but I'm not sure this will really tell you what you want to know on whether I'll freeze up or not. In a sparring match, I know I'm going to be attacked. It's not a surprise."

Ronnie massaged the back of my skull with his talented fingers. "I do agree with you there, angel. At least this will give you a little more confidence against someone other than me, where you have the comfort of knowing I won't fully hit. I'm pretty sure this guy is a cocky motherfucker, and will try to get away with things you wouldn't expect from me. It's good in that regard, but rest assured," he turned my head, "if he makes one wrong move, he will be answering to me."

Of that I had no doubt. "Set it up for whenever. I'll follow Ronnie's lead on this." I had a vague sense of unease that settled, and clearly Jax was not a fan of this idea.

"I'll be going with as well." He gave Ronnie a hard look. Ronnie just nodded at Jax.

I had a feeling that they all would be going. "Airy, sweets, if you aren't comfortable with this, say so," Mags told me.

"I'm fine Mags, I trust Ronnie's judgment," I told her as his hand tightened in my hair.

"So do I, it's this other guy that has me on edge,"

Jax added. "Especially if he used what Ronnie called an unconventional move to get the drop on Ronnie."

"He did Krav Maga," Ronnie's curt tone cut in.

"Are you fucking kidding me?" Jax shot to his feet.

"I knew what to expect after that, and he didn't get the drop on me again," Ronnie defended his decision. "I also told him that with her it would be straight boxing, nothing else, and I let him know that I would be there."

"Jax, it's okay." I reached out for his hand. He let me take it and he sat back down, moving closer to me. "I agree with Aedan that I need to be tested. I also know that with any of you, you won't push me. It's fine."

"It's not fine, I can feel the feeling you just tried to push down," Jax said into my ear, loud enough for Ronnie to hear, but not the others.

"That feeling is the reason I need to do it," I said softly. I looked back up at the group, "Set it up. Tomorrow is fine, or whenever."

Aedan gave a nod and took his phone and walked out of the room. "Are you sure, baby girl? This is completely your call to make. Ronnie and I were against it at first. I agree with Aedan, and I agree with your hesitation," Smitty reasoned with me.

"It's worth a try, right? Better than hiring someone to attack me out on the street unexpectedly," I countered.

"That would never happen on my watch," Ronnie said menacingly.

I stood up. "How about cake?"

Mags squealed in delight. "Yes! I've been eyeballing that beauty all day! Bring me the cake!"

She was perfect in getting the night back on track. I laughed and headed into the kitchen, Jax on my heels. "Can you get plates and forks?" I turned to ask, but he was directly behind me, close.

"Siren, I don't know why, but this sparring thing is scaring me. I know it had some reaction in you. I saw it in your eyes and I could feel the unease. Tell me, are you doing this just to pacify Aedan?"

I put my fingers on his face and he instantly relaxed

into me. "No Atlas, I'm not. I do think it's a good idea for me to practice with an unknown person in order to hone what I've learned. I am uneasy, I'm not going to lie, but I think I would be even if this was Ronnie's idea and not Aedan's."

"Atlas, not Zeus?" he smiled at me, hugging me.

"Well, right now you seem to be carrying the weight of the world again. Let it go and you'll be Zeus," I said and kissed him lightly.

Then he took control and that heat that he brings set me on fire as he deepened the kiss, demanding a response with his tongue and lips leaving me breathless and wobbly. "How about now?"

"Definitely Zeus," I whispered, my body burning and aching for him.

He let me go and grabbed the plates and spoons instead of forks, and got the ice cream. "Need spoons if we are having ice cream, and I know that hungry mama out there wants ice cream." He grinned.

Damn but that man had some power over me to send my heart into weird beats every time he smiled like that. "Did we ever find candles?" I couldn't even remember my own name right now, he had me so flustered.

"In my pocket, want to check?" he goaded me.

I'm never one to back down from a challenge and I watched his eyes darken as he realized I was going to reach down into his pocket. "Be careful what you wish for, Zeus," I answered wickedly.

I slid my hand in his pocket along his legs, letting my fingers nudge against a rapidly swelling cock and I smiled at him as I heard him suck air in between his teeth. "You're going to be the death of me."

"What a way to go," I pulled my hand out and stretched to kiss him.

"Damn it, now I can't walk out there yet," he grumbled.

I took the ice cream from him and held it against his crotch as his eyes bugged out at the sudden cold. "That should do the trick," I winked handing it back to him. I grabbed the cake and a knife to cut it and walked back out.

Ronnie gave me a knowing smile and I whispered in his ear as I leaned over, "Nothing a little ice cream in the crotch couldn't fix."

He looked at Jax's pained expression and burst out laughing. "My day has been made now."

The others looked at us in confusion while Jax glared at Ronnie, fighting a smile. "Jax, could you get the candles out of your pocket please?" I asked sweetly.

He couldn't hold back anymore and bent over laughing. "To save myself from freezing balls again, I will happily do it for you."

Mags was the first to put it together and she started giggling. "Best birthday, ever."

We sang while she clapped along, and then I let her cut the cake so she could take as big of a piece as she wanted while Aedan scooped the ice cream. It was quiet while we ate the cake, then Smitty and Ronnie cleaned up again.

"Presents! Time for presents!" Mags jumped up.

Jax still wasn't feeling okay about the sparring match Aedan had confirmed was now tomorrow, but he still felt lighthearted after Airiella stuck ice cream in his crotch. Brilliant move on her part in that it worked, also devious. He loved her to pieces.

They filed into the TV room where the others had piled their gifts for Mags along with his. Aedan had made a movie for her of pictures and videos he's collected over the years. They started off with that. Mags was beaming, she loved it.

Then Aedan gave her a small box. She opened it and found a jeweled pendant with their birthstones, and the ones for when the babies will be born. Jax knew that the doctors said they wouldn't wait past the due date if she hadn't gone into labor because her frame was so small. So the month they would be born was already known.

She opened the one from Airiella next to find a basket full of soaps she'd made and had her friend mail here, along with bath salts and other spa goodies that Airiella had made and stocked up. She'd thrown in some exfoliating gloves and a pair of fluffy slippers. Jax smiled at the look on Mags' face. She was ecstatic.

She opened Smitty's next, which turned out to be a split framed photo of the sand sculpture she'd made and a photo of Airiella hugging Mags which turned out great. She had tears in her eyes and ran her fingers over the picture and hugged Smitty.

Ronnie handed her his, which was hilarious to Jax, because it was gift certificates for various restaurants that delivered. He told her he figured while they were all out on shoot locations she wouldn't even have to go anywhere or do anything.

Then it came time for Jax. He picked up the stack of wrapped gifts and handed one to everyone except Aedan. They all gave him a questioning look and he just shrugged. "Open them."

Jax glued his eyes to Airiella, that was the reaction he wanted to see the most. He heard Mags gasp how beautiful it was, but he didn't look at the others until he saw what he wanted. Her eyes were wide and she touched her fingers to the picture he'd gotten of her.

The one where she was sitting in the sand, her wings outlined by the spray of the water, the sun showing the glow they all saw when they looked at her. Her hair flowing with the breeze. It had been a stunning picture that needed no editing at all. Easily, one of the best photo's Jax had ever taken.

He glanced around then, they all had tears in their eyes. When he looked back at her, she was staring at him, completely still. She must have put her walls up because he couldn't get a good read on her emotions and her eyes were shimmering pools of amber.

"This is what we see when we look at you." He kneeled before her. "I wanted you to see through my eyes," Jax bared his heart and he swore another one of those broken pieces of his was just put into place.

She still hadn't said anything, she just stared at him, a few tears slipping down her face that he caught with his finger. Then she was in his arms, holding him so tight her arms shook. "I'm speechless, I don't know what to say," she cried in his ear, tucking her face between his neck and shoulder.

"You don't need to say anything. I just wanted you to see through my eyes, show you what a gift you are to me," he whispered back. "To the world."

She pressed her lips to his neck. "Thank you, Zeus."

Mags flung herself at him once Airiella was back on the couch. "This is perfect! Absolutely beautiful, Jax."

Ronnie and Smitty both had expressions of awe. "You nailed it, man. This, this is love," Smitty said quietly.

Ronnie didn't say anything, the emotions on his face said everything Jax needed to hear. The way that Ronnie pulled Airiella up onto his lap and held her spoke volumes more than either of them could ever say to each other. They were united in this one woman.

Jax stood back up, "I know it's Mags birthday, I just wanted everyone to have a copy. Happy birthday nag, I mean Mags." Jax grinned at her.

"The love in this room, right now, is the perfect gift. Thank you everyone for making my day amazing!" Mags exclaimed, warming Jax's heart because she still clutched the picture to her chest.

"Oh, one more thing to share, but this was not for Mags," Jax said and pulled his shirt off and turned around.

"Holy fucking balls, man," Ronnie stood, Airiella in his arms. He put her down on her feet and walked over to Jax. "You covered the demon wings. Are these Airiella's wings?"

"Yeah, the sight of them is imprinted on my brain, so I drew them first, then went and had them done in sessions," Jax explained. He didn't share the raven though. Ronnie would see it at some point, he was sure.

"Her name is in the negative space," he heard Mags say quietly, he felt her touch it, pointing it out to Aedan.

"Jax you could be an artist."

"So could you, Mags," Jax replied quickly.

He looked over at Airiella standing there, still and quiet, her emotions still walled off. He put his shirt back on and stepped away from Ronnie and Mags, closer to Airiella. She didn't move away, her eyes followed him though. Those pools of shifting color centered on him.

"You okay, siren?" he said so only she could hear.

She nodded numbly at him as Smitty pulled him away to talk to him about an idea he had for a tattoo to incorporate Airiella's wings on him in a smaller version. He was only half listening to Smitty, watching as Airiella gave Mags a hug and then walked out of the room.

"She's okay, bro," Smitty told him, his gaze following Jax's. "I think the picture overwhelmed her emotions, it's not bad emotions. She's just trying to make herself believe she could really be as beautiful as what you captured. That's what I am picking up anyway."

Jax looked at Smitty. "Nothing bad?"

"Nope. She's crazy, mad in love you. That love that Mags said she felt in the room was her. Believe me, nothing could have made her see what we do, more than that picture. It rocked her. Give her a few minutes. Check with Ronnie if you don't believe me."

"No, I believe you. Her response just worried me." Jax bit his lip.

"Because you just single-handedly did what we all have been trying to do since we met her." Ronnie came up alongside him. "You just changed the way she saw herself."

Chapter Twenty-Six

I sat on my bed cross legged and stared down at the serenely beautiful photo Jax had taken. It was really me. I touched the glass again tracing the figure with my nail. I'd never seen myself like this and my brain and heart were arguing whether it was real or not. When had I turned into this?

I knew one of those deep cracks inside me filled when I saw the picture and it filled with Jax's love that he couldn't speak out loud. Instead he handed me a picture showing me. Whoever I thought I was, has been replaced with this image.

It was scary, letting go of those familiar feelings of self-loathing and accepting that the beautiful creature in this photo was me. I was in uncharted waters now, treading water desperately, looking for something stable to land on.

They walked in then. The stability I had been looking for to keep me from drowning. Ronnie settled on one side of me, Jax on the other. "This is really me," I repeated out loud.

"Unedited, siren," Jax said as if he were reading my thoughts.

"In my mind, when I saw this, I saw me, the other

me. I mean, I saw the old me, the one I always see when I see me. She waved goodbye to me. I saw me go, she left. Now I see this, this creature that my brain refuses to accept is me, but it is. It's really me." My voice broke as I whispered the fumbled words.

Ronnie picked the photo up and put it on the nightstand, then pulled me down so I lay on the bed, those men I loved so desperately on either side of me, holding my hands, letting me come to terms with this new vision of myself.

I rolled to my side, facing Jax, Ronnie rolling with me, spooning me. I slid my hand across Jax's rippled abs and over to where I knew the raven tattoo was, my heart feeling like it was going to burst with all the emotions tumbling around. Jax covered my hand with his, interlocking our fingers.

I didn't try to hold back the tears that fell, they were healing tears. I didn't know how these two knew so much about me without me having to tell them, yet I was grateful beyond reason for it. They'd made me a believer in love at first sight, even against overwhelming odds. They let me shatter, and lovingly helped me rebuild with no judgment.

"Can we stay together tonight?" I asked them both once the tears stopped.

"I'll leave that up to Jax," Ronnie said gently.

"It's fine with me," Jax added.

"Perfect. Strip then, both of you." I sat up, waiting for them to stand.

"Um, angel, I don't think Jax is ready for that," Ronnie's voice was hesitant.

"I just want no barriers between us," I clarified. "Not sex."

I felt the tension leave Jax and he stood, Ronnie following suit. I was able to get up then and stripped off all my clothes, not feeling self-conscious for the first time that I could remember. I heard Jax swear under his breath and glanced over as I picked up my clothes to put in the laundry basket.

"Sorry, siren. I can't help my reaction to you," Jax

apologized.

"Don't be sorry, remember last time? I'll do that again." I smiled a promise at him.

"What was last time? And I'm definitely not sorry," Ronnie said, proudly standing at attention.

"I helped Jax without the burden of making that connection permanent yet." My eyes couldn't stop from swiveling between the two men.

"I'm down," Ronnie immediately said, grabbing some Kleenex from the nightstand and handing them to Jax and taking some for himself.

Jax couldn't hide the grin that lit his face as he walked over to shut the light off and guided me to the bed, his hands on my hips. "In you go, siren. Hope you can multitask."

"Oh, I've got no problems with that," I said, my phone sex voice coming out.

I laughed as they both swore and settled on their backs on either side of me. I sat up to get the right angle with both of them, teasing them first until they both couldn't stand it anymore and started stroking, the feel of both of them hard, hot and heavy in my hands an incredible turn on.

Maybe it was because they had an audience in each other, or it was something else, but neither lasted very long. It also could be that I used that horny energy that built in me and pushed it back into them through the connection that tingled their skin everywhere my hand touched.

They cleaned up with their tissues, then Ronnie played me like a violin with his magic fingers while Jax kissed me senseless. Mutually satisfied all around we all fell asleep woven together, the feeling of our shared connection lending us a sense of safety.

Ronnie was tense. Damn it, he hated this. He paced around the ring walking Airiella through a warm up to make sure she was stretched before starting. The others all sat back against the wall on the other side of the ring, Jax being the most tense, Smitty a close second.

He knew Airiella was nervous about Jax, even if he didn't feel her through the connection. The glances she kept throwing his way an obvious tell. He stopped the warm up. "Go drink some water," he told her.

He watched as she slipped between the ropes and headed straight for Smitty, whispering in his ear. Ronnie saw the look cross Smitty's face and the tight nod he gave her. She went over and sat next to Jax and held his hand, whispering to him now.

Did she feel something off? The texted message relayed through Mags from Winnie flitting across his mind. That thought put his teeth on edge. There was nothing in this situation that was in his control except for himself. Even then, if something happened to her, he didn't think he'd be in control. He cussed out Aedan in his mind, fully knowing it wasn't Aedan's fault, but this had been his idea.

Jax had a wary expression on his face as she talked to him and Ronnie noticed the tension set in his jaw. Damn it, she was talking him down. He was out between the ropes of the ring and in front of Jax in three steps.

"Jax, you in control?" Ronnie drilled him.

"Yes. I feel off, though." Jax got points for the honesty, a testament to how far he'd come in a short while.

"He's doing great," Airiella told him softly. "He's fighting back."

Ronnie nodded and motioned Smitty with his head. He stood and moved away from the group. "What did she make you promise?"

"How do you now she made me promise anything?" Smitty gave him a cool look.

"I know her, and I know you. I saw the look that went across your face," Ronnie challenged.

"She made me promise that if something went sideways to get him out of here." Smitty didn't look happy at that.

"Why does that make that look come on your face?" Ronnie was genuinely confused.

"Because I know that if something happens, it will be to her. And instead of me helping her, she made me promise to take care of him." Ronnie got it now.

"I've got her," Ronnie promised.

"I know. I worry that I won't be enough to get him out of here though," Smitty added.

"Use Aedan. Mags can probably talk him down too," Ronnie thought out loud.

"She thinks something is going on. She said she's got a weird feeling in her stomach that she doesn't think is nerves," Smitty said carefully.

"Fuck. I feel it too. It's making me feel like a caged lion," Ronnie paced a few steps. "If you need to get to Jax, keep reminding him to fight. Over and over."

"That's what she said, too." Smitty huffed out a breath. "Nothing like going in blind, right?"

"Yeah, this isn't an investigation though," Ronnie muttered. He saw Matt approaching them from the other end of the gym. "Looks like the show is about to start."

Smitty clapped him on the back and headed back to sit next to Jax. Airiella came up to him resting her fingers on his arm. "I know you've got my back; I'm worried about him though."

"I know angel. I feel it too." Ronnie looped his elbow around her neck and pulled her into him. "Stay on your game. I can't keep him from hitting you as this is sparring, and it's what happens. Do not let your guard down."

She nodded. The fear a shadow across her features making the butterflies in Ronnie's stomach turn into a hoard of stampeding rhino's. He didn't doubt her instincts at all, they just didn't know what form was going to happen. "I can't pull from him if he loses control. I won't risk his life," came her quiet warning.

Ronnie wanted to puke. "We'll figure it out. I'll knock him out if I have to."

She gave him an unreadable look that felt like she saw right through him. "No, you won't. I won't let it come to that."

Matt came up and introduced himself to Airiella, interrupting anything Ronnie might have said. "You are my partner for this match? Nice to meet you, I'm Matt."

"Airiella," was her simple reply. Her even tone sending warning bells through Ronnie's head.

She held her hands out to Ronnie who got her gloves in place and she opened her mouth for the guard. She rested her bare skin against his arm and he felt her pushing love at him. She stepped into the ring and waited.

"Do not injure her," was the only warning Ronnie gave, his tone deadly and cold.

"Chill, man. Not my first rodeo," Matt fired back at him as he climbed in the ring. A gym employee counted them off and they started.

Not a sound came from the group behind him, and he never once took his eyes off the two sparring. Airiella took a few hits in the beginning, then seemed to find her rhythm and was able to dodge most of the rest he threw. They made it through the first round relatively okay.

"Is he hitting too hard?" he asked her quietly, checking her over.

She shook her head no, and gestured at the mouth guard. He pulled it out of her mouth, making a sucking noise. "He's hitting, I don't think it's full force though," she was slightly winded. He held a water bottle for her to drink some.

"You are doing fine, though it's all defense. If you see an opening, strike. I know we focused on defensive moves mostly, but you know how to push back. In order to stop the threat, you either need to run and run fast, or disable him in some way until you have an opportunity to get away. I've seen a few openings I don't think he's aware of, or he's just being sloppy. Go for a kidney shot. Nice big hook, either side," Ronnie coached.

She nodded. He put the guard back in her mouth and kissed her nose. He turned her back around and they counted them down again. She was doing great, and had even taken a couple of shots when Matt switched it up on her like he did Ronnie, and threw a Krav Maga move in knocking her feet straight out from under her.

Ronnie was through the ropes in a heartbeat. "No. You do that shit, you and I will go a few rounds in here with me not holding back. Make the smart move, Matt." He was so angry that he was digging his fingernails into his palms.

She got back up warily, rubbing her glove over her tailbone. He knew Jax had stood up by the look on her face as she glanced behind them. He didn't turn. He held Matt's eyes until he conceded. Only then did Ronnie back out of the ring and held a hand out behind him to say he had it under control.

He didn't though. He felt the tension thicken in the air and saw Airiella's posture stiffen. Ronnie didn't relax when she didn't drop her guard, and he noticed that the hits against her were coming harder and faster. His temper was fraying fast.

Suddenly she froze and her head swung around to look back at Jax, Ronnie saw the panic in her eyes and realized that Jax was losing control. It happened at the same time that Matt threw a nasty punch that had harmful intent behind it. There was no mistaking the movement or the look on Matt's face.

Ronnie heard the shouts from Mags and Smitty, and the roar that tore through Jax in the same moment he hurdled over the ropes into the ring. He didn't make it in time and the punch caught her in the shoulder with a sickening crack that sent her launching backwards.

Slow motion took place in Ronnie's mind, he was three inches too far away to catch her and she slammed into floor of the ring, her face contorted into fear and pain. He saw Smitty leap at Jax who was way too close to the ring for comfort, and he saw a second punch coming straight for him.

Ronnie reacted the only way he could. He snapped out a jab that broke Matt's nose and sent him sprawling, blood spraying all over. "What did I tell you?" Ronnie snarled out, squatting down to check on Airiella.

She was shaking and ghostly pale, her shoulder clearly dislocated. He helped her sit up and winced as she bit her lip and raised her arm, the snap of it making him want to puke again as she put it back in place. He didn't want to know how she knew that trick.

His blood turned to ice as Matt stood, a vacant look on his face and something other than his voice boomed out, "You are a natural. A simple, beautiful disaster, but you are no match for me. I will kill him slowly and make you watch."

Airiella stood, gritting her teeth in pain. She boldly turned her back on Matt looking at Jax. "Fight it, Jax. You've got this. Whoever this motherfucker thinks he is, he has nothing on you. Fight it, baby."

Ronnie felt the temperature in the room drop to arctic levels. "Who are you?" he demanded. This sparring match had turned into a scene from a nightmare investigation. Matt wasn't Matt anymore.

"I'm the one who will stop at nothing to destroy this beast you call an angel," he advanced at Ronnie.

Of course, she stood in the way. "Take your best shot," she bit out, her fighting stance perfect. The challenge in her voice irresistible to whatever energy the room was filling rapidly with.

Ronnie tried to move and found he was stuck, once again, her powers freezing them all in place. Matt, or whoever he was, leapt at her and Ronnie was absurdly proud at the front kick she delivered while he was still in the air, straight to his balls.

It knocked Matt down but didn't stop him. This wasn't human, or the body was, but whatever was in it wasn't. That kick to the balls would have dropped any man. It also wasn't the darkness that was in Jax. Ronnie didn't know what she was battling. It was clear to him that her attention was divided, though. That couldn't be good.

Ronnie heard thunder and saw a flash of lightning reflected in the mirrors. Shit. He needed to move. The cackle of laughter that sent chills up his spine echoed through the gym, letting him know in no uncertain terms Winnie's warning had become reality.

"You can't kill me. It's laughable that you are even

trying to stop me. Watch as I take him down." Matt's face changed to a sinister grin as he focused on Jax.

Airiella started to glow and Ronnie watched in horror and fascination as the bystanders in the gym all dropped while Jax managed to break free from whatever hold she had on the energy in the room. To Ronnie's amazement, Jax was Jax.

The darkness didn't have him, but it did look like it was trying to take him over. "Fight it, Jax," he heard her tell him. "Raven, I need your guidance," she whispered.

Ronnie was suddenly free to move though she stilled him with a hand motion. He moved to Jax's side instead, and grabbed a hold of his arm. "Fight it, Jax. Leap of faith, bro. I don't know what she's doing, but he will never get to you."

"I'm worried about her, not me," Jax ground out, his voice hoarse.

"Me too," Ronnie said uncomfortably. Whatever was happening was nothing they had experienced with her before. She was far stronger, not to mention glowing.

Airiella was glowing brighter by the second, and Ronnie was terrified that she was going to die. Flashbacks of last time echoing in his head, that was the only time he'd ever seen her glow like this. He couldn't define the feeling he felt building in Airiella, but he felt the flow of energy rushing into her, it was almost painful through the connection.

"Who are you?" she demanded, her tone hard and powerful.

"My name is of no consequence to you. You won't win. That energy that lives in him will be mine. I will take it and harness it," Matt cackled again. "You have no future here."

"Airiella," Jax said strong and clear. "Love wins."

"Look in my eyes," she said, her voice melodious and mesmerizing. Like she was trying to hypnotize it or something. "What do you see?"

"I've already told you, a natural, beautiful, disaster," came the evil grinning voice from Matt.

Ronnie felt the flow of energy change, air swirling like mad, tearing through the gym. The floor trembling under his feet. Jax's skin went icy under his hand. "Stay with me, Jax," Ronnie muttered, fighting his own fear at what was taking place.

"Funny thing about natural disasters. They typically come from nature when there's an imbalance that needs to be corrected." Her melodious tone didn't match the menace in her words, and Ronnie felt powerful fear then. She was changing the game. "You just threatened those I love. Put these innocent people here in danger. You possessed someone that I assume was unwilling."

"He was willing," Matt spit. "These pathetic humans are often willing when you offer them what they want. I didn't take him by force."

"I don't care," she said and she took a step forward. "You are on the wrong side of the fence on this one. These people here are innocent. You still threatened those I love. Whether or not I am a disaster, remains to be seen. I may not be able to kill you, and maybe I can, we will soon see." The ground trembled again and her glow turned an electric blue. "I am the storm that nature called to reset the balance."

Her tone was cold and she stepped into him and clasped a glowing hand around his arm. It was like she had become the lightning she calls. Living lightning. Divine Justice. The scream that tore from Matt's lips was chilling in a way Ronnie had never heard. The room turned pitch black and Ronnie heard two bodies hit the floor of the ring.

A few seconds later it was like nothing had ever happened. People started moving around again, she looked normal, Matt looked normal, except neither of them were moving. Not one person outside his little group even remembered anything happening, except both them dropping from sustained hits.

Jax and Ronnie reached her at the same time, Ronnie lifting her limp body in his arms. "She's breathing," he announced, his body giving into the shakes as Jax helped him out of the ring. "You fought it off?" he thought to ask Jax.

"Not at first." Jax paled. "Some part of me thought about losing her, and that helped. I thought of the picture I took, and I was able to get control. Hurt though. I feel sick."

"What the hell was that?" Aedan shrieked. "Why are all these people acting like nothing happened?"

"Is she okay?" Mags crowded in and stroked Airiella's face. "She doesn't look like she did when I saw her in the hotel that first time."

"No, she didn't pull the energy from Jax. I have no idea what that was, but she's a hell of a lot stronger now than she was before," Ronnie said quietly as the filed out of the gym.

"Let me look her over," Jax demanded. Ronnie stopped and between Jax and Mags, they checked for signs of injury, but it simply looked like she was sleeping.

Aedan was freaking out and trying to hide it, while Smitty was talking quietly into his phone. Aedan knelt down next to them, "Airiella?" he went to touch her, but pulled his hand back as if she was going to hurt him.

"Taklishim is on the way," Smitty broke in, "said to get her home and watch her. Also, Degataga said that we have the most unconventional angel in history."

"What the hell does that mean?" Jax asked angrily.

Ronnie looked down once again at the limp angel in his arms. "Shit just got more serious, didn't it?"

Smitty nodded mutely holding the door open for Ronnie while they all got in and raced for home. "I love you angel," he whispered to her, his eyes tracking the raven that flew alongside them.

Note from the Author

Domestic abuse and sexual assault are very real issues that have become extremely prevalent in our society. It's happening way too often, and could be a lot closer than you think.

That friend that suddenly flinches when someone lifts their hand to wave, the family member who suddenly withdraws, the friend who wears clothes that cover every part of their body, or the one who apologizes for everything.

Abuse comes in many forms, not just physical. If you find yourself or a loved one in this situation, please get help.

Reach out, whether it's to family, a friend, law enforcement or a crisis help line, it's a step in the right direction. There is always someone willing to listen and help.

Don't give up, you are worth your own effort to get out, you are worth so much more.

National Domestic Violence Hotline – 800-799-SAFE
Suicide Prevention Hotline – 800-273-8255
National Sexual Assault Hotline – 800-656-4673
National Emotional Abuse Text Hotline – Text HELLO to 741741